A PLUME BOOK

TASSY MORGAN'S BLUFF

Educated at Harvard, Yale, and UCLA, JIM STINSON has taught film production at Art Center College of Design, media history and criticism at California State University, Los Angeles, and video production at La Cañada High School. He's written for academia, published four mystery novels, made feature and instructional films (gems like *Electrical Hazards in the Coronary Care Unit*), and spent twelve years as a columnist and contributing editor at *Videomaker* magazine. Today, when not writing fiction, he is constantly revising his popular textbook on video production to keep pace with exploding media technology. Though born and bred in Pittsburgh, Pennsylvania, he has spent all his adult life in California and Oregon, where he now lives with his wife, Sue. He dotes on his two adult children and is pleased to report that they remain at large.

JIM STINSON

Tassy Morgan's Bluff

a novel

A PLUME BOOK

PLUME
Published by the Penguin Group
Penguin Group (USA) Inc., 375 Hudson Street, New York, New York 10014, U.S.A. •
Penguin Group (Canada), 90 Eglinton Avenue East, Suite 700, Toronto, Ontario, Canada
M4P 2Y3 (a division of Pearson Penguin Canada Inc.) • Penguin Books Ltd., 80 Strand,
London WC2R 0RL, England • Penguin Ireland, 25 St. Stephen's Green, Dublin 2,
Ireland (a division of Penguin Books Ltd.) • Penguin Group (Australia), 250 Camberwell
Road, Camberwell, Victoria 3124, Australia (a division of Pearson Australia Group Pty.
Ltd.) • Penguin Books India Pvt. Ltd., 11 Community Centre, Panchsheel Park, New
Delhi – 110 017, India • Penguin Group (NZ), 67 Apollo Drive, Rosedale, North Shore
0632, New Zealand (a division of Pearson New Zealand Ltd.) • Penguin Books (South
Africa) (Pty.) Ltd., 24 Sturdee Avenue, Rosebank, Johannesburg 2196, South Africa

Penguin Books Ltd., Registered Offices: 80 Strand, London WC2R 0RL, England

First published by Plume, a member of Penguin Group (USA) Inc.

 REGISTERED TRADEMARK—MARCA REGISTRADA

LIBRARY OF CONGRESS CATALOGING-IN-PUBLICATION DATA

Stinson, Jim.
  Tassy Morgan's Bluff : a novel / Jim Stinson.
    p. cm.
  ISBN 978-0-452-29724-1 (pbk.) 1. San Andreas (Calif.)—Fiction. 2. City
and town life—California—Fiction. I. Title.
  PS3569.T53T37   2011
  813'.54—dc22   2010050125

Set in Caslon 540 Roman • Designed by Eve L. Kirch

PUBLISHER'S NOTE
This is a work of fiction. Names, characters, places, and incidents are either the product
of the author's imagination or are used fictitiously, and any resemblance to actual persons,
living or dead, business establishments, events, or locales is entirely coincidental.

147204767

Always for Sue

ACKNOWLEDGMENTS

Special thanks to my Constant Weeders: Dunbar and Annegret Ogden, Louanne Ferree, Mairi and Juergen Panoscha, and Sue, Alex, and Lillie Stinson, as well as my agent, Al Zuckerman, and my editor, Laura Tisdel.

ACKNOWLEDGMENTS

It is a truth universally acknowledged, that a single man in possession of a good fortune must be in want of a wife.

—Jane Austen

Tassy Morgan's Bluff

1

*L*incoln Ellis left his house with a plastic grocery bag holding a big steel can that faintly resembled a Thermos jug. He lugged it along the bluff-top street, around the switchback, and down toward the little harbor, trudging past great stacks of crab pots topped with loafing seagulls. He didn't hear their squabbling or feel the late-May sunshine or see the blue Pacific. He didn't notice the fishing charter posters on the wall of the harborside bait shop.

Inside the little shack, he asked, "Can I borrow a boat?"

"Depends." The owner affected a Down East terseness appropriate for a Bar Harbor lobsterman. In fact, he'd been born right here on the Redwood Coast, about an hour south of Oregon.

"On?" Linc could do the laconic thing too.

"Kinda boat, fer how long. Ever run a boat, Linc?"

Linc had not, but he'd watched the locals start outboards. How hard could it be? "I just need twenty minutes—half an hour, tops."

The man stared a moment, then shrugged. "C'mon."

San Andreas didn't rate a marina, but the tiny town maintained a long wooden pier to service the commercial crab boats, now retired for the summer while their skippers said fervent prayers that the few remaining Dungeness crabs were all down there breeding like fruit flies. The two men climbed down to the water-level dock, and the bait shop guy pointed to a skiff with a small greasy outboard. "Squeeze the bulb, turn the key, pop the choke, pull the rope."

He turned and disappeared up the ladder, the bastard. Okay, Linc would figure it out himself. He'd once crafted intricate movie contracts at a thousand dollars an hour and an idiot could run an outboard motor, as boating statistics attested. Key, choke, rope: right.

Many sweaty minutes later, Linc stopped yanking the starter lanyard. Could the damn thing be out of gas? That would just fit the bait shop guy's sense of humor. Linc hefted the red plastic can: plenty of fuel. Blocked fuel line? It snaked from tank to motor like the tube on a blood pressure thingy. . . . Aha! He grabbed the plump rubber bulb bisecting the fuel line and squeezed repeatedly until it was too hard to compress anymore.

Now the motor started on one pull. Linc pushed in the choke and twisted the throttle. The prop churned the water white but the skiff just sat there. Wait: A handle stuck up with a two-ended arrow painted beside it. He shoved the lever back and sure enough, the boat started backward.

For about three feet, then the dock line yanked tight, the skiff stopped short, and Linc nearly toppled out.

Okay, untie the boat first; he knew that. He did so and backed out. He pulled the handle forward and the skiff went ahead, pushed the handle back and the skiff reversed. After repeating this several times (forgetting the neutral spot in the center) Linc felt confident enough to take the little craft out. He sideswiped the pier only twice on the way.

Linc figured out that when you pushed the motor handle one way the boat went the *other* way; then he discovered that the push had to be gentle to prevent tacking back and forth like a sailboat. A few minutes' practice and he felt ready to venture beyond the boats at their moorings. He chugged along at a cautious five miles per hour until he'd cleared the harbor breakwater, then caught his breath as the first wind waves slapped the seaward side of the skiff.

Okay, this was "at sea" enough, wasn't it? After all, the whole damn ocean was sea, including the harbor. He turned to—port, was it?—eased back into sheltered water, and struck out parallel to the little beach, away from the hazard of the other boats.

At what looked like a safe distance, he turned the throttle all the way down to idle, but the skiff, still in forward, kept moving. He didn't dare kill the motor—what if he couldn't restart it?—so he pushed the handle, tiller, whatever, to one side and held it with his knee. The skiff began a slow, tight corkscrew pattern.

Eighty yards away and twenty yards higher, Tassy Morgan spied the dinghy from her studio window. Tassy's studio spanned the harbor side of her shack above the beach. She painted on a large flat board instead of an easel because she used a wet-paper watercolor technique and water persisted in running downhill.

With yet another corny seascape finished, she was resting her eyes on the harbor view when she saw something moving out beyond the pier and the moored pleasure boats. Tassy grabbed her brass telescope and swung it around on its tripod. It was her neighbor from across the street, out in a flimsy skiff. She focused the long yellow tube and started tracking the boat, which was sketching small spastic circles in the afternoon chop. Its behavior seemed a bit weird, but then so did her neighbor—from what little she knew of him.

Unlike Tassy Morgan in the shack looming over him, Erik Halvorsen didn't notice the skiff. Walking the beach below her, he was looking up at the bluff that lifted her shack fifty feet above high tide. Tassy's front deck was propped up by a tangle of braces and pilings improvised ad-lib as the bluff slowly crumbled from under it. At its glacial pace, erosion would take a thousand years to eat the little town on its plateau, but Tassy's cottage was first on the menu and the ocean was nibbling away.

Stupid white people, what did they expect? Erik's own forebears had built houses of wide cedar planks lashed with vines and deer sinew that could be dismantled and moved in one day. They'd used this sacred stretch of beach as a fish camp, summer after summer for hundreds of years. He could imagine sleek cedar log canoes pulled up on warm sand, fish drying on woven racks, dogs and bare-ass kids running into the surf. Unhappily, none of it remained—not so much as a single bead.

Now it was white people's dogs running loose on the beach— shitting on the ancestral home of his people. He glared down the long swath of sand at a stocky dog that was nosing the washed-up kelp. As if in response, the dog looked up at Erik and barked twice: *bark*, pause, *bark*, as if to greet him. The white people needed that beach for their tourism. Without it, White San Andreas was just another rural backwater, ignored and slowly dying.

Erik Halvorsen was Narowa, a full-blooded Native American except for the itinerant logger who had absentmindedly sired his great-great-grandfather and thereby started a family with Viking names. Erik wore his hair in a long black braid but was otherwise dressed in a crisp broadcloth shirt and expensive, well-pressed slacks, now stuffed into calf-high barn boots. Handsome and self-assured, he resembled a Saudi business executive. Shaking his head over Tassy's rickety shack, he continued shooting the bluff, the beach, and the foot-high surf with a shirt-pocket camera.

Gradually, the irregular noise of an outboard caught his attention, a faint-loud-faint-loud pattern that didn't sound normal. Sure enough, one of the bait shop skiffs was out there bouncing around in incompetent circles. Erik couldn't quite see who was in it—a tourist, maybe, or one of the new invaders. San Andreas had too many white people already without all the boomers pushing in.

They took over the town government because the locals couldn't be bothered with it. They forced locals out of the housing market by paying insane prices for shacks like the one above him.

The only thing white people didn't steal was local jobs, because there weren't any.

Except at the casino. Erik smiled briefly; the Narowa owned the casino.

And Erik's grandmother owned the Narowa—maybe *owned* was too strong, but she'd been tribal chair as long as he could remember—and what Grandmother Halvorsen wanted, she got. And like any entrenched sovereign or CEO, she did not condescend to explain things. She'd simply said, "Go take pictures with that little camera of yours. Make it look good." Well, that wasn't hard. With its sweep of warm sand, gentle surf, and sparkling tide pools, the San Andreas beach was gorgeous.

Fifty yards out in the water, Linc was still running the skiff in circles and grumbling at his ridiculous task. Burial at sea had sounded romantic when he and Ellen discussed it two decades ago; at thirty you're still immortal. But aneurysms could bloom at any age—in Ellen's case, forty-eight. The little seacoast village had an ambulance, but her arterial blossom had opened and killed her before she'd reached the hospital thirty miles south. Nearly half an hour in that big red can screaming Code 3 all the way down US 101, holding Ellen's hand, fighting to keep his seat on the side bench and stay out of the paramedics' way, wondering was it hypocritical to pray? Stumbling into Emergency, then sitting, sitting, memorizing fake wood grain on the admitting counter front, sitting, sitting. When they finally came out their expressions said it all.

Back in his little skiff, Linc tried a deep breath, but his ribs and diaphragm were clamped and he had to suck the air in little sips. Okay, okay: to the job at hand.

With Ellen's mother warehoused in a Florida care factory and her sister lost in some personal fog, arrangements had been up to her husband alone. When Linc had agreed to cremation, he'd been too stunned to realize he'd be stuck with a jug full of ashes. What the hell did you do with it, display it like a golf trophy, stash it in a closet, throw it in the trash? He'd kept the damn can under his bed for over six months now.

Ellen really had talked of burial at sea, and San Andreas had been her dream: owning a B and B in redwood country, overlooking a stunning blue bay where gray whales romped around sea stacks and harbor seals honked at low tide. She'd had her wish for just six weeks, and now she would sleep with the whales.

Linc extracted the urn from the grocery bag and stuffed the plastic into a pocket. He studied the steel can until he'd figured out the latch. Pulling the lid, he discovered gray ash and a few larger chips.

Aw jeez. He sat there staring at the powdery mess. The skiff chugged round and round while Linc tried to summon memories of Ellen. But the sorrow, the grief were still so strong that they scooped out all the details of their lives together and left nothing inside.

After several minutes he sighed and stood up. The skiff lurched and Linc sat down again fast while the motor, freed from his knee, centered and pushed the boat forward. He dropped the urn, snatched it up to keep it from spilling, lost the lid, grabbed the tiller, pushed it over, and trapped it again with his knee. The boat resumed its tight spirals.

Time to get serious. He would wait for the right point in the boat's circular path to dump the ashes on the landward side so the sea breeze could not blow them back. He'd have to stay seated and lean out over the knee locking the tiller.

The plan worked, more or less. The little skiff waggled alarmingly, but settled as a small sad cloud of Ellen floated to the water. Linc thought he should say something but couldn't think of a damn thing except *Good-bye.* His chest felt filled again with that thick, clogging stuff that stopped his breathing. Okay, then, good-bye, Ellen. Good-bye. He sat some more but the suffocating clog wouldn't go away.

Shit: Gray ash coated the boat's edge. Holding the urn, he leaned over past his knee again to dip up water for washing it down. Too far to reach. He slid closer on the seat and tried again. Abruptly, the skiff tipped Linc and his tin can into the drink.

Linc flailed around, and as his clothes and shoes dragged him under he wondered, Why not just keep going on down? But his lungs disagreed and he sputtered to the surface in time to see the motor, re-centering again, push the boat away toward the beach. What had Dorothy Parker said? *You might as well live.*

Up on the beach, Erik Halvorsen turned when he heard a yell and a change in the outboard sound. The idiot tourist was flailing around in the water, holding up something shiny. Erik started toward the surf line, then stopped as the guy slowly rose out of the water, which turned out to be maybe four feet deep. Shrugging, Erik resumed work with his tiny Nikon.

After a few minutes the tourist plodded into view, sopping wet and sandy up to the knees. Erik paid him no attention. The man looked around in a dazed kind of way, then shambled over.

He said, "Is there any way off this beach?"

Erik studied him impassively. Now he recognized him: not a tourist but a new invader, one of the boomers.

The man gazed around vaguely. "How did you get down here?" He appeared wiped. His hands were shaking and his face seemed on the verge of breaking up. Drugs, maybe?

Erik pointed at the sandy bluff. "There's an access path there."

The dripping man peered at the faint indentation that wavered up the bluff face. "That's a path? Is there no other way?"

Erik shook his head. "That's it. Be careful."

The guy stared blankly at the perilous climb, then shrugged indifferently and shuffled off toward it.

In the house at the top of that path, Tassy wondered about this neighbor, whom she called the Zombie. She'd noticed him several times, lurching up the road past her house—not really lurching, of course; just sort of plodding. He could have been good-looking in a mildly weathered way, but his blank zombie face looked dead and dug up.

Twenty yards up the gently sloping street, he would turn into the walk of the big old house across the way and disappear inside. The house was appropriately gothic. It had briefly been a B and B, but now no one entered or left but the Zombie.

When her neighbor fell out of his boat Tassy wondered what to do about the accident. She was reaching for her phone when the Zombie reemerged from the depths. More and then more of him rose up out of the ocean until . . .

He started wading through water that didn't reach his hips, and Tassy burst into delighted laughter, a honking guffaw that made some people smile but had always irritated her ex-husband and mortified their daughter.

The memory was enough to kill Tassy's mood. Two years now and the past could still chop her into pieces. It wasn't her laugh or any other one thing that had been judged unacceptable. It was her self, her whole self, and she still couldn't really guess why. When her husband had explained it, the individual sentences made sense but she just couldn't add them together. No matter how he put it, it seemed to boil down to one thing: Somehow, Tassy wasn't likable; people didn't like her.

Okay, deal with it. Let's see, three o'clock, so the mail had arrived, another big excitement in an already big day. She wandered through the great room—if an awkward ten-by-twenty space could be called "great"—and opened the front door.

As she pulled stuff out of her mailbox the Zombie rose slowly into view again, this time in the gap between her house and the next one. He was sopping wet, of course, but his eyes were alive now and his look was puzzled. He moved a few feet forward along the side of her house. "Am I trespassing?"

"Not really." Tassy smiled and crossed toward him. "I'm Tassy Morgan."

"Linc Ellis," he said absently, then, "Tassy?"

"Mm-hm, Anastasia. You run the B and B, don't you?"

"Not anymore." She waited until the silence drove him to add, "What do you do?"

"I paint—mostly seascapes for tourists."

A blunt gray dog—a stranger to Tassy—appeared over the lip of the bluff and trotted forward with what she could swear was a smile on its face. It wagged its tail briefly at the two of them, but since the tail was curled into a tight upright spiral over its back, each wag amounted to just a two-inch vertical twitch.

"Don't strain yourself," Tassy said, smiling at the dog, and its own smile widened into a downright grin. It offered her two more underdone wags and loped off.

As if none of this had happened, Linc said, "Paint. Paint is good." She had the feeling that he was operating his mouth by remote control. "Painting is good." The distant controller pulled his mouth into a smile. She had a strong impulse to gather him to her and rock him.

"Well . . ." he said vaguely, "thanks." She raised her eyebrows and he added, "For the free passage."

Erik Halvorsen climbed into view on the beach path and walked past them. "Hey, Tassy."

"Hi, Erik."

Erik headed for a van labeled "Okega Casino" parked at the curb.

"Do you know Erik Halvorsen?"

As if he hadn't heard, Linc said, "Is the path some kind of easement?"

Tassy nodded at the next house over. "My property goes all the way to that rental, give or take. Why do you ask?"

"Pure reflex; I'm an attorney."

His conversation was as damp as his clothes, but he was clearly suffering from who knew what—and suffering instantly triggered Tassy's mothering mode. Besides, there was something else about him that made her want to hold him there. "What's the fancy can?"

Linc looked at it as if he'd forgotten, then: "Cremation urn—bottom half, anyway," and the life leaked out of his face. He absently waved good-bye with the can and started off.

Tassy stared after him, connecting the dots to his antics in the boat. Though she didn't pay attention to village gossip, she recalled somehow that he'd lost his wife. She thought, better to die than walk out on you, then hated herself at once and wondered if she could do anything for him. Tassy watched Linc plod up the street as she opened a letter.

She scanned it.

"Sonovabitch!" she remarked.

~

Erik snaked the van along a two-lane road lined with ancient coast redwoods pierced by shafts of sunlight—a stretch that had starred in fifty car commercials. Though he'd walked or driven through this venerable grove since childhood, these tallest of all living things never failed to make him shiver with something he would not quite admit was fear. The enormous trees were so very old, so implacably *uncaring*. Time out of mind, his people had lived in the narrow band between the indifferent sea on one side and the silent redwoods on the other.

The casino was only a mile north of town, but signs every two hundred feet assured customers that they were almost there. He swept up the welcoming drive, rolled past the thousand-car parking lot, stopped in front of the big glass doors, and surrendered the van to a man in a Windbreaker with the Okega logo.

The building was perhaps the most tasteful casino in North America, all redwood and glass and tubular steel beams that echoed cedar logs without trying to imitate them. Erik pushed through the doors, passed the gift shop full of Indian souvenirs (all third-world made and none of them Narowa culture), crossed a field of slots and blackjack tables, and entered his grandmother's office. As chair, she kept her official office in the tribe's administrative center, but Grandmother found the casino more convenient, especially its excellent restaurant.

Aside from a few of the Narowa's antique (and now priceless) baskets, her office decor was 1970 government issue, retained from the years Grandmother had spent as an Indian Affairs attorney at the county seat. She still wore the careful face and clothes that seem to mark public servants from clerks to commissioners, and her handsome Indian features had grown beautiful with age and authority.

The Narowa did not have chiefs as such, but as chair Grandmother was theoretically first among equals. In fact she was boss, plain and simple.

Erik kissed her on the forehead. "There's white people on our beach again."

Grandmother smiled. "Not our beach, Erik, not yet. It still belongs to the county."

"It's our ancestral summer village."

Grandmother gazed at him stone-faced until he felt put in his place. "Focus, Erik. Did you get pictures?" He nodded. "Then pick out the best shots and make color prints—make big ones, for a council presentation."

"The tribal council?"

Patiently, "No, the county."

"I thought the city owned the beach."

Grandmother shook her head. "It's unincorporated county. We don't have their attention yet, but their budget's down three million this year. They could make it all up by selling us one little beach nobody uses." She grunted in frustration. "So far, we're getting nowhere with them."

2

The inland side of San Andreas was not picturesque. THE NO-FAULT CITY said the sign below the freeway off-ramp, which puzzled the too-infrequent tourists, mostly Dutch or German, who didn't get the joke. The Pacific was invisible, and a regrettable trailer park masked the perky tourist shops beyond it. The gas station and market were new and clean—which was more drawback than asset because too many tourists gassed up, bought deli subs, and got right back on the freeway to resume their inspection of giant coast redwoods, to the despair of the city council, the chamber of commerce, the merchants association, the beautification committee, and the visitors bureau. All five had essentially the same members, but each cherished its own name and letterhead stationery because the residents, especially the newbies, liked being presidents and treasurers. Besides, in a village of five hundred souls, the talent pool was a puddle.

The ocean side of town was more attractive, mostly businesses in shingled cottages painted tasteful colors and set about with cheerful potted plants.

Tassy Morgan paid the buildings no attention. Long hair flying, long legs pumping, she charged past the Seaside Café and the Good Vibrations Internet and latte parlor, past the Sea Breeze boutique and the Ocean's Bounty tchotchke shop, and up the walk of a tidy bungalow, where she jumped three steps to the porch and rattled the brass ship's bell. The sign beside it said WELLESLEY GALLERY.

The eponymous owner opened the door, bowing slightly. "You rang, madam?" He looked elegant in designer jeans and sockless Top-Siders. The jeans had a sixty-inch waist and his open-necked blue oxford button-down was custom tailored to contain him. Of course Wellesley's nickname was Orson.

Tassy shook the letter in his face. "Orson, you wrote this!"

"Correction: The planning commission wrote it—well, the majority did. *I* voted against it. They decreed that you can't tear down your disreputable shack, darling. It's a disreputable historical monument—or something." Through twenty-five years of West Coast exile, Orson had cherished his W. F. Buckley drawl.

"Monument to what? It's a cheesy, sixty-year-old beach house built by some local speculator who ordered the plans by mail—the worst kind of postwar ticky-tacky—and now it's a hopeless wreck!"

"It's a *midcentury classic*, quote-unquote, though it does indeed run down the neighborhood."

"I'll appeal."

"The commission meets again in six months." Though he savored emotional scenes, Orson was not unsympathetic. "Darling, I did my best for you."

"The bluff it's on won't last six months. It's crumbling. I wake up at night to the sound of tiny landslides under my bedroom."

He nodded. "Sands of time and all that."

"*Orson, what do I do with my house?*"

"*I* don't know, darling; paint it?"

"*Paint it?*"

To sidetrack her, Orson swept a thick arm around Tassy's shoulders and guided her over to a gallery wall. "Notice anything different?"

She studied her four big watercolors, matted and glazed on the burlap surface. "Hey, three of these are new. Why'd you replace my other ones?"

"For some unfathomable reason, the buyer wanted to take what he'd paid for."

"All three?"

"Nine hundred dollars' worth." He squeezed her shoulders. "Cheer up, sweetie; the tourists love you and so does Orson."

"But my house . . ."

"Now, go paint redwoods for me. I can sell *tons* of redwoods."

Tassy returned home still angry but somehow comforted. Orson had that effect on people.

～

Linc Ellis was staring into space out his front parlor window when his neighbor came steaming up the other side of the street. She paused at her house but instead of turning in, started pacing back and forth, looking at it. Intrigued in spite of himself, he watched her. It didn't hurt that her work shirt suggested major convexities, her hips rambled nicely, and her thick hair swung in the sunset breeze. He wondered what her legs were like inside those jeans—long enough, he could tell that much; she had to reach nearly six feet. She stomped up and down, up and down, waving her arms as if having a fight on a mobile headset. Linc wished he had that much energy—wished he had any, for that matter.

Then she froze as if struck by some kind of brainstorm. She checked the demure, pretty cottages flanking her eyesore, then shifted and stared at the B and B. Linc retreated from the window but she turned away as if she hadn't seen him. Another moment of staring at her walls and then she disappeared inside. What was her name? Tassy.

Inside her shack Tassy headed straight for the yellow pages in her studio. She'd driven past the Ace Hardware store at the county seat, but she needed to find out how early they opened. She was half-way across the room when she saw the animal on her rickety deck, sitting quietly outside the glass door. It was the chunky gray dog she'd seen coming up from the beach.

She unlatched the door and slid it back. "Hey, dog. How'd you get up here?" Tassy smiled and squatted but did not reach out. The dog smiled back at her. "Are you friendly? You look friendly." The dog rose and approached her, then sat down within petting distance. It watched her with a steady, self-possessed calm that was almost unnerving. "You look like you're smiling, but I know that's just an accident, like dolphins." The dog opened its mouth into a full grin. "Or is it? Are you laughing at me?" The dog advanced until they were nose to nose, then licked her. Just once. No slobbering, no lap-lap-lap stuff; just a quick canine smooch.

Without thinking, Tassy wrapped her long arms around the dog and hugged it. It burrowed in as if it enjoyed this and then stayed quiet. She buried her nose in the thick, gray ruff at its neck. Its smooth coat smelled slightly of salt and a hint of—what?—kelp, maybe, but not of dog, though the animal was fairly wet.

Whoa, what was happening? She felt like she was hugging her long-lost Gran or some lover just home from a war. She unwrapped herself and stood. How could she feel so strongly, so suddenly, about a strange dog?

"Well." Tassy steadied her voice. "Well, you want to come visit a bit?" She stood up and backed away from the door and the dog paced into the studio. Then it stood still, as if waiting in a starting gate: head high, pointed ears pricked, burly chest thrust forward, fluffy tail still curled in that vertical snail that mussed up the fur on its back.

It looked like a husky that had been shortened, front to back, by squeezing, with the excess shoved into its chest. But instead of uncanny blue husky eyes, its eyes were deep, liquid brown and each was bordered with a thin black line that extended back across the temple, as if the dog were made up as Cleopatra.

What was he, some kind of spitz? Was he a *he*? Yes, he was—or at least had been, before his sad but responsible loss. She said, "I'm going to sit in the living room. Want to come?" When she turned and walked off the dog followed, and when she sat, the dog sat erect on the floor in front of her. Tassy held a hand over the adjacent couch pillow and snapped her fingers. The dog jumped up and curled beside her.

What she could feel through his heavy coat didn't seem undernourished. She rotated his collar until she could read his tags: a current county dog license and a disc stamped "Beowulf," with a phone number. She scratched under his off-side ear and he laid his head on her thigh.

"Beowulf?" He raised his head and looked at her. "Oh, don't give me that yearning look, but aren't you a love!" She knew better than to follow that thought, so she added hastily, "Better get you back home."

But when she dialed the number on her cell phone, she got a disconnect message. Well, okay, the county could look up the owner by the tag number. Too late to call them today, though. She could be in love with Beowulf for just this one night.

~

By the next morning, Beowulf had disappeared through the sliding door left open for him. Probably just as well, though she couldn't help feeling disappointed. On the thirty-mile drive down to Ace Hardware, she told herself sternly she shouldn't worry about every loose dog in the world; but she bought a double dog bowl and a grooming rake like a short length of coarse band-saw blade with a handle at each end. She checked again when she got home, but still no Beowulf. Well, she could always take the stuff back.

By the time she was ready to start, the morning fog had burned off, which was good if you were using water-based paint. Tassy pried the lid off the gallon can and studied the contents approvingly. She was prepped to go in paint-spotted jeans and an oversize man's shirt, her long hair trapped in a ponytail and covered in front with a calico do-rag. She deployed drop cloth, paint tray, and roller on her tiny front stoop, then poured the succulent pigment. Excellent!

Half an hour later, Tassy was too absorbed in her painting to notice the giant white SUV that rolled slowly up, paused across the street, and then, in silky silence, rolled on. If she'd looked, Tassy would have seen that the driver was a woman with a beautiful Asian face, a vicious American scowl, and a ladies-who-lunch scarf, who was just lifting a phone to her ear.

It wasn't ten minutes more until big Jack Millhouse barreled through Linc Ellis's kitchen door, yanked him away from his coffee, hustled him into the front parlor, and shoved his nose against the window. "Look at her, look!"

Linc glanced sideways at him. "Where'd you come from?"

"I—well, Margaret Nam called me and—never mind, look!"

Across the street, Tassy had paint-rolled half her narrow housefront a pulsating purple and was now applying a vomity green to the window trim, working carefully, like the artist she was.

"Ya gotta stop her, Linc." Millhouse's voice, always damp somehow, sounded downright sweaty.

Linc tried to keep a straight face. "Me?"

"You're city attorney, aren't you?" Puffing from his run, Millhouse ran plump fingers through thinning carroty hair.

Linc smiled out at the lush woman in ratty clothes who was finishing one of her windows. "Only pro bono. You want the police force."

"Willard's off today. Look, Margaret Nam says the ordinance is clear: gray or blue colors, pastels preferred."

"You're the mayor; *you* do it."

Millhouse blanched. With elections six months off, he viewed controversy—*any* controversy—as a ticking bomb. His safest course was to delegate, then hide. It rarely failed. After visibly straining to think of a plausible evasion, he came up with, "You want a purple house in your view? What'll your guests think?"

"I don't have guests." Still gazing out, Linc wondered what it was about the woman that just made him smile. And when had he last smiled, anyway?

Millhouse embroidered his plea. "You'll have guests; you'll re-open. Besides, the town needs this B and B."

"*You* need it to help fill your coffee shop."

"*Restaurant.*" The mayor's Seaside Café was just around the corner and Ellen's guests had been generous spenders. Linc had thought of them as *her* guests, as if he just roomed at the B and B they'd both owned.

The mayor's round face shone with sincerity. "Linc, the town's counting on you." Millhouse was another immigrant who had re-treated to this micro-city because he could be a big shot here. He and others like him farmed the municipal power structure, such as it was, watering, weeding, manuring their local influence. Linc was city attorney only because he'd volunteered to work for free back when he and Ellen had wanted to become part of things. He'd grown bored with it even before her death, and close to seven months afterward, only inertia kept him in the job.

But the woman who'd swept purple paint across her housefront gave off a kind of—what?—almost electricity and Linc felt like some sort of dimly sentient battery that knew it was almost discharged. It might be intriguing to learn what she was up to. Linc nodded okay to Millhouse, whereupon the mayor snuck out through the kitchen, sidled across three backyards, and disappeared toward the safety of the next street.

~

When Tassy caught sight of Linc she had just started on the other half of the housefront. Her technique involved slopping a long upright slash with as much paint as she could and then rapidly spreading it with lateral roller strokes. She'd laid on the first up-and-down swash and pushed paint out to the right with a vigorous swipe across its top when Linc entered her peripheral vision.

"Morning, uh, Tassy." He looked woebegone, as usual, though the tips of his mouth were curled slightly. What had once been a business shirt hung free of his pants, its front a history of recent meals. The pants themselves had been quality goods in some remote time before their fall. This moldy ensemble was bracketed by a three-day beard at one end and flip-flops at the other. The man looked like a wino who'd once been an uptown broker.

"Linc, isn't it?" She glanced at her own grubby clothes. "I think you win."

He didn't seem to notice. "New paint?" As a conversation starter that had to rank right up there with *Hot enough fer ya?* so Tassy waited. "Purple," Linc ventured, besting even his previous try. "It's, um, lively."

Okay, she'd rescue him. "Brightens up the joint, don't you think?"

He paused a long moment, then shrugged. "Thing is, I have to tell you purple's unacceptable."

Tassy looked suddenly dangerous. "To you or your guests?"

"To the city. I don't have guests. There's a color code—part of the Beautification Initiative." When she snickered he added, "I didn't name it—or write it."

"And you would be?"

"Volunteer city attorney—for now, anyway."

"Look, volunteer city attorney for now, I'm damn sick of being told what I can't do with my own house."

"Right, yeah." He seemed at a loss. "I sympathize, but we—well, *they*—can take you to court."

"Let 'em."

"Aw, don't make it hard. . . ."

Tassy surged from warm to boiling. "Make it hard? Try *this* on!" With violent sweeps of the roller, she added a lower crossbar to her vertical, then swooshed a big arc to the right of it. Two roller *bonks* for punctuation and the wall screamed "F.U." in three-foot vibrating DayGlo capitals.

Linc felt energized by this big, vital woman. She had to be fairly close to his age but she moved with an almost violent force, slashing out the big *F*, pouncing and bending on the *U*, jabbing the painted periods. When she turned to confront him her face was red and the rag across her forehead had slipped to a pirate tilt. She cocked her fists on her hips, still holding the roller.

He paused, feeling electricity in the air, then said, "You're dripping on the porch."

"Fuck the porch."

"That's not my kink."

Tassy froze, then erupted in laughter, great honks like some baritone goose; and without knowing it, Linc started laughing too, feeble *heh-heh-hehs* compared to her bugling, but his very first laugh nonetheless.

Just to keep things going, he said, "Maybe we could talk this— you know . . ."

"Okay, I'm done"—she aimed her roller at him—"for *now*." She docked the roller in its tray. "You better come in." Tassy walked into the house, leaving the door open. Linc followed.

The skinny front room had a thrift shop dinette to the right with a micro-kitchen beyond it, an open door on the left that revealed a rumpled bed, and a short center hall, through which Tassy led him to the big studio in the back. The cottage had clearly been built for this space. Its size and shape mirrored the front room, but rather than stingy windows flanking an entrance, five-foot glass panoramas filled the three outside walls, framing neighbor cottages, endless blue sea, and the green shoreline sweeping off into haze miles away. The ocean view was always spectacular, but day by day you got used to it. Presenting it in huge windows made it fresh again and Linc was reminded that San Andreas was, after all, an amazing place to live. He wandered toward the sliding glass door to the deck.

"Don't go out there; it's not safe. I'm losing the ground underneath it."

"Can't you fix that?" Linc continued to wander, looking at things, picking things up, putting things down.

Tassy perched on a high work stool. "This trash pile? Be better to tear it down. *Then* I could get a construction loan—you know, big enough to rebuild from scratch, do it right."

"But?"

"The town denied permission. Another of your rules."

"Not *my*—"

"I know, I know, but you're their enforcer, aren't you? You're the guy who breaks knees."

"I just do a little free legal work, and I only started eight months ago."

"Why do you do it?"

Linc considered the question while he stared at the restless ocean. Finally, "Originally—" He broke off and thought some more. "I guess it gives me something to do. Anyway, I promised them a year. I like your seascapes."

Tassy looked at him as if she'd caught his evasion, but she said only, "How about I trade you the paint color for a go-ahead on the building?"

He didn't respond.

"It would be the right thing to do."

Linc sighed. "The law's not about right and wrong; it's about legal and illegal."

Tassy sang in a doubtful contralto:

The Law is the true embodiment
Of everything that's excellent.
It has no kind of fault or flaw,
And I, Milords, embody the Law.

Linc grinned. "*Iolanthe.*"

"More or less. You like Gilbert and Sullivan?"

"I did it in college—played the Mikado and the Pirate King."

Tassy cocked her head, grinning back. "Somehow, I can't picture that—a corporate pirate king."

"Long ago. I wasn't always this way, you know." He frowned. "But then, nobody is." He wandered back toward the living room.

Tassy called, "How about my trade-off, counselor?"

"Not in the cards—citizen." When she strode angrily up to him, Linc added, "Of course, no law says you have to erase what you've already done."

Tassy frowned, puzzled. "Which side are you on?"

"Frankly, my dear, I don't give a damn."

"Except for the law."

"Except for the law." He meandered out the door and off the stoop.

As she watched Linc trudging homeward, she noticed Beowulf trotting down the street past him. When the dog spotted her he broke into a lope, and Tassy felt a little surge of pleasure. Hey, tomorrow would be soon enough to call the county about his owner.

3

By two p.m. everyone in San Andreas knew about Tassy Morgan's editorial, and three tourists had shot it with small cameras. The locals debated whether it was a gag or not, and if it was, whether or not it was funny. They didn't divide into pro and con groups—the town was too balkanized for that. The few wilted remnants of flower power thought it was groovy. The artist community applauded, but then they relished *any* controversy they could find and made them up when they couldn't. The old power elite, who had once run the town and still owned half of it, were now too feeble to notice.

On the blue-collar side, the crabber clans had better things to think of, like paying the rent in these lean summer months. The upholler libertarians who drove pickups into town to sell dope or find day work were similarly distracted, and the longtime resident working folks were mostly too cranky to give a shit.

The affluent immigrants, however, were not about to take it lying down. They hadn't finagled for years to co-opt the town just to have it trashed by some rogue artist type who wouldn't get with the program.

At the market's one checkout the topic soon faded, but it held up longer at the Hair Place, where Jimi worked big magic. Jimi'd lived in San Andreas for years, although she was a Paris-class stylist and so rich she didn't have to earn a living in San Andreas *or* Paris.

Jimi washed and cut and tinted hair because it was her métier. Like Tassy, she was one of the most talented artists in the area and the least self-important. Jimi's own hair was a pert, defiantly bottle-red bob, and her matching lipstick was always blotched by the cigarettes she sneaked between clients.

She scissored men too—or at least those men who refused to drive thirty miles to a barbershop that would make them resemble new-mown sheep. That included Mayor Millhouse, who cherished his wispy remnants enough to brave what he still called "the beauty parlor." Besides, the Hair Place was the switchboard for the San Andreas gossip lines and the mayor liked to tap them when he could. "Just a little off the top, Jimi."

Out of sight behind him, Jimi grinned. She could cut Jack's hair with about three snips, but the shop conversation was interesting enough to keep him in the chair awhile by snipping slowly.

Margaret Nam was in from her real estate office, getting her nails done yet again. That was good, though: Angela, the manicurist, needed the money, though Margaret wasn't big in the tip department. Jimi gave Angela extra from the till, on the pretense that she, too, had a stake in the shop, but even this quiet charity left her far south of the poverty line.

Angela did nails when she wasn't too pregnant to reach them. The pedicures went off at seven months but she could hang on to hands until nearly full term. Four kids in that shack off the old county road and now a fifth nearly baked; but Jimi thought, hell, it wasn't her business.

Extending her arm like a dainty pope, Margaret Nam allowed Angela to work on her fingernails—nails that were perfectly matched and neither long enough to look vulgar nor short enough to suggest manual labor. In due course, Angela would paint them a subtle shade chosen to signal both power and sex. *An executive siren*, Margaret Nam thought; the perfect balance.

The female children of Korean immigrants often drove their parents crazy with their fearsome energy and disdain for docile obedience. Korean drive and talent were equal in both genders, but only in America could the girls strike out alone. For Margaret, this had meant fleeing easy comfort and inevitable marriage in La Cañada, California, to build her business and her power here, though her mother kept phoning to describe suitable husbands in L.A. Her father, who had strictly forbidden her departure, wouldn't speak to his daughter at all, though she could feel his disapproval all the way up here, next to Oregon.

But when she finally got him to visit—and she would—he would find the most successful business and the most respected person in San Andreas. With her wealth and position secure, she could turn full-time to remaking her adopted town, a project already firmly in hand; and when people obstructed her she would recruit them or defeat them as needed. It was, after all, for their good.

Obstacle one was this noodle of a mayor, looking silly under a pink sheet while Jimi dawdled over his vanishing top hair.

Noticing Margaret's glance, Jimi said, "Saw you had clients, Margaret."

"They wanted to see the Sullivan place until they found out what 'distant ocean views' meant, so I drove them down to those beachfront houses—one of those darling rentals is for sale." Margaret looked severely at Millhouse. "And guess what they saw, Jack?"

Could Millhouse be as dumb as he looked, or was he simply stalling? He started, "Ah . . ."

"Half a purple slum, Jack. Right in between two beautiful properties: half a bright purple falling-down shack. I thought you took care of that this morning."

"Ah . . ."

"But when I drove back this afternoon—with clients, Jack—you had not taken care of it."

"Well . . ."

"Something else they saw too. Something added *after* you failed to take care of it. They saw 'F.U.' in purple letters, Jack, *big* purple letters." Her voice remained soft and silky.

The manicurist looked puzzled. "Somebody's initials?"

Jimi interrupted. "What'd you tell them, Margaret?"

Margaret waved a delicate hand, which Angela had stopped painting just in time. "I told them the town was taking care of that eyesore, but they just looked at each other and I knew I'd lost them. So what are you doing about it, Jack?"

"Ah . . ."

"You mean you can't make that Tassy Morgan clean up her house? I would be . . . *surprised* at that, Jack. I think everyone else would be surprised too."

"I'm working on it, Margaret." With unexpected grace, Millhouse signaled Jimi, left the chair, yanked off the pink sheet, and put a bill on the register shelf.

"Are you going to tell her?"

"A meeting." Jack hustled out the Hair Place door. "I called everybody—left you a message."

Another meeting at which Margaret would run things, as usual, but it would waste less time if she could do so officially, as mayor. Well, she'd have to be patient for six more months, until the elections. Margaret's beautiful face remained calm as she extended her hand again.

~

Norman Stihl wore the ruin of a romance hero face. His lean brown jaw wasn't lean anymore along the ridge line and his thick lion mane was graying, but his soulful eyes were only improved by the laugh crinkles, and his construction business kept his six-foot-three frame trim. Women often tried to take him to bed, and if they were even fairly presentable they succeeded. His accommodating attitude had lost him two wives so far, but Norman had lost them stoically, in the discharge of what he saw as almost a duty.

Now, Tassy here was a real good prospect even if she was almost his age: strong and tall and well upholstered. Norman watched her paint swiftly on a big sheet of wet paper edge-taped to a board. Yeah, she hadn't yet come on to him, but most women would in time, and if she didn't, she was choice enough to shift him out of neutral.

Norman had come into her studio after checking her sick front deck, which was almost a dead loss—hell, it could hardly hold his weight anymore. He'd also have to restore the bluff below it before building a replacement. He said, "I'd give it six months, tops."

"I still don't have thirty K." Tassy swirled a brush in her cleaning water and wiped it with a rag.

"Could be a cheaper solution—hell, there's *always* a cheaper solution. Trick is to think it up." Norman rescued houses for a living, and there was lots of work on the bluff above the beach and those crumbly hills behind it. "But that's a lot of planning to do—on spec, I mean." He dropped a pause in here but Tassy didn't fill it. "We could talk it over, though." Another unfilled pause. "You know, discuss it informally—make plans." Absently, Norman registered on the dog under the worktable. It looked like Beowulf.

Tassy straightened up, wincing slightly, and studied him over her glasses. "Thank you for the offer, Norman." With that odd little smile on her, he couldn't tell whether that was a yes or a no, or even which offer she meant.

Norman leaned back against a table edge and casually folded his arms like his role model, George Clooney. "I like watching you work. You're a real pro."

"You're pretty smooth yourself."

She didn't look up again, so the Clooney pose was a loss, but

Norman could be patient; and anyway, Margaret Nam was already scratching his itch these days.

~

Meanwhile, Linc Ellis had joined San Andreas's leading citizens in the Seaside Café, Mayor Jack Millhouse, Prop. This ad hoc gathering was standard procedure; half the town business was conducted without the inconvenience of the public meetings required by state law. The only eight-place booth was plenty for the five members of the . . . well, what? Dottie Franklyn, who owned the tchotchke shop, was secretary of the city council but announced that she was darned if she'd take minutes for the chamber of commerce, the beautification committee, the merchants association, or the visitors bureau, whichever. Dottie was a skinny, daft woman wound so tight that she'd twang if you plucked her.

"This isn't a meeting, Dottie." Millhouse sat at one end, where he could signal the only waitress on at four o'clock. He stirred his index finger in a circle above the table and mimed pouring coffee. "We're still in fact-finding mode."

"*Fact-finding?* Just which facts are we missing?" Margaret Nam's newly enameled fingers rested on the tabletop. "Shall I go take a picture for the record?" She waited until the girl had poured everyone coffee, then said, "I'm sorry, I'd rather have tea."

Smiling, smiling, the waitress removed the mug.

"Earl Grey."

"Fine."

"Decaf."

"Fine." And the waitress went off with the mug.

Sitting beside Margaret, Linc studied her serene beauty, her plu-perfect business suit, her signature scarf—Thai silk, or something like that; Ellen had never been able to teach him about clothes. He noticed that Margaret's laced fingers tensed and relaxed, tensed and relaxed, like a small animal breathing. Well, he was edgy himself, though he couldn't quite think why. Hidden under the table, his right hand was fingering the Rachmaninoff *Paganini Variations* on his thigh, with the virtual keyboard sliding left or right as needed.

"Sorry I'm late." Wheezing slightly, Orson Wellesley aimed his behind at the remaining outside seat, causing a hasty general side-shuffle to cede him most of the booth. "Chardonnay, please, darling." The waitress had followed him over and her smile for him was real.

Linc said, "There's nothing on the books to make her erase it."

Margaret nodded. "Yes there is: 'General Unsightly Condition.' "

Orson chuckled richly. "That covers half the town, Margaret. Think of Bill the Fixer's front yard carvings and that old car on blocks in Dave's driveway." He accepted his chardonnay.

"But they're not on a *Visitor-Designated Street*. That *woman* is, and every home but hers is *perfect*—picture perfect."

Linc was oddly pleased to realize that Margaret was pissing him off. Maybe emotions did come back, but gradually, like pain after an anesthetic wore off. Or maybe he was starting to feel proprietary about his whirlwind neighbor. He moved to sidetrack the issue: "Jack, how about Orson and I talk this over? He knows Tassy better than anyone. We'll approach her—you know—indirectly."

Hearing a subcommittee forming, Millhouse was eager to delegate. "Fine, Linc. Then I guess we're through here." He vacated his end so Dottie and Margaret could slide out. "Keep us posted."

Orson saluted with his wineglass and Linc nodded solemnly. "Will do, Jack."

As the others filed out, Orson Wellesley drained his glass. "Why do I drink this turtle piss?" He clicked his tongue as if at a bitter cough syrup. "What did you get me into, dear boy?"

"Orson, this situation is truly dumb."

The gallery owner nodded agreement.

"How'd you let it happen?"

"How did *you*? We're both on the planning commission."

"Well, true."

"But three of a kind still beats a pair." Orson shrugged. "You and I do what we can, but . . ." He smiled at the waitress and held up two fingers.

"What happened? I must have missed that."

For nearly seven months Linc had "missed" things at meetings while sitting right in them, but Orson knew why, so he just said, "She wanted permission to replace her house, which is indeed falling down, but is also a protected structure. She wouldn't take advice."

"How so?"

"In San Andreas, you don't replace anything; you *restore* it."

"That shack?"

Orson waved this away. "Show some drawings to the county building office—napkin sketches if you're Norman Stihl—which vaguely resemble the actual house. You promise honor-bright to preserve the whole structure, except, of course, for the few trifling bits that are too far gone to save. The county issues your 'restoration' permit and you tippy-toe back to San Andreas."

"But *all* of that structure . . ."

"Of course." The waitress delivered a tall plate of deep-fried onion rings and another chardonnay. Orson resumed with his mouth full. "By the time Norman's done, why, mercy sakes! Only one percent of the old house has proved savable—say, a foot of trim or something. Have a ring? No? This offer will not be repeated. The county comes out, signs off on the 'restoration,' and goes away. Norman returns, replaces the trim, and *voila!* a completely new house. Happens all the time."

"Seems unnecessarily—"

"Dear boy, this whole crappy town's on one list or another. If we didn't fib to the county and the coastal commission, we couldn't build *anything*."

"But Tassy didn't know this."

"Alas, no, and she wouldn't let me tell her. She has a thing about independence." Orson sighed. "Understandably."

"You know her well?"

Orson paused a moment, then, "Why?" He consulted his chardonnay.

Linc noted the watchful intelligence behind the airy manner. "I need to know how to approach her; I'd like to get her out of this."

Orson stopped in mid-munch. "You would? Hm." He considered this gravely, then nodded as if making a decision, leaned as far in as his convexity permitted, and shifted to deep-dish mode. "She's an absolutely classic trophy discard: Tassy bears the heir and puts up with her master's career obsession. So, after twenty-five years he has his big office, his McMansion, his perks and toys, and his bombproof portfolio." Orson paused to refuel with rings. "And, major surprise, he proceeds to pluck a twenty-six-year-old Ivy League diva—well, probably she plucked him." He propped his elbows on the table, laced plump fingers beneath his chin, and batted blue eyes at Linc. "'I am so tired of boys, y'know? I don't think a man grows up until he's forty.'

"Well, whoever plucked whom, the WASP beauty of this maiden is unspoiled by character and unblemished by thought. Her manners are good, her taste is trained, her legs are long, and her breasts expensive." Orson saluted this tidy summation with wine and caused the final onion rings to vanish. "Like most of them, she's got no hips to speak of, but childbearing isn't in her job description. The girl has one of those names like Lindsay—in fact, I think it is Lindsay."

Linc sighed. "How'd Tassy handle this?"

"The way she tells it, she stuck it out for weeks and weeks, hoping—well, you know how people hope. But when the daughter—

they only had one kid—lined up with the father, he of the bottomless bank account, Tassy finally picked up and left.

"Which was just *peachy* for the husband. In exchange for an uncontested divorce, the rat gave her a crummy beach shack and enough cash to not quite live on for not quite two years."

Linc's inner lawyer bridled instantly. "That's *all*? What'd the rat do, stick it to her with some kind of pre-nup?"

"*Qui sache?* Maybe just her dramatic gesture. You know, 'Give me a bankroll and someplace to live and I'm outta here'—Tassy does that kind of damn-fool thing."

"So she moved up here and started painting."

"Oh no!" Orson polished off his wine. "She was Chicago Art Institute, you know, a serious pro, but she mostly shelved it for the wife-and-mother thing."

"She's good."

Orson shook his head. "*Too* good for tourist seascapes, but not quite ready for New York. I wish I could find a niche for her."

Linc said, "It seems you care about her."

Orson smiled and nodded. "I do take care of her. She's my favorite pet."

"Will she see reason?"

"Tassy Morgan doesn't play well with others. Given her recent history, who could blame her?" Orson pushed away the empty plate and looked meaningfully at Linc. "Charm might work."

"From me? Then it's hopeless."

"Oh, I don't know. Tassy has a sensitive crap detector, and for a shyster—"

"I'm retired."

"For a shyster emeritus, you seem straightforward."

"That's why I'm emeritus."

An approving nod. "You operate sans crap." Orson inspected the check. "Wouldn't you know it: Millhouse hit me for a tea and four coffees."

Watching Linc leave the coffee shop, Orson sighed at his empty glass. He was all too aware that the good men were married or straight. Or in his friend Linc's case, mourning dead wives.

4

Sunset was kind to the ex–B and B. The warm light bathed the extravagant gables, wrapped around the three-story corner turret, and threw scrollwork shadows on the veranda. Linc's wife had had it painted soft gray and soft blue, set off with cream trim. As Victorians went, the house was a stunner, even in a county where tarted up Vickies were common as grazing deer.

Inside, Linc Ellis poured a Jack Daniel's, the first of two and two only, and tonight he would stick to it, so he splashed in some extra, just an inch or maybe two. He sat on the parlor window seat to watch the sunset, and if the sun was setting behind Tassy's house tonight, well, that was merely an accident of the solar calendar.

The sun retired reliably, and when the street had turned black and her windows had lit, he got up, stiff from sitting, and lit lamps of his own. He poured his second Jack, with just an extra inch or two—or had he done that with the first one? Whatever.

Rather than Victorian, Ellen had designed the parlor in mixed New England–Morris-Prairie: spare but comfortable furniture, Shaker for spare and Craftsman for comfortable. The lamps were Frank Lloyd Wright, and like the chairs and tables, they were copies, but good ones. The four bed-and-bath suites were similar. She'd been skilled at choosing pictures and she avoided lace curtains and cutesy collectibles. The effect was cozy but not with a capital *C*.

For well over six months Linc had been blind to it all. Now, in the glow of glass lampshades and whiskey, the parlor began to light up again.

Nice room; nice house; nice business; all hers. T'hell was he going to do with it? One good thing: she never had much chance to really live in the place, so it was still more her project than her home. Without an emotional link to Ellen it was nothing but *stuff*. Just give it to Goodwill.

Then what? He'd avoided *then what?* for months now. For a time, Linc had wished he could howl, rend his garment, do something, *anything* that would clear the stifling clot that so often filled his chest and hurt his heart and sent him stumbling around with his eyes not seeing. Now the squeeze on his heart had begun to relax—who knew why? Had he poured his second drink? He thought he hadn't. Had he already drunk that extra inch? Probably not. Ice clinked; whiskey chuckled from the bottle neck; good stuff.

Tassy's front room lights went out and Linc stared at their yellow afterimage. Off to bed early. She lived alone. She'd have her habits, her routines, her work—self-sufficient. Why couldn't he? Set the alarm tonight; get his ass out of bed in the morning. Monday, laundry; Tuesday, shopping; Wednesday, well, something else. Lay out the week, keep a schedule.

Bullshit. He couldn't even fill one day. Tassy painted, worked hard enough to sell them. What did *he* do? Pissant legal stuff for San Andreas. Have to deal with that paint job of hers. Tight-ass Margaret was right: *Unsightly condition* would cover it. There had to be a better way. Maybe if the town sprang for a repaint job . . . Fat chance!

Even so, *repaint* was an idea to play with.

Linc sank down on the window seat, tipped an ice cube out of his empty glass, and chewed it absently. He'd once been a world-class negotiator, resolving vicious conflicts, wheedling agreements, building baroque contract structures that made impossible movie deals possible. He couldn't have lost it completely—or could he? Linc crunched another ice cube.

~

The next morning Linc watched silently as Orson conjured what he called a "simple" breakfast. A superb cook, his friend held open kitchen for just a few special people, like Tassy and Linc, who could drop in whenever and did, though their visits had not yet coincided.

"Dear boy, you roped me into this." Orson swished a crepe like a fragrant platter out of the pan and poured another. "As her dealer, and, I might add, her only friend around here"—Linc raised a hand like a student in class—"all right, *almost* her only friend, I won't manipulate her."

Linc nodded sympathetically. "I just need one day, Orson—even a long afternoon." Having quit last night after three drinks (plus six inches) he felt almost okay this morning—better, in fact, than he'd felt in a while. Maybe it was Orson's bright kitchen or the late-May sunshine or the smell of breakfast. He watched the big man move with the dainty grace of Oliver Hardy, whipping batter, cooking crepes, deploying homemade jam.

"No more for me; I'll bust," Linc said.

"You're such a wuss." Orson dealt another skinny pancake.

Linc asked, "Any bright ideas?"

Orson pursed his lips and reviewed his crepe, then opened his phone and speed-dialed. "Tassy, darling, guess who. . . . Very funny. Listen, sweetie, I need a tiny favor: I'm running low on Spray Mount and foam core board. . . . No hurry, but whenever you happen . . . No no no, tomorrow's fine—better, in fact. . . . Hm? Well, I don't mean *better* better; that's just a way of speaking. . . . Get me two cans and some twenty-four-by-thirty-sixes. You're a pussycat. Bye, dear." He holstered the phone. "She's going into town tomorrow at lunchtime."

Linc considered: With punishing gas prices and a sixty-mile round-trip to the county seat, San Andreas folk tended to make long lists and consolidate shopping. He'd have all afternoon. "Thanks, Orson. By the way, can I have her cell number?"

Orson recited it and Linc punched it into his own phone.

"So, here's the deal."

"No no no! I want nothing to do with these shenanigans, whatever they turn out to be. Tassy'd wring my neck if I did." As if surprised at his own vehemence, Orson reined himself in. "You sure you won't have just one more crepe?"

Linc mimed feeling stuffed.

"At least some more jam, then."

~

Linc strolled down the non-tourist street where Bill the Fixer resided next to DayGlo Dave. The old friends' two cottages were tidy and well painted, though Bill's yard was invisible under a redwood army of carvings and Dave's was a sort of shrine to the Chrysler Corp. The eccentric front yards, plus the lack of curtains in the windows and flowers in the empty beds, betrayed these as all-male establishments. Bill's wife was long gone and Dave, well, somehow Dave never could get lucky.

The locals called him DayGlo Dave (though not to his face) because a long-past construction job at an old nuclear power plant had dosed him with enough stray rads to eventually give him cancer. It was more or less in remission now, but as always . . . who knew? He worked as a plumber, logger, carpenter, painter, yard man, paver, driver—usually one or two days at a time, like the other folks scrabbling to live in this remote small place where the big trees were gone, the crabs were going, and the tourists didn't need skilled labor. Dave was just fifty, but gnarled and weathered by punishing outdoor work, and his illness had burnt away all his body fat.

Linc found him in his tiny front yard, sitting on a concrete block next to his beloved 1970 Dodge Charger, which was sitting on several others. "Morning, Dave."

"Hey, um . . ."

"I'm Linc—from the B and B?" Dave had trouble with names sometimes and, after all, Linc was a newbie.

"Oh, yeah; 't'sup?"

"I've got some work, for you and—I don't know—maybe three others."

Dave spread his arms as if asking, *Do I look busy?*

"It's light work and I'll pay the full-day rate for four hours."

Dave stood up, a short, slight man in mechanic's coveralls, his thinning hair starting high on his head. "Can't beat that." His smile lit his gentle face.

"Who could you get to help?"

"Yo, for sure; he's always around." Yo was the local Source and since he dealt only weed, Police Chief (and total force) Willard wouldn't bust him because there was no place to hold him and the paperwork would take vital law enforcement off the street for hours—not that anyone had ever actually seen Willard on the street. Yo took his name from his usual greeting, and waggish clients would sometimes answer, "Yo, Yo."

Dave continued, "I think those kids in the van are still there." Flower-power microbuses, now as rare as cougars, still roamed the North Coast, overnighting in scenic highway pull-offs—sometimes for weeks. Since their drivers flaunted white-bread dreadlocks and lived without visible sources of income, the locals dismissed them as Trustafarians. Though they never worked, they would make an exception for Yo and his high-class ganja.

"Whatever you say. We'll need paint and tools, Dave, so you tell me what to get." Dave's forehead creased as he geared up for thinking.

Later, as Linc wearily drove the sixty-mile round-trip for supplies, he asked himself what he'd been thinking. Why was he roused to his biggest effort in months over a paint job he cared little about and the municipal bozos about whom he cared less? Because of her, obviously, but because of her *why*?

When Tassy drove off at noon the next day, Linc turned from his window stakeout and telephoned DayGlo Dave. Within twenty minutes, Linc, Dave, Yo, and a VW bus so old that it had the original tiny windows rendezvoused in front of Tassy's house. Yo was tall and thin and stood in a shallow S-curve. The van disgorged two young adults—loosely speaking—both blond and ripe smelling in matching rags and dreads, plus a toddler of uncertain age and sex. Dave carried two ladders and Linc supplied paint and tools from the hardware store.

He'd established a sliding pay scale proportional to speed, and the results were astonishing. Three dudes and a dudess who never moved faster than a mellow slouch launched themselves into an unrehearsed close-order speed drill. Yo and the Rasta man wielded rollers like short swords, while slow, careful Dave painted window trim. The girl, who worked with a sort of dazed intensity, was meticulous, painting the door. The kiddie went on walkabout, though no one seemed to notice.

Within an hour the visible sides and trim of the one-story house were repainted. California's environmentally correct paint wouldn't hide with a single coat, so they had to wait forty minutes. Dave unwrapped a sandwich, Yo and the couple climbed down out of sight for recreational inhaling on the perilous beach path, and Linc went out on a neighborhood sweep for the couple's free-range baby, who had long since disappeared. He finally found him two streets away, accompanied by a blunt gray dog with a wolf's face and a permanent smile. Linc watched as the dog herded the kid up to the frontage street, turned him downhill, and gently chivied him toward his parents.

Linc asked DayGlo Dave, "Who's the dog?"

Dave smiled. "Oh, that's Beowulf. Real smart dog."

Back on the job site Linc wondered vaguely where the dog belonged, but Beowulf was keeping the toddler busy—enduring the animal torture a two-year-old can inflict—so Linc turned to supervising a second coat of paint.

The street was unusually empty. There never were many tourists on a late-May Tuesday, but the locals too were absent, because Mayor Millhouse at one end and Constable Willard—caught in a surprise raid on police headquarters—at the other, were practicing ad hoc traffic control.

At about four fifteen, Dottie Franklyn, who was lurking in front of the Hair Place, in sight of the freeway off-ramp, spotted Tassy's little Ford and called Linc on her mobile phone. By that time, the recoat was dry and the tools and spare paint had been donated to Adam and Eve, who would probably use them to repaint their bus yet again. Linc had distributed greenbacks, some of which the young couple slipped at once to Yo. At Dottie's heads-up, Dave carried off his ladders, Yo melted away as was his wont, the VW wheezed out of sight, and Linc retreated to his parlor stakeout.

A few moments later Tassy rolled into view, parked, left the car, walked around to the curb, started toward her door—and then froze. Her house was suddenly blue, violently blue, the hard, bright blue of the Aegean Sea, and the wood trim was blinding Greek-whitewash white. Shock, amazement, fury—so many programs fought to open at once that her brain froze and crashed. When her phone rang, she opened it but was unable to speak.

After a moment she heard, "Tassy?"

Silence.

"Tassy?"

Finally she grunted.

"Hi," Linc said in a fake chipper tone, "this is Linc—across the street?"

She continued to stare at her house.

"Tassy?"

After almost a full minute, she shut her phone, pocketed it, turned, and paced slowly up the road.

When she arrived at the B and B porch, Linc was in his open doorway. "Say, do you have time to come in a minute?" His offhand delivery would have been funny if she'd noticed it.

Tassy nodded twice, slowly, and discovered a small, hoarse voice: "Oh, yes. Yes, I have time." Linc stood aside as she stalked into the parlor. She turned back toward him, still locked in a helpless stasis.

Now it was Linc's turn to stare, as if trying to read her reaction. He asked, "Drink? Iced tea, Steelhead ale, chardonnay?"

Silence.

"Jack Daniel's?"

More silence.

"That's about it."

"Steelhead."

Linc raced to the kitchen, clinked things, and raced back as if afraid to leave her alone. He held out a glass and the ale, but Tassy took just the long-necked bottle. She tipped back her head and drained it, the muscles in her strong neck moving as she swallowed.

Linc was starting a sigh of relief when Tassy shifted her grip to the bottle neck, swiveled at the hips, and fired a vicious underhand pitch at the parlor window. The tempered glass shattered, scattering sparkly crumbles on the floor and the porch outside.

When she turned back toward the frozen Linc, she felt almost functional. "Thanks. Like they say, I needed that."

Linc looked at the window, nodded several times, and then shrugged. "Let's talk."

"Let's *explain*."

"Let's negotiate." He cleared a chess set off a game table and they sat down facing each other.

"You sonovabitch; it was you, of course."

"Mm, and about seven others—eight if you count the rug rat."

"I think I'll call the police."

"Report vandalism? That's a municipal offense, so police equals Willard. You think he'd arrest the city council?"

"*All* of you?"

"Let the record show that Orson Wellesley disapproved and took no part."

"That's a relief. I'd have to burn down his gallery."

Linc sighed and studied her, then, "Tassy, let me lay it out for you—please."

She gave him an unreadable stare.

"The city was going to take you to court."

"Oh, *now* I'm scared."

Linc nodded. "The ordinance is so weak, you might win. But legal fees could get pretty high. I work for free, Tassy; who pays *your* lawyer?"

She reflected that her bank balance hovered in the low three figures and puffed out her cheeks.

He said, "Another ale?"

"Why not?"

"I'll bring it in a paper cup."

She couldn't help grinning and Linc smiled back. He went into the kitchen and returned with another bottle.

"You're trusting me with that?"

Linc smiled again and sat across from her. "Let's go all the way back to the start. You set out to paint your house purple. Problem is, the ordinance says blue or gray; no purple. Okay, so why not compromise? Paint it blue—hell, that's *almost* purple—but an *intense* blue, you know, like a Greek islands travel poster. The town gets its blue and you get your bright color."

"But I didn't say you could."

"Um, true. I thought if you lived with it a bit, you might come around. Hey, you got a free paint job—two coats, no less."

"On a shack that won't last six months." Tassy cocked her head and studied him. "I still can't figure which side you're on."

"The side of peace and quiet."

She stood up. "And I still didn't say you could."

Linc looked up at her. "Live with it a week, Tassy. If you still don't approve, I'll personally take the white trim paint and roll a new F.U. on your wall."

She looked at him.

"Ten percent larger."

She smiled inside, but countered, "Twenty percent."

"Fifteen."

"Done." She held his look. What was it about this guy? Though she was still pissed at the situation, he'd somehow deflected her anger away from himself. In some weird way, she was enjoying him. Tassy cast around for a reason to stay. "Got anything to eat in here?"

"Leftover takeout. How about that Beach House place?"

"Good. I won't have to change. Got any money?"

"Oodles."

"Even better." She couldn't decide whether *oodles* was literal or joking, not that she cared, but she liked the way he took her up on it—just like that.

~

The Beach House restaurant distilled every surf-side cliché: plank walls, fishnets, floats, crossed oars, seashells, rusty bollards, brass barometers, signal flags, rope trim, sailing prints—all soaked in the odors of grease from the kitchen at one end and booze from the bar at the other.

The view across the beach was the reason for coming. The surf was channeled by angular sea stacks thrusting thirty feet in the air and forcing the waves into spectacular crashes and swirling patterns of froth. Near sunset, the backlit spray spread gold lace patterns against the sky. Gulls wheeled, cormorants dove into the shallows, and stately pelicans swept by in tight formations. Fifty feet out, a clan of harbor seals festooned a flat rock just above the spray. Fat and indolent, they claimed the beach like nature's idle rich.

But that about covered the restaurant's charms. The food was underwhelming, so the tables were uncrowded, though they had fewer seats than the bar, where the patrons kept the stools warm and the well drinks pouring. Mainly locals, they continued the running conversations of old friends—or rivals or enemies; it didn't really matter—so the noise was a moderate buzz. Tassy and Linc found a free banquette whose vinyl had seen better years.

Then they waited for drinks to arrive. Tassy was still too upset to say much, so she studied the plastic menu with a care it didn't require.

After a long silence, Linc said, "I wonder what a bend is?"

"A turn in the road. Why?"

He pointed at the display hung above the back of the booth: a demonstration board of seafaring knots that had once been white but had turned the color of old clothesline. "See there in the center? A 'fisherman's bend.' What's it for?"

"Mm, and there's a sheet bend. Doesn't look like a bent sheet. Clove hitch, figure eight . . . bowline! I can do that one. My dad taught me years ago."

"Are your parents living?"

Tassy looked at her water glass. "No. I don't have anyone—now."

Jeez, that sounded so mawkish. She lifted her chin. "Free as a bird and liking it."

Linc cocked his head slightly, as if he didn't quite buy that.

The drinks arrived—Jack Daniel's and more Steelhead ale— furnishing safe conversation. Though neither Linc nor Tassy knew or cared much about drinks, discussing them sustained limp small talk until their orders had been taken—a chicken Caesar salad for Tassy and a seafood combo for Linc.

Then things slowed to a stop.

While Linc was inspecting the tablecloth thread by thread, Tassy took time to study him. He really was quite good-looking for a man of, what, fifty? He'd changed into an outfit that she thought of as casual prep. The shirt, pants, and shoes were expensive and he wore a blazer and open collar as though the Beach House was his country club. The watch on his left wrist had the classy finish that only the Swiss can deliver. His absent wedding band had left a deep dent and a ring of white skin. His right hand was invisible because . . . "What are you doing under the table?"

"I . . . what?"

"You're doing something with your hand under there." He looked so disconcerted that Tassy couldn't help laughing, and her goose-call honk had heads at the bar turning toward them.

Linc looked at her as if sorting out something complicated and then relaxed into a smile. "I was playing—"

"Do I want to hear this?"

"Scarlatti. A keyboard sonata."

"Under the table."

He demonstrated on the tablecloth, his fingers wriggling like a crab at a square dance.

"You play, then?"

Linc shook his head. "Not really. A little, long ago. Too impatient to keep it up."

Now, *that* was weird. "An impatient attorney. You must have been a trial lawyer."

Another shake. "Entertainment law—motion pictures. Contracts, mainly, for twenty wretched years."

"Why'd you stay with it?"

"Same reason Willie Sutton robbed banks. It's where the money was." It was his turn to smile. "It seemed like a good plan at the time. I made buckets of loot and invested a lot of it. We lived carefully—well, by Rodeo Drive standards. Ellen worked too."

Okay, he was willing to talk about his dead wife. "What'd she do?"

"Hotel management. Her dream was to buy a big old Victorian up here and open a B and B."

"Your dream too?"

"I thought so, but after she died—it was sudden—I realized I had no interest in it. Truth is, I never did."

"What *are* you interested in?"

"Haven't thought about that. Excuse me." Linc slid out of the booth and headed for the men's room. Tassy suspected he wanted to slide out of the conversation too.

Linc returned to the banquette to find dinner on the table. He signaled for more drinks and sat down.

His plate was a Heart Association wanted poster piled with clams, scallops, and shrimp deep-fried in batter that was optimized for retaining fat, plus french fries and a basket of bread and butter. A side dish of slaw made a feeble bow to the vegetable kingdom, but even it looked greasy.

Tassy ogled his plate. "Ooh, how I envy you." She patted her belly with her palm. "I have to watch every bite."

"Oh, I won't eat half of this."

"Well, don't ask for a doggy bag. I might mug you for it on the way back." She started on her Caesar salad.

Linc watched Tassy as she ate. Her shape seemed better than fine to him, though so unlike Ellen's. His wife had been neat, compact, as organized as a Swiss Army knife; his orderly soul had cherished that. Tassy was exuberantly large, and her big gestures and forceful aura captured even more space around her. Her laugh was as warm and raucous as the rest of her. Some of this warmth flowed over him and it felt good, like a wood fire after a long, cold walk.

She quizzed him about his life and work without any tact at all, and Linc found himself retelling anecdotes about the inanities of studios and the shenanigans of the sacred monsters who made movies. She laughed at everything and asked for more.

"You really like this stuff."

"Enough to watch the gossip channels and read the celebrity rags at the Hair Place."

"They're big spoiled kids, you know."

"But they have so much energy."

He suddenly realized that he'd loved dealing with those crazy people, loved the risk of being swept up in the whirlwind of their self-regard. Tassy was not unlike a movie star, but with the unpleasant parts left out. Maybe that's why she attracted him so much. By the time she'd finished her salad and stolen most of the fries off his plate, they were somehow friends of a sort, and an almost-buried part of Linc hoped they might be more.

5

Margaret Nam trapped Jack Millhouse behind his cash register, where he was organizing green breakfast tickets, and decreed that the paint job had failed.

"It's just as bad as purple—maybe worse because there's so much more of it." She said this quietly, pleasantly, knowing that her calm, tidy beauty was having its usual effect.

Poor wishy-washy Millhouse looked anxious, as well he might. "Ahh, Margaret . . ."

She continued, almost murmuring: "The wording's very clear, Jack: pastel blue or gray." Margaret took care to never raise her voice, use bad language, or crack her expression of calm politeness. She knew that a dozing leopard looked like a plus-size pussycat, but the natives would never risk waking it.

"Well, Margaret, I'm just as upset as you are." He half-placed a ticket on a stack, then picked it up as if he'd lost his count. "And I consulted our attorney immediately. Linc pointed out that it reads 'pastels *preferred*.' He says we can't take her to court over a preference."

Margaret was tired of pulling the strings of the people who pulled the strings. It was more than time to stop operating the mayor and start operating *as* mayor. She was making the stupid man so nervous that he picked up all his tickets and started over. All right. As always, she'd have to do it herself. "Do we have a book of city ordinances, Jack?"

The mayor's anxious look faded. "More like a binder, but yeah. I keep it in back with my gavel and stuff. Why?"

"I want to borrow it."

His cautious tone returned. "Oh, I'd hate to let it—"

Purring, "Are you telling me there's only one copy, Jack?"

"No! What I mean—I'm *not* telling you that."

"Well, then?"

Millhouse took a deep breath and actually sucked in his gut a bit. "Margaret, I think we got a good compromise here, and that house sure looks better than it did."

"Better, Jack, but not *good*. We'll never make this town a romantic vacation spot until it looks like a real seacoast village."

"Or a theme park."

She ignored this timid protest. "The ordinance book."

Margaret watched rusty wheels going round in his head, and then Millhouse improvised, "I'm, ah, tied up now, Margaret; I'll bring it to your office."

"Today, Jack."

"For sure, Margaret." She gave him her sun-emerging-from-clouds smile, turned, and clicked out in her elegant pumps. Margaret knew he was watching. She never wore pantsuits, because her legs were too good—and too good to waste.

~

In Latin America, *ranchería* meant the part of a *rancho* where the workers, largely Indian, were housed. As with so many other words, California co-opted and changed it to mean "a small area set aside for Native Americans." About a third are considered full-fledged reservations by the federal government. Hence, the humble San Andreas Rancheria of the Narowa functioned as independently as the great Navajo Nation, though the Navajos' slightly larger domain had hundreds of times as many people and thousands of times as much land.

Thirty years ago, the tiny tribal enclave north of San Andreas had held a haphazard collection of rotting trailers, barns, and sheds more or less separated by ad-lib kitchen gardens. The casino revenue had replaced this rural slum with tidy houses, some tribal built and others that were double-wide constructions posh enough to be designated "manufactured homes."

Grandmother Halvorsen's house, however, was made of real cedar logs, ordered as a kit from Connecticut. It wasn't an authentic Narowa house, of course, but nobody lived in those anyway nowadays, and besides, Grandmother was too old and too wide to crawl through a circular ground-level entrance cut small enough to exclude bears, and she had no problem conceding the superiority of the white man's bathroom, of which she had two-point-five. In fact, Grandmother had lived and worked all her life in the great outer world, returning to the rancheria only when she could retire in the style to which she was accustomed.

Erik found her in her greenhouse, an elaborate prefab of pipes and translucent panels, puttering with pots and plants and other stuff he never paid attention to. "Morning, Grandmother."

"It may be for you, but the rest of us call it lunchtime." She submitted to a cheek kiss.

"I had a late shift at the casino."

"And you didn't sleep well; I can tell." Grandmother rinsed her hands in the greenhouse sink and dried them on a festive kitchen towel. "Come have some iced tea."

"Can I have a soda?"

"That junk full of sugar? You'll drink my herbal and like it. Made it up yesterday."

In her Lincoln Log living room, she cleared two Harlequin romances off a chair and waved Erik into it. "Now—what's on your mind?"

Erik was used to her direct approach. "The beach thing. You said I'd have more to do."

"Not yet. Your pictures didn't do squat with the county board of supervisors."

"I still don't get why we have to take over that beach."

Grandmother sighed. Erik's father was barely smart enough to run the casino, and as for the boy himself . . . she feared that the long tribal reign of Halvorsens might be winding down. Patiently, she re-filled his iced tea glass. "Erik, what is our next big investment?"

"The resort?"

"One hundred and fifty luxury suites in the heart of beautiful redwood country."

"It'll take out the Johnsons' double-wide."

Still patiently, "And many others, but the rancheria's small and the ocean-view lots are few. The Johnsons will be taken care of, be-lieve me." Grandmother sipped her own muddy tea. "Now, why are we displacing tribal members to house a bunch of rich white people?"

"So they'll gamble."

"*Game* is the word of choice, but yes."

Grandmother stood and started pacing, as if in a courtroom. Though she was short and broad in the beam, her bone density was excellent for a lady her age and she carried herself with the inbred dignity of a social grande dame, which, of course, she was. "But we can't say that, Erik. 'Hey, rich white people: Come stay at our resort and eat too much and booze it up and blow your bankroll.' That's why it's called a 'resort.' We say, 'Come spa, play tennis, ride horse-back.' And now we want to say, 'Come get an Indian tan on our Indian tribal beach.'" The old lady smiled. "Most of them won't, of course. They'll just booze and eat and lose money."

"Why can't it still be the county beach?"

"Because then it wouldn't be our beach. We are going to have that land, grandson; we are going to own it again, the way we did before they stole it from us."

"But that was a hundred and fifty years ago."

Grandmother's glare was so fierce that Erik took refuge in his tea, then regretted it at once. Blinking tears, he changed the subject. "What's wrong with the board of supervisors?"

Grandmother looked suddenly grim. "Somehow, someone spilled the beans on our resort plans."

"Why would they object? We'll bring more tourists in."

"To *us*, grandson, not them. It's bad enough that our uppity redskin casino steals all the tourist dollars. Adding an executive-class resort—well, we might as well name it Custer's Last Stand." Erik's stern grandmother surprised him with a dry chuckle.

~

DayGlo Dave was attending an art preview in the yard of Bill the Fixer, one house up from his own. People really did address him as Bill the Fixer, because that was on his business cards, two thousand of which he had ordered in 1989 from a one-inch ad in the back of *Popular Science*. Like Dave, Bill would turn his hand to any job around, but unlike his best friend, he specialized in small engine, machine, and appliance repairs. He also excelled at carving redwood with chain saws, and his yard was populated with bears, eagles, and leaping salmon, plus totem poles (which belonged to cultures hundreds of miles north) and a sideline in little wood windmills with noisemakers to liven up boring front yards.

Bill had just finished his most ambitious work to date, a full-scale Narowa Indian holding a salmon net. The detail was perfect, down to the fisherman's basket-weave hat, which was amazing, considering that Bill claimed to carve with nothing but chain saws, the smallest of which was a lethal electric job with a ten-inch bar.

"How 'bout his net, Bill?"

"That's why I asked you to look. Think it's cheating?"

Dave studied it. The netting part was woven hemp and its rim was an undulating steel armature threaded with wooden beads to look like line, knots, and floats. Anchored inside the sculpture's wooden arm, the steel hoop held the net in midair. "I'll buy it," Dave said.

Bill took him literally. "You can't afford it. I'm hoping for an artistic tourist."

Dave knew that Bill's business sense didn't equal his carving talent, so year by year, his yard and drive and sidewalk filled to overflowing with unsold sculptures. "Maybe Orson Wellesley could sell some for ya."

Bill the Fixer snorted. "And take thirty percent?"

As things stood, Bill's take was now zero percent on a good day, but Dave was diplomatic in his quiet way, so he hunted around for a change of subject. "I made good money on that paint job; two hundred bucks for an afternoon."

Of course, everyone knew which job he meant. Bill the Fixer nodded. "Chances are, you'll get another two hundred for a repaint." When Dave looked puzzled, Bill added, "Some a the new folks want to make her change it. Willard told me."

"You *saw* Willard? Right out here on the street?"

Bill shook his head. "In the market." He thought a moment, then said, "Buying Copenhagen snuff."

Dave returned to the repaint topic. "Can they make her do that?"

"Who the hell knows? They got everything so fancied up—rules for this, rules for that. Use to be this was a quiet place."

Bill tended to heat up about stuff, so Dave switched the subject back again. "Anyhow, that's your best carving yet." Bill nodded thanks. "You oughta get five hundred bucks for that."

"Yeah, I should." He looked like the thought cheered him up some, which was good. Dave liked cheerful folks, liked to *make* them cheerful.

~

Two streets away, Tassy was also judging a large artwork: her house. She walked uphill toward the B and B, turned, and studied the shack with the shining sea and the late afternoon sun behind it, a perfect picture postcard. Back in front of the house, she inspected the blinding white trim. Repainted without being scraped, it made the place look raffishly cheerful, like a house in a Mexican village. How picturesque could you get?

Exactly! All the house needed was a whitewashed anchor in the damn front yard and a Sailors' Rest geezer whittling scrimshaw on the porch. Her shack had been tacky but at least it was real. Now it was as fake as the Indian jewelry in the tchotchke shop. Tassy started pacing. And Orson wanted paintings of redwoods! Jeez! How long before she started cranking out old mills and flower-covered cottages? A wannabe Thomas Kinkade!

She walked inside to find Beowulf on her living room rug, front legs in sphinx position, rear legs splayed out flat behind him as if he were a frog. She bent to stroke his smooth coat. "How can you *do* that?" she asked, and Beowulf sat up to deliver his one-lick salutation. "Yeah, I'm glad to see you too. C'mon, let's see what's up for eats." The dog trotted behind her to the kitchen area, all of ten feet away. Tomorrow would be soon enough to call county animal control. "Where you been all day?" Beowulf grinned.

As she poured newly bought dog chow into the bowl, Tassy returned to the house topic. She'd promised Linc to give it a week. Maybe the colors would grow on her, ho ho.

And what about Linc? He was still on the wrong side, of course, but she couldn't help liking him. Morose but funny, homely but handsome, serious and yet frivolous . . . Tassy sighed. One day his shirt was rotting off him; the next it was clean and starched. Starched! Who even did that anymore? Then he was back to grubby again. She supposed he intrigued her just because he was complicated, like no one else around here except her art dealer, and Orson didn't offer romantic possibilities.

Whoa! Where had *that* come from? She was on the slippery slope to fifty, goddammit, and she hadn't felt romantic in . . . well, the divorce was two years old, but face it, the champagne had gone flat long before. She was through with romance, not for lack of interest, but out of self-protection. She'd been ripped to shreds and scattered and no one was going to repeat that. She felt safe in San Andreas, where the dating pool was stocked with fish like that chain saw guy and his odd little friend. Not that there weren't any sharks at all. Norman Stihl was circling and he wasn't unattractive, but he didn't seem to be trying that hard. She guessed she just wasn't live enough bait.

But dinner last night had been fun and Linc was her neighbor and she'd be smart to stay on the good side of the temporary acting city attorney. Perfectly sound reasons. It didn't mean getting involved, for chrissake! She might just invite him for dinner; after all, it was her turn.

Funny, though: How could he keep looking more attractive without really changing anything?

~

Linc was finishing supper in the B and B kitchen, to which he'd added a microwave and a toaster oven. The big Wolf range and stainless fixtures were painful reminders of what Ellen had planned to create here, but he couldn't stand the dining room or parlor anymore, and he didn't want crumbs in his bedroom at the back.

Inspecting the scraps on the microwave tray, he wondered if he should get a dog. He could take cats or leave them—and cats returned the compliment. But some kind of dog. A cheerful Lab or a dignified boxer. No, a shelter dog: couple years old, past chewing and peeing on carpets, some poor abandoned bastard. A female (well, that would be a bitch). He got on better with females somehow, just liked their company. Ellen had filled that need for twenty-five years, and for nearly seven months afterward he hadn't felt it anymore. Now somehow he did again. Maybe it was all part of emotions coming back, like getting pissed at Margaret that day.

Or maybe it was his outrageous neighbor. He'd sensed Tassy's energy and glow right off, and dinner at the Beach House had shown a lot more. Her humor was sardonic but not cruel, and most often aimed at herself. She paid attention to politics and the arts. As for sports, she shared his bewilderment that otherwise rational people would purposely get hot, sweaty, tired, and achy in pursuit of recreation.

He scraped the leavings into the organic-garbage pail and stashed the tray in the scrap cardboard bin beside the separate containers for green, brown, and clear glass bottles. Good thing the kitchen was big. Something more about Tassy, though—what was it? He guessed you had to call it maturity: that *together* kind of self that took decades to integrate. Though she could be impulsive as a girl, Tassy was a grown-up. Did a wet paper towel go with newspaper or garbage? Oh well.

Not to mention her mama-bear sexiness.

Whenas in shorts my Tassy goes,
Then, then (methinks) how sweetly flows . . .

Well, that didn't work, did it?

Next, when I cast mine eyes, and see
That brave vibration each way free

Hell, he would not—*could* not—go there. The hole left by Ellen was still mostly empty and he was wary of filling it with whatever came to hand, however choice the filling.

Linc wandered off toward whiskey and TV.

~

Norman Stihl thought Margaret Nam too was sexy, all flowing lines and slender contours. After thirty-eight years her breasts were still pert cones with brown button nipples, and the clefted sweep from the small of her back down her perfect behind was enough to make a man smile like an idiot.

Lying on his back in her bed, Norman did smile at the butt planted on his pelvis while its owner knelt astride him, facing his feet and taking her weight on her knees. They had finished, but were allowing him to wilt at leisure. Margaret usually made love with the same attitude that she brought to playing tennis. Since Norman, too, considered sex a sport, they understood each other perfectly. They had an arrangement, not a relationship, and that suited him great.

Still, tonight had been different somehow: less, oh, less athletic and more kind of . . . he couldn't put his finger on it. He felt kind of guilty, but he couldn't help comparing the tight butt before him with Tassy's sexy backside, which his X-ray vision had stripped of its shorts. Damn! Tassy was one fine figure of a woman, like his daddy used to say.

Margaret uncoupled, climbed off, and instantly made for the bathroom in her uptight way, reminding him in passing that the rest of her was as slick and tight as her butt. With Margaret so available and hassle-free, why did he keep thinking about Tassy? Was she that special or was it just his usual knee-jerk letch? He wished Margaret would let him smoke in her house.

"Norman?" The toilet flushed and she reappeared, hair brushed, face perfect, body peek-a-booing in some kind of lingerie thing—he didn't know what it was called. She lay down beside him and studied the ceiling. "What do you know about the bluff in front of Tassy Morgan's house?"

"That it's not in front anymore." Why'n hell would she bring that up? Margaret's brain was as twisty as a river through a delta.

"You mean it's some kind of hazard?"

Norman knew—who didn't?—that the town was on Tassy's case about her house. He also knew he wasn't slick, but he *was* plenty sharp enough to stall. "I dunno; why?"

"The city has the right to stabilize the bluff, doesn't it?"

"I guess. Yeah."

"Even if it means taking out a house."

Aha! Well, Norman wasn't having any of *that*, first because the construction business was in the toilet and he expected a big job rescuing Tassy's shack, and second because rescuing Tassy was a big part of his plan to get her into the sack. "Bluff's okay for a pretty good while."

"How long?"

Keep it light, real light: "Hard to tell. Awhile."

She studied the ceiling some more. "Then I've got one more option. It's not as good, but I'll make it work."

Norman wondered if he should warn Tassy. He'd get points for it. On the other hand, Margaret's real estate office had sent him lots of referrals; and, hey, he had *her* in the sack already and, he had to admit, Margaret's sack was getting better. If she wasn't so damn irritating sometimes, she'd make an okay wife. Then he reviewed memories of wives one and two and came to his senses again.

Why didn't people take life easy like he did? Damn!

6

The next morning Linc dragged himself to another illegal coffee shop meeting of the city council. Presiding as usual through preemptive strike, Margaret Nam opened the mayor's municipal binder at a page flagged with a yellow sticky. The page contained an ordinance, drafted by Linc's predecessor, covering the "general appropriateness" of buildings and the town's governance thereof. She moved that they cite Tassy, and Dottie Franklyn seconded.

Linc shook his head, called the ordinance squishy soft, and opined that enforcement would be dicey.

Undeterred, Margaret called the vote. Dottie voted with her, after a monologue that veered through ten topics of no discernible relevance and in no detectable order, but delivered so breathlessly that no one could interrupt.

When Dottie'd stopped vibrating, Jack Millhouse looked instinctively at Margaret Nam, who returned an eloquent smile—her Mona Lisa model. The mayor's gaze locked and so did the smile, until they seemed to be holding some silent contest. Finally, Millhouse fumbled through a few empty sentences before allowing as how he'd promised to be a "proactive" mayor, and since intervention was proactive, he was voting with the ladies—um, women.

Linc knew the real reason was fear of Margaret Nam, who had once again flattened Millhouse with her feather-light steamroller. As a survivor of numberless studio meetings, Linc could admire her gift for invisible bullying.

He and Orson voted no but the usual three-to-two majority won; resolution carried; illegal meeting adjourned. Millhouse even banged his coffee mug like a gavel. With an impatient glance at her watch, Margaret slid out of the booth—she could do even that gracefully—and left. Dottie Franklyn and Millhouse followed.

Linc watched the proactive trio depart. "Orson, why is our mayor so shit-scared of Margaret?"

Orson paused in the mission of leaving no french fry behind. "He's terrified she'll run for mayor—probably win too."

Linc's gesture said, *So?*

"Poor Jack thinks if he lets her run the town *through* him, she won't need to bear the heavy yoke of office." He couldn't suppress a snicker.

"It doesn't work that way."

"Of course not, dear boy. Margaret wants to be Lord Mayor of San Andreas—her *amour propre* demands it. Politically speaking, Jack's a walking dead man."

With a grimace of distaste for this foolishness, Linc left the booth and strolled over to Millhouse at the cash register. "What are you going to do now, Jack?"

"Well, *you* are, Linc."

"You're still unclear on the concept: I'm counsel, not enforcement."

"But you'll write the citation—summons—whatever."

"In my professional opinion, the rule is unenforceable in court."

"But it'll never *get* to court." Then, anxiously, "Will it?" Before Linc could answer, Millhouse added, "And if it does, you'll handle it."

Linc shook his head. "Pro bono gets you just so far, Jack, and then I go on a *very big* clock. I'm warning you: This one is a turkey and turkeys do not fly." He started away, then turned back. "You might try talking Margaret around, or maybe change your own vote." When Millhouse seemed even more distressed, Linc added, "You know, our voting was invalid anyway because it wasn't a legal meeting."

The mayor looked blank.

"The State of California says you cannot vote on municipal business in private." Linc waited until the implications penetrated, then walked out into the sunshine. That Millhouse would grab these lifelines was just too much to hope for.

Linc hiked the fifty yards seaward to his own street, turned left, and started up the gentle slope. The morning fog had lifted and sun sparkles capered on the wavelets in the harbor. Gulls wheeled, surf sloshed, and the clear air revealed the sweep of evergreen coast all the way down to the smoke cloud above the pulp plant at the county seat.

Nearing Tassy's house he realized that the immense Lincoln Navigator parked at the curb was Margaret's impress-the-clients land yacht. The woman wasted no time. Feeling not unlike Jack Millhouse, Linc snuck past the giant SUV and tiptoed toward home.

~

Margaret had been disconcerted when Tassy answered her knock, grunted "Come," and fled toward the back of the house, leaving her in the puny great room. She recovered fast enough to case the house with a Realtor's eye. Pathetic, really—almost a squatter's cabin—the kind of shack people threw up as summer places back when beachfront land was cheap. Margaret had never met a house she didn't like—or at least couldn't sell—but Tassy's place had to come close.

Making her way toward the ocean side, she found Tassy working on a painting in her studio, slashing and dabbing paint strokes, wiggling brushes in water, lifting bits of pigment off the paper with the edges of a cloth. "Got to keep going or it dries. Sorry."

Margaret smiled her best professional smile. "I hope I'm not interrupting."

"Only if I let you and I won't." Tassy's tone was cheerful.

"You have a lovely place here."

"Except for the view it's a dump, but it was all I could afford." Obviously the woman made a fetish of candor, probably part of her "artist" posture; but Margaret had years of practice with clients who were impolite, ignorant, arrogant, vague, dismissive—you name it. There wasn't an attitude she couldn't deal with, including artistic temperament. She watched in silence for several minutes with the patience that came of waiting in foyers while prospects took just one more teeny peek at the master bedroom closets.

The paintings on the land-side wall drew her attention: very different from the stuff in Orson's gallery. They were nonrepresentational but evidently seascapes, though Margaret couldn't explain how she knew it. The large expanses of toothed paper opposed violence and serenity, energy and peace in a way she admitted appealed to her. She genuinely envied Tassy's talent. Margaret herself had chewed methodically through every art and craft from sand painting to macramé before grudgingly conceding that her creativity lay in management and civic vision.

Finally, Tassy jugged all her brushes and unbent herself, wincing slightly.

Margaret pointed at the wall. "I like your paintings."

"Thank you. I can't seem to sell that style."

"You could in a more, well, urban market. What I like is they're not too—what?—too *bold* to live with."

Lips curving slightly, Tassy looked over the top of her glasses. "I'll take that as a compliment."

"In fact, they're giving me ideas. I have two summer rentals to decorate—seaside motif, of course. Maybe you could paint four or five for me."

"I don't match other people's color schemes."

Margaret winced at this hint of patronizing, but kept her smile friendly. "Yes, I noticed." Couldn't the woman tell a real compliment when she got one?

Tassy looked puzzled, then chuckled. "You mean the house color. Well, Linc chose that."

"Mm, I wish he'd consulted me first—oh, and you too, of course."

"Of course." Tassy looked speculatively at her guest. "I take it you're not happy about that."

"It's just that we're trying *so* hard for the seaside village look."

"But New England seaside, not Crete." Tassy nodded toward the Pacific outside. "More *authentic*."

Margaret detected the slightly dry tone but couldn't see any reason for it. She pushed on: "Now, if it'd been just the ocean side . . ."

"Where people couldn't see it."

Margaret brightened at this apparent progress. "Well, yes, in fact."

"If people don't see it, it's okay."

"I don't know why not. Look, we really, *really* want to be friendly about this. . . ."

" 'We'?"

Tassy's tone was dangerous but Margaret's face stayed calm as a Zen garden. "The council. There is an ordinance on the books, of course, but we hoped we could deal with all this like neighbors."

Tassy nodded without expression. "But if not, there *is* an ordinance. Why am I not surprised?"

Margaret stopped trying to get through to the woman. "Well, you know small towns," she said, and gathered herself to go.

Tassy's deadpan held. "I'm learning."

Margaret wiggled fingers in a small feminine wave and headed for the front door. She let herself out and climbed into her Navigator, looking even more petite against her white behemoth.

As soon as the SUV had rolled out of sight like the final float in a short parade, Tassy set out for the B and B at close to a dead run. Linc wasn't in the parlor, the big dining room, or the even bigger kitchen, but Tassy heard music and followed it to a twelve-by-twelve back room bulging with a bed, dresser, computer desk, file cabinet, fifty-inch flat screen, big audio speakers, and Linc in a rocking chair. With its cheery windows and French doors to the kitchen, it had clearly once been a breakfast room. It looked like he lived his whole life here.

When Linc glanced up and saw her, he prepared his mind for the worst.

"So you have an ordinance, do you?"

"Aw, jeez." He just knew something like this would happen.

"Gonna bust me, are you?"

Knew it the minute he saw Margaret's SUV. "Course not. Let's go in the kitchen." He rose and half-muted the music with a remote. When he started toward her, Tassy didn't move, so he kept on coming until he was herding her back through the doorway.

"First she talks about buying four or five of the paintings I can't sell." Tassy was literally backpedaling. "Then she wants this California village to look like *Our Town*, which is in Maine."

"New Hampshire."

"Whatever. Then she wants to work it out *like neighbors*." Tassy batted her eyes with exaggerated innocence. "Then she threatens me with your goddamn ordinance." She huffed down onto a kitchen chair. "Margaret Nam is one stone bitch."

Linc was aware, in a dim male way, that certain women hated one another on sight, and exhibit A was seated in his kitchen. He was seasoned enough to admit that he didn't understand this phenomenon and never would, so he kept his big mouth shut.

The water was hot in the electric kettle, so he built two mugs of tea instead and shared what insights he did have. "Margaret's a special type: a star. I used to be faced with divas like her." He extracted two tea bags and dunked. "Some stars develop—or maybe just have—a genius for deceit. They sound reasonable; they speak politely; they're not high-handed." He carried the mugs to Tassy at the table. "But they are utterly sure that they deserve to get their way in absolutely everything." Linc wandered back to find spoons. "Somehow they usually do it, and they do so because they're like Speedy Gonzalez: come and gone before you know you've been screwed. That's Margaret."

Sitting down, Linc pushed a silver caddy toward her, a superb two-chambered piece holding brown sugar and Splenda.

She scooped sugar lavishly. "Pretty."

"She is that. Petite."

"No, the sugar dish thing."

This woman kept shifting gears on him. "Ellen had a good eye." Tassy resumed hastily, "Well, I'm *not* changing the paint."

Linc couldn't suppress a smile. "Decided you liked the blue, did you?" She puffed up like a rooster. "Uh uh uh, take it easy. Anyway, you're not going to get busted." Not as long as he stayed city attorney. "How's your tea?"

"Fine. The woman graciously offered to permit my unsuitable color as long as it couldn't be seen. Can you imagine?"

Yes he could, having dropped the germ of that very idea into the illegal council meeting. He nodded, meditating. "Who knows? She may be on to something." Linc sat and watched her patiently.

"How about this: I'll post a big sign that says, 'Avert eyes until past house.' Get real, Linc."

"Suppose you masked the paint job—concealed it."

"With what, magic shrubs?"

"A fence. You're allowed a fence."

"Come *on*!"

"Think about it. Your street side doesn't have any view to block."

She nodded. "Except for people looking *in*. I can't get from my bedroom to my kitchen without mooning the neighborhood."

Linc grinned. "That does it: I'm buying binoculars."

"Not much to see," she grumbled, but her little smile held a hint of pleasure.

"Oh yes there is, and I'll finance the fence."

"*What?*" She banged her mug down, slopping tea on the hardwood table. "Why?"

Linc automatically applied a paper napkin. Why? Because he knew Tassy was broke. Because he didn't want her hassled or hurt. Couldn't say that, though, so he put on his best negotiator's face. "I guess I'm selfish."

Another "What?"

Linc hemmed and hawed convincingly, then made his tone reluctant. "If you must know, it's to get me off the hook. They *will* use that ordinance to take you to court and it's so poorly drawn that they'll lose and you'll win."

"Works for me."

"But not for me. I'll put in days on a hopeless case and they'll never pay me for it."

"You don't need the money. Hell, you want to buy the damn fence!"

There was his opening. "I didn't say that. For one thing, you'd never accept a gift—"

"Damn straight!"

"And I wouldn't insult you. By 'financing,' I meant I want to buy two of your paintings, the abstracts in your studio."

"You too?"

"Sure. Say, twelve hundred each."

"On condition that I buy a fence with the money. That's the second bribe I've been offered today."

Linc dialed up his best showbiz sincerity: "This may be the wrong time to say it, but I wanted those paintings the first time I saw them—the middle pair."

Tassy stared at him suspiciously.

Linc nodded. "Wrong time to say it, I know. Okay, I'll buy the paintings, no strings. How you handle the house is your business."

It was a pleasure to watch thoughts and feelings chase across her face. After a long struggle she sighed. "That was damn slippery. You know I'll have to get a fence now."

"I'm a shyster, remember?"

"How do I get a fence?"

"From DayGlo Dave and Bill the Fixer."

"Those guys with the cool front yards? Okay." She nodded. "Okay, I'll do it.

The conversation was over but she didn't seem to want to leave any more than he wanted her to. She cocked her head toward the little bedroom. "What's that music?"

"Berlioz, *Harold in Italy*; Toscanini and the NBC Symphony."

"Soloist?"

"William Primrose, 1939."

"Impressive."

"January second."

"Wow!"

"Live broadcast."

Tassy looked at him as if waiting for more. Linc wanted to say more, things like *sit here with me; you look lovely in sunshine; you're a fascinating, crazy woman; put your hands on my face; I want you.* But he couldn't get the words out, and when the silence threatened to grow embarrassing, she got up with unnecessary bustle. "I'll go see Bill the Fixer, then."

Pause. "Great."

Another pause, as if she were giving him one last chance, then, "I'll let myself out." She turned abruptly and left.

She fit so well in that kitchen—would fit anywhere in this house. Why couldn't he have Tassy in his bedroom instead of Berlioz? He snatched the tea mugs and walked them to the sink. She didn't want to go. Why couldn't he see that in time? Why was he so stiff necked? Why . . . ? Linc banged the mugs on the drainboard.

~

The retreating bluff face had not really reached Tassy's bedroom, but as she lay staring at the dark again the creaks and ticks expected of any aging house sounded like the clock of doom. Today, she'd had to shim up the ocean side of her painting board with wood scraps because the water and paint were now running downhill. The studio, at least, had lurched off level and though she couldn't be sure, she thought the bedroom was sagging as well. A front yard fence: talk about rearranging deck chairs on the *Titanic*!

Good thing Linc was buying. No! It was her paintings he'd bought, not the fence; and how she spent the money was her choice. Instead of a fence, she could repaint the house, and for a fraction of the cost. Why keep up this fight? She had better ways to spend her energy.

For the damn principle, that's why. For twenty-five years she'd gone with the flow, as they used to say, and it wasn't until her family had *outgrown her*, in her husband's tired phrase, that she noticed where that flow, like a glacier depositing debris, had left her. Low and dry was where. She'd realized that if she didn't finally take command, the sticks and leaves of her life would go right on decaying into mulch. But there were seeds, too, in that deposit and she was determined to root again and grow. No more going with the flow.

Only now the house was doing it for her. Tassy rolled onto her side and finally dozed off, unaware that she was sleeping with her teeth clenched.

At the foot of the bed, however, Beowulf slept the sleep of the just.

7

The next morning Tassy found Bill the Fixer in a torrent of noise and a blizzard of sawdust, sculpting. Terrified of distracting a man with a chain saw, she crept cautiously sideways into his field of vision, and after several surgical thrusts with the saw, he killed his lethal tool and nodded at her. She took an instant liking to this thick, cheerful man with his shock of gray hair and five-day beard, both half-buried in sawdust. "Hi, Bill, I'm Tassy Morgan."

"That you are." He put down the saw and spritzed his work with an air hose. His face reminded her of potatoes: his nose of small russet, his skin classic Idaho.

"Linc Ellis sent me over; said you and Dave could build me a fence."

Bill glanced at the sculpture. "Whaddaya think?"

Tassy examined the piece, a six-foot depiction of Paul Bunyan, complete with bushy beard and woolen watch cap, minutely rendered in wood. Like the totem poles nearby, it belonged to a mythology hundreds of miles distant, but she imagined the tourists weren't fussy, and she sympathized with a fellow artist who had to produce what sold.

"You cheated," she said, grinning to take the edge off. "You shaped these details around the eyes and nose with chisels." She explored them with gentle fingers. "Beautiful work. Feels like you *really* broke the rules and sanded." When he beamed at the compliment, she added, "You do any pieces just for yourself?"

"Not anymore. Might as well, though; nobody buys this stuff either."

"You should go back to it." Indicating the chain saw, "Even with that thing, you know how to go where the wood takes you."

Bill's face stayed still while he thought about that, then broke out another warm smile. He cocked his head as if sizing her up. "A fence." He ruffled his thatch of hair, releasing a gnat cloud of sawdust. "Well." Bill stared at her, abstracted.

By now, Tassy knew enough to not take offense. Some folks around here—some of the pre-boomer folks—left air in their conversations, partly to think of just what to say and partly to think of what not to.

Finally, "Tell you what, Tassy, Dave's who you want."

"Your partner?"

Bill shook his head. "Just a neighbor, next house down. He'll buy all the stuff, build the fence, and finish it for you. Make you a good price."

"Don't you want half of this?"

"Sure I would." Bill cocked a thumb at Paul Bunyan. "But I'm real backed up on work."

She looked around the yard bulging with unsold sculptures. "Do you have commissions waiting?"

He tapped his sweaty forehead. "Just from me."

Tassy nodded, smiling. She could relate to a man whose art was more important than earning a living.

Bill changed the subject back. "Besides, Dave needs to get his mind off things."

"What kind of things?"

Apparently this poked through some membrane of male privacy, because Bill just stood and looked blank.

Getting the message, Tassy said, "Thanks. All right."

When she turned to go she saw Beowulf sitting on the sidewalk, well out of chain saw range. She turned back. "Bill, do you know this dog?"

"Sure. Hi, Wolfie!" The dog replied *bark*, pause, *bark* but stayed planted on the sidewalk. "Everyone knows him; he's all over the place. Norwegian elkhound, purebred."

"I wondered about that. What about his owner?"

Bill scratched his thatch of hair again, launching another sawdust cloud. "That'd be John Ankers, down the coast road. Died about a month back."

"Then who takes care of Beowulf?"

"Everyone in town, I guess. Wolfie goes where he pleases."

"He's sort of attaching himself to me now."

Bill the Fixer shot her an appreciative grin. "I always thought that dog had good sense."

Tassy decided on a subject change and nodded at Paul Bunyan. "You ought to do more figures."

He studied her, deadpan. "Nudes, maybe."

"Need a model?"

His blush was bright enough to penetrate beard and sawdust. He stared at her without expression, then said abruptly, "See Dave, next house down."

As she strolled out Bill the Fixer's front gate, Tassy wondered why she'd said that about modeling. By the time she'd passed Dave's rusty car next door, she knew why: Bill's Paul Bunyan was so beautiful and so heroically rendered that she wondered what she'd look like under his hand—well, saw. She knocked on Dave's door and waited.

~

Later, after a lunch of plain yogurt that was separating in its cup but still tasted okay—well, it tasted rancid, but it was all she had—Tassy hauled Linc's paintings over to the B and B. At nearly three by four feet each, they were heavy and clumsy, even in their simple frames, and she wished she'd made two trips.

"I'd've helped you." Linc took a painting as she lugged them up onto his porch. His face looked handsome when he smiled.

"The price includes delivery." On the way in she noted that someone—Bill or Dave?—had reglazed the window.

Linc had removed three big prints from the fireplace wall in the parlor—pictures installed so recently that they left no outlines on the wallpaper. He set one of her paintings there on the floor and Tassy placed the other by it. Linc handed her a check. She said thanks. They stood there.

Linc said, "I could use some help hanging them—you know, placement." He unclipped a yellow tape from his belt.

They worked together, measuring, calculating, driving nails, cursing, adjusting, cursing, readjusting. The frames were fitted with small sawtooth hangers and one of the pictures persisted in drifting off level.

Finally Tassy said, "Show you a trick." She found a tiny headless brad in Linc's mason jar of nails, held the picture straight, and tacked the brad invisibly against the side that wanted to drift upward.

She studied the effect. He'd given her big watercolors the place of honor opposite the windows, displacing artwork chosen by his wife. And he was right: Her paintings gave the parlor what it needed, a pair of unique statements amid all the catalog reproductions. All by themselves, her watercolors changed the character of the room.

That was worth thinking about. She dismissed her touristy sea-scapes for Orson as financial necessities; on the other hand, these paintings revealed, in their new setting, where she was going—or wanted to go. Their powerful effect on the room showed she was getting there. Wasn't that something: A couple more sales like this one and she might start painting what she wanted to paint!

Linc stood there a long time, then finally said, "Very fine. Very fine, indeed." He smiled again, this time in a way she hadn't seen before. He looked trim and energetic today—looked that way more often now, come to think of it.

Tassy glanced around, then studied Linc again and knew that something in her had shifted somehow. Maybe her warm little surge of confidence was coloring him as well as the paintings.

"I talked to Dave," she said. "Bill sent me to him. He'll work out fine. Bill wants me to model nude for him."

Linc blinked as if wondering where the hell *that'd* come from.

"I'm tempted. What do *you* think?"

Link inventoried her quickly from stern to stems and then said slowly, "You have a lush physique. . . ."

"I'm fat?"

"No, no! Victorian painters would have loved your body: They could paint it nude and get away with it by calling it a classical subject."

"Hang me in a saloon."

"More like in a grand salon. An odalisque by Ingres."

"Wow! That's pretty heavy stuff."

"Poor choice of words. You're beautiful, Tassy. Deal with it."

That something inside Tassy shifted further—hell, it damn near lurched!

~

The first part of the week brought an eighty-degree heat wave, a temperature unprecedented in the annals of San Andreas. Unfiltered by the usual fog, the sun treated the town almost like the rest of California while residents stayed inside and complained. Still, the few tourists who ventured past the trailer park were charmed by the scene that sparkled in the late-spring sun. Though it looked nothing like the Maine village of Margaret Nam's ambition, the little town had its own funky character. Some of the houses might want a paint job and the little gardens might need more care than their overworked owners could give them, but the houses looked lived in, the businesses looked worked in, and the town bustled in the sunshine with an honest purpose that no Disneyland village could simulate.

DayGlo Dave could not bustle these days, even though his chemo was over, but his dogged application was steadily building a six-foot palisade of raw cedar planks around Tassy's front and side yards. Dave had upheld Bill the Fixer's faith in him. Though he seemed a touch slow on the uptake, he asked good questions, took Tassy with him to select materials at the lumberyard, and let her pay for them without extra markup. Then he went to work digging postholes, pouring concrete, setting posts, and fitting rails. When he got to the cedar planks, Tassy worked with him. With her handing boards and Dave setting them with his pneumatic nail gun, they finished three sides of the fence by lunch on Wednesday.

Dave was resting a minute, like he was forced to do nowadays, when Tassy showed up with a jug of iced tea. She sat with him, watching the ocean through the fence rails on the unfinished side. "You're really good at this," she said. "Are you a full-time carpenter?"

He'd been an industrial pipe fitter, but that was a while back. Dave shook his head and smiled.

"What *is* your main business, then?"

"Disability, I guess." He studied her reaction to that. When she just looked puzzled, he added, "I get around okay, but after workdays like this I go to bed right after dinner."

Her look turned sympathetic. This lady had a way of looking at you like she was interested, like she cared. Last couple days, he'd noticed that, noticed how easy she was about helping out, how easy she was to work with. Now he found himself talking more than usual. He told about the power plant, the radiation, the cancer thing. The more he talked, the more she gave him this, well, real nice look, and so he talked some more. When he couldn't think of any more to say, he watched the ocean.

"That's quite a story," she said.

How about that! She didn't say how sorry she was or "You poor thing" or anything. She just showed she listened and paid attention. This woman knew how to act. "Another hour, maybe," Dave said, nodding at the fence. "Better get on it."

"It's going to be beautiful, Dave." She grinned at him and, hell, after a grin like that he hated to even take her money.

~

By Thursday the town had returned to respectable temperatures, though the sunshine and ocean sparkles continued. Tassy's new fence didn't ignite instant outrage, but everybody noticed it and was ready to weigh in with a comment if asked, or in Dottie Franklyn's case, whether consulted or not. Enthroned in the sole chair at the Hair Place, she said, "A fence may be legal, far as I know, but it seems kind of, well, *you* know . . ."

Jimi was tinting Dottie's hair palomino, using three different colors to layer it and make it blend when the dirty white roots reappeared. "What are you saying?"

"I guess, I mean, I don't know. Margaret Nam's handling that."

"*Handling*, is she? Has Margaret seen it?"

"She's been down in San Francisco—some kind of real estate thing. She said she'd be back this evening. I did tell her about it, though. We talk on the phone, you know. Margaret and I are close."

Jimi changed the subject diplomatically. "Angela had her baby: an eight-pound girl."

"Well."

"She'll be back in a couple weeks."

"Well." That about wore out Dottie's interest in the absent manicurist. "Margaret said on the phone she was concerned about that woman's fence, very *concerned*."

"Sounds like she's got it in for her."

"Now, why would you ever say that?"

Jimi didn't reply. She learned everything about everyone from the people who sat in her chair, and she tried not to take sides. She also knew village herd behavior only too well. Once, when old Mrs. Lagan thought Jimi's color job had made her hair fall out—though at eighty-nine she was lucky to have any—she'd spread it around the garden club and business had dropped off for weeks. Not that Jimi needed the income, but she hated to be idle. She patiently lifted and painted hair strands, thinking good thoughts about Tassy Morgan and keeping her own counsel.

~

Tassy was in her studio rounding up her work board, pad, pastel box, and stool to head for Reuben's Last Creek. North Coast weather changed about every two miles, and this morning the fog pattern bumping along the shoreline hinted at clear skies inland. She wouldn't paint stupid redwoods; who wanted art a foot wide and four tall? Yeah, well, some people actually did but she wasn't about to supply it. She loved doing landscapes, though, and Orson wanted variety.

She walked out her door toward her car. She was about to throw her junk in the backseat to join all the other junk there when she noticed Linc sitting on the top step of his front porch. He was looking at her. She stared back a moment and then he waved—wagged his hand a little, really, but she took it as a wave and strolled over. "Hey, Linc."

"Howdy. I like your outfit." She'd thrown on a saggy baggy sweater, denim shorts, and hiking boots with white socks. She knew she could get away with it because her legs were so much of her six-foot height and they hadn't yet had a visit from the saddlebag fairy. Linc looked her up and down appreciatively.

She glowed a bit. "How's the old saloon girl holding up?"

Linc waggled Groucho eyebrows and mimed flicking a cigar.

Okay, time to change the subject. "What are you doing there?"

Linc looked serious. "I'm holding down this step." She cocked her head. "Weather report says wind late this afternoon and this step's loose, so I'm sitting on it."

"It's ten a.m." There was a gag on the way.

"I like to be prepared."

"Why not nail it down?"

"Too much skill involved. I'd have to find a nail, then I'd have to find a hammer, then I'd have to drive the nail all the way into this top board without bending the nail *or* making big dents in the wood. Sitting's a nonskilled occupation."

Tassy nodded thoughtfully. "Half the town does the same kind of work." They looked at each other for a moment and she saw that Linc had no more clue than she did about where to go next. "Want to drive out to Reuben's Last Creek with me?"

"What's out there?"

"Scenery." She held up her painting kit.

"Scenery." Linc's look left no doubt about which vista he meant. "Fine plan!" With uncharacteristic energy, he heaved a big chair off the porch and started down the steps.

"What about that step?"

"Oh, right." He turned toward the porch. "Down! Stay! Good step!"

She studied his oversize seat. "Don't you have a folding chair?"

"Nah."

"Don't you want a hat or sunscreen or something?"

"Nah. Let's stop at the market, though, load up on grease and beer."

When they reached Tassy's little Ford, Linc looked at the stuff piled in the back. "I see what you meant about the chair. Why don't we take my truck?"

Linc had a truck? Come *on*! But the North Coast suffered the highest fuel prices in the country and she grabbed any chance to not drive, so okay, bring on the truck. Tassy smiled and nodded.

The odd vehicle he backed down his driveway was half truck and half luxury four-door. Linc opened a contraption protecting a truncated truck bed and heaved the lawn chair into it while Tassy established herself in a glove leather captain's chair inside. Before he could put up the tailgate again, Beowulf appeared out of nowhere and jumped into the bed.

"Hey!" Linc stared nonplussed at the dog, who grinned back at him. "Hey!"

Tassy opened the passenger door and looked back. "Oh, that's Beowulf. Hi, Wolfie."

The dog answered with his usual *bark*, pause, *bark*.

"I know who he is," Linc said, "but why the sudden interest in me?"

"I'm the one he's interested in. Let him come."

"I don't think dogs are supposed to ride in back."

"No one around here cares. Let's go."

Linc looked doubtfully at Beowulf, who already had his muzzle aimed toward the delicious smells that would assault his nose. Linc got in the truck.

~

Two hours later, Linc was wanting a nap. He'd stuffed himself with hot wings and coleslaw, well irrigated with Steelhead ale, and was lounging in his Adirondack chair from Crate and Barrel while Tassy perched on a folding stool with a work board on her bare knees and her fingers—which were filthy with pastel dust—darting swiftly across a big paper pad.

Out in front of her, Reuben's Last Creek wandered off in docile perspective, its banks as green as only Ireland and the Redwood Coast could be green. Tendrils of fog advanced and retreated, changing the light from hard-shadowed sunshine to softest diffusion and back again in five minutes. The great silent trees beyond the meadows seemed to come and go with the fog like immense grazing animals.

Nearer, on the opposite bank, three Jersey heifers had strolled into the view and were also grazing, while Tassy added them quickly before they strolled out again. Beowulf had expressed a professional interest in bovine management, but Tassy had told him to stay and he'd obeyed her. Linc was impressed.

He watched her sketch the slanting sunlight on the cows' knobby caramel hips. Amazing what you could suggest with a couple of dots and smudges. The whole effect was so classic that Linc half-expected a kid from a Winslow Homer painting to come round up the livestock.

To make conversation he asked, "Why's it called Reuben's Last Creek?"

"Reuben was an explorer—well, he really cared more about gold. Hold still, Bossy, one more minute. These little rivers start up in the Trinity Alps and there was gold in most of them, in one place or another. He and his party worked their way up the coast, hunting them."

"You enjoy local history?"

"I forget where I read this. Anyway, half his party wanted to split off and follow this creek toward the gold but the other half didn't. They arbitrated the dispute in the usual male fashion, and when the

mud settled, Reuben's remains sort of floated to the surface. So this
was—"

"His last discovery." Linc studied the gnats in the sunbeams.
"You must like it up here."

"You mean San Andreas? How could a painter not love this?
Jury's still out on the people, though. How about you?"

"I never thought it through. It was Ellen's dream and I'd kept
her in L.A. while I built my very big career. After twenty-five years
she more than deserved what she'd waited for, whatever that turned
out to be. Turned out to be here. Now . . . ?" Linc inspected the gnats
another moment, then said, "Maybe I should try fly-fishing."

Tassy thought about Linc while her fingers did magic tricks
with pastels. Had she asked him out here because he could use
TLC? Well, he could, of course, but it was something more than
just that, a growing feeling of—what? Fitting, matching—*rightness*.
That was it.

Well, that was just great! *Mr. Right?* After all those dry decades
had she found Mr. Right? Too late, Mr. Right, too damn *late*! Disgusted, she threw down her chalk and shaded her eyes with her
hand. Stop it! Get a grip. She took her hand down and looked at
Linc. "About all I can do on this. Ready to go?" Her voice was not
quite calm.

"Sure." He looked at her mildly. "You've got green war paint on
your forehead." Linc stood up, approached her with a clean tissue
from his shirt pocket, touched the tip of his tongue to it, and wiped
at the pastel fallout. His concentration on the cleanup job was almost
funny, but his warm left palm and fingers on her opposite cheek sent
a different message entirely and she felt . . . she felt . . .

Jesus, the next thing to a sexual rush, or maybe not even the
next thing! Unconsciously, she pulled her thighs together. Her
hands were trembling slightly. When he smiled and turned her loose,
Tassy thought, amazing! Like riding a bicycle, you never forgot how.

She took deep, unobtrusive breaths and cast about for a different focus—anything.

Beowulf's smile was almost knowing. *Get a grip*, she thought again fiercely and strode away toward the truck. "Come, Wolfie, let's go riding."

8

That evening, Margaret Nam drove home from the airport, swinging past Tassy's house while there was still enough twilight to inspect the fence. It was clearly as bad as Dottie had said, a small wooden fort filling, simply *filling*, the yard. All it needed was corner towers and the U.S. Cavalry inside. The fence just had to go, but she knew she'd wrung all she could out of the city council—or the building commission or whichever committee spineless Millhouse had called on.

Why couldn't people see how important the town's appearance was? Tourists and home buyers wanted a picture-book seaside village. And it wasn't just for business. Margaret really liked San Andreas, liked the people, wanted the best for her adopted home, and, yes, wanted credit for imagining the best and making it so.

None of which was solving the problem of Fort Morgan. Meditating on it, she recalled that the county building inspector was due to sign off on renovations to one of her rental properties. Tomorrow, in fact. John Hansen had once been her lover, briefly, and she could still sweet-talk him a little. Perhaps she would drive him past that unacceptable fence and see what he could come up with.

~

In the apartment behind the gallery, Orson hovered with a bottle of good red. "So Linc bought both those paintings. Top you up?"

"Why not?" Tassy smiled at him. She couldn't get a handle on Orson's kitchen. It didn't boast Viking and Sub-Zero toys, didn't have granite counters, didn't belong in *Architectural Digest*, but it was warm and comfortable and it exuded an air of unquantifiable chic. She watched him bustle over spaghetti alla Bolognese. "I owe you a commission."

Orson shook his head. "I refused those paintings, remember? They were too good for my clientele."

"You're still my dealer."

He launched into Disney Italian: "I no sell-a da goods, I no take-a da commish." Pouring sauce over the spaghetti, he sang "O Sole Mio" in a corny basso.

Tassy barked her outsize laugh. "And me without my accordion. Stop! Too much, Orson! I'll never eat all this."

"Oh, struggle with it, darling." Orson sat at the table with her and smiled.

She looked at the big man who took such care of her. "I love you, Orson; why aren't you available?"

Lightly, "I know the flip side of *that* one: All the good men are taken or straight."

She said, only half-joking, "We could still set up housekeeping."

"What would you call that, a *hookup blanc*? That's the best offer I've had in—well." He smiled quietly but shook his head again.

They ate in silence awhile, then Orson paused and watched her. When she noticed and stopped too, he said, "Besides, you've got a thing for Linc going."

Whoa! "I beg your pardon?"

"Well, starting, anyhow. I noticed the way you talked about your picnic today." He returned to his pasta, letting that one float in midair.

Tassy thought of Linc's hand on her cheek and nodded ruefully. "There's—I don't know—just something about him that attracts me."

"You've got it backwards, darling. You're not attracted to him because 'there's something about him.' He acquires a 'something about
him' *because* you're attracted to him. It always works that way; God
knows why."

She half-hoped Orson would talk her out of it. "Maybe a bad
idea. He's on the city side in this stupid fence thing."

"Think Montague and Capulet. Besides, he's been voting with
me on this one. And he's not fond of Margaret Nam."

Tassy pushed her empty plate away. "What's with that woman
anyway?"

"I admit that she can be unpleasant." Orson sighed and thought
a moment. "Underneath, I suspect she's frightened of—well, I guess
that's her little secret."

"Everyone's frightened of something. It sure doesn't make her
a sweetie pie."

"Speaking of which—dessert?"

"Ogod, I'll be too fat to move."

He gracefully harvested plates. "Never, dear; trust Orson on
that."

~

It was Monday morning before County Building Inspector John
Hansen parked his official-business-only hybrid subcompact in front
of Tassy's house, unlatched her new gate, and knocked on her door.
His fieldwork started at eight a.m. and it was now eight a.m., 08:00:00.
With an average of five miles between job sites, punctuality and efficiency were important to Hansen, whose standards were unusual
in the county and unheard of among its public servants. A local joke
held that a prompt response to a 911 call was anytime the same day.

It was 08:01:30 before Tassy opened the door dressed entirely
in a T-shirt that was too long but almost not too-long enough, with
her hair a bright cloud around her and a coffee mug in her fist. She

surveyed the tidy man in twills with the county logo on his pocket. "Yes?"

"Good morning—Ms. Morgan?"

Tassy nodded.

"John Hansen, county building department."

Building department: That couldn't be good.

"I'm here about your fence."

Not good. "That would be permits, right?"

He nodded.

She kept a poker face but grinned inside. She was all over this one. "That fence didn't need a permit. I checked the city website."

"Permit or not, it has to conform to code."

"That's exactly what I checked." Feeling a bit paranoid, she'd spent an hour lip-reading her way through an endless PDF of zoning regulations.

The man sighed as if this kind of thing was familiar. "I can't tell what you checked, but this fence is on your front lot line."

"Which is allowed."

"For fences up to three feet high. Yours is six."

"But it said six. I read it carefully."

"Six is permissible on the side and back lot lines. In front, the minimum setback for that height's twenty feet. Here, I'll show you." He started to open his briefcase.

"Aw come *on*! I don't *have* twenty feet of front yard. The fence would have to run through my damn living room."

The man almost cracked a smile. "That's about right, yes."

"I'm thinking six feet high on the sides but three across the front would look pretty dorky."

Hansen shrugged noncommittally.

"So what do I have to do?"

For the first time he seemed unsure of himself. "You don't *have* to do anything. You won't be cited unless someone enters a complaint."

"No one has?"

Hansen shook his head.

"Then why'd you drive all the way up here to tell me?"

"I just happened to be going by. . . ."

"At eight a.m., thirty miles from your office, you just *happened*?"

Since he was standing six inches below the doorsill, his eyes were lower than Tassy's. Now they seemed to dip even farther. "I'm here as a courtesy—completely informal."

"Sort of a warning." Her soft tone was ominous.

His eye level sank another inch. "I just thought you'd want to know."

Tassy tried to keep her voice calm. "What I want to *know* is who put you onto this."

"Completely informal. Here as a courtesy."

She checked herself just in time. No point killing the messenger. "Then an equally courteous good-bye, Inspector." And she did close the door gently.

Tassy mulled the problem while she dressed and brushed her hair, then strolled up one street and turned down the non-designated row to the house of her new friend DayGlo Dave.

Damn! She wished Orson hadn't told her that nickname. It was horrible, but she couldn't get it out of her head. She found him on a cinder block seat, drinking coffee and watching the morning go by.

When she said hi, he answered with his usual shy smile. They made small talk for a few minutes, but neither was good at it and conversation threatened to dry up; so Tassy said casually, "Ever run into John Hansen, the building guy?"

"John? Sure, all the time."

"Recently?"

"Recently what?"

"Have you seen him recently?"

Dave gave the question his usual slow care, then, "Couple days ago. He did a final on a room addition I worked on."

"Oh?"

"Yeah."

Patience, patience. "Where was that, Dave?"

"The old Patton place off Seacoast Lane."

"I don't know any Pattons."

"We just call it that. I guess it should be the Nam place now." He pondered a moment, then shook his head. "Except Margaret Nam doesn't live in it."

"Ah. Mind if I pull up a cinder block?"

Dave hauled one into position, then stood there, then brightened. "Want coffee?"

Tassy nodded at his mug. "Smells good."

He hustled into the house with more speed than usual and, she thought, a bigger smile than the occasion called for. More and more folks seemed to actually like her. It was unprecedented.

Back to the problem at hand. Two days ago, that inspector talked to Margaret Nam and this morning he hit her with some damn technical infraction. She guessed she could add two and two.

Dave brought her a mug and sat back down. Then they watched the morning together—or Tassy pretended to. Inside, her anger started spinning like a tropical storm sucking power and speed from the ocean below it. It was hard to think clearly through the haze of outrage, so she focused on coffee and morning sunshine and her brain whirled away on its own.

Ten minutes later the coffee was gone and the rage was fueling a plan. "Think Bill's home?" she asked.

Dave nodded.

She gave him her mug and stood up. "Well, as long as I'm visiting neighbors, I might just look in on him too."

"Oh," Dave said. "Okay."

"I need a loan from him." Tassy patted Dave on the shoulder and he smiled broadly. "And a lesson. Thanks for the coffee."

~

Linc was in his big steel kitchen, deciding what to nuke for lunch, when he heard the unmistakable *ga-ruff—ga-ruff—ga-ROWRRRRR!* of a chain saw starting. Funny, there weren't any trees this close to the shore. When the wind was right he could hear Bill the Fixer sculpting, but Bill didn't sound so close. Curious, Linc strolled through his parlor and out onto the front porch. From his high vantage point he could see part of the far side of Tassy's new fence over the top of the front, and as the howl of the saw continued, that far side commenced to waver and sag. He started down his steps just as Jack Millhouse, in an uncharacteristic white apron, bustled up from the direction of his coffee shop. Halfway to Tassy's property, Millhouse popped open his cell phone. Linc figured he'd better get over there.

~

Tassy heaved up the big orange saw. It was heavy and deafening and it stank of oil and two-stroke exhaust. It also scared her shitless, but its big motor and twenty-inch bar were just what the surgeon ordered. With its rear handle tight in her right hand and the side of its yoke gripped in her left, she kept the bar horizontal as Bill the Fixer had taught her. Move it slow and steady and don't cut with the front tip of the bar; okay! The first six feet of fence palisades were sheared off at the knees and now she faced the first major upright. Slow and steady, she chewed smoothly through the four-by-four post, and the cut section sagged even more, but didn't fall to the ground.

That was a problem. She let the saw idle while she thought.

At that point someone shouted something loud enough to hear

and she turned to find Millhouse close behind her. As the saw swung around he started to say—

ROWRRRRR! She gunned the saw and Millhouse pranced backward. She took a step toward him and he scampered all the way to the opposite curb.

The problem was the horizontal things—rails, weren't they?—still supporting the cut-off boards. Heaving up her ungainly weapon, she gunned it again and sawed downward. Jeez, it was heavy! The first fence section fell into her yard. Exhilarated by her own terror and the joy of big destruction, she attacked the second section, her arms jerking spastically as she and the saw fought their way across the fence. When she'd severed the boards and posts all the way to the front, she locked the chain as Bill had showed her and rested a moment.

This time it was Linc coming up behind her, and he looked furious. Screw him. It was her fence on her property. . . .

"Tassy! What are you doing? You're not wearing gloves or long pants; you don't have goggles; you need a hard hat and steel shoes. Christ, that thing'll cut your leg off!"

Forgetting that the chain was locked, she revved the motor again and the saw died. Linc looked relieved until she yanked the starter rope, knocked the yoke forward to unlock the chain, and answered *ROWRRR* with the saw.

Tassy went to work on the front fence. (Sweet how he worried about her safety.) From post to post to post she slaughtered the boards, straight across the front gate, which collapsed completely, around the uphill corner, then from post to post again, ripping and splintering all the way to the ocean side and back across to the house. What little she could hear above the racketing chain sounded like the groans of a building collapsing.

Finished, she pushed down the red slider thing to kill the motor and set down the big Husqvarna saw. Her shoulders were screaming, her arms trembled uncontrollably, her fingers would never uncurl, and her ears still howled in the silence. Tassy looked at the splinters and bleeding scratches on her thighs. A small enough price to pay. She'd have peed her shorts in terror too if she hadn't been focused so tightly. She made her shaking legs carry her out to the curb.

By now her audience included Millhouse, Linc, Bill and Dave (with Beowulf planted between them), Dottie Franklyn, Sharon Morning Sky from the Good Vibrations latte parlor, and Jimi from the Hair Place. She spotted Orson Wellesley puffing toward the group, and even the bait shop guy was trotting up the hill from the pier. Nobody said anything. They were probably deaf as she was. She felt Linc's arm go around her and thought vaguely how nice it felt.

Margaret Nam's giant white SUV rolled up across the street and stopped. Freeing herself from Linc, Tassy strolled across the road toward the Lincoln, while Margaret hastily powered up her window. Tassy rapped smartly on the glass and Margaret lowered it a finger width. "Yes?"

"Thirty-six inches," said Tassy loudly. "Give or take, here and there. You send back your tame building inspector; check it out." The window whispered closed, the big car whispered off, and Tassy turned away.

Still shaking, she walked to the high corner of her lot and surveyed her handiwork. The front was a junkyard of expensive kindling. Great stretches of fence sprawled on the ground or yawed at steep angles, prevented somehow from falling. The remaining low fence screamed for orthodontics: boards snaggling forward and back, jagged top edges bristling with splinters. All in all, a pretty good job. A damn fine job! A statement in front of everyone that even Linc couldn't counter.

Linc was talking quietly to Bill and Dave while the rest of the audience melted away, except for Beowulf and Jimi the hair genius, who bear-hugged Tassy, nearly setting her hair on fire with her cigarette. "Come in for a free cut," Jimi murmured. She looked at the wood chips in Tassy's hair. "Shampoo too." Jimi patted Tassy's shoulder, turned, and ambled off. Dave and Bill and the saw left too.

Linc cocked his head toward the B and B. "Bridal suite's got a big Jacuzzi. C'mon."

Tassy couldn't figure what was going on but was just too shot to bother. Nodding, she followed him up and across to the B and B.

9

$\mathcal{M}$argaret Nam rode her great white whale of a car to the corner, swung inland past Millhouse's coffee shop, rolled past the boutique and Dottie's tchotchke palace and seashell bazaar and the Good Vibrations latte parlor, turned right past the trailer park and the filling station and the market and Jimi's Hair Place, and she didn't see any of them. She surged up the northbound freeway ramp, merged with traffic, set cruise control, and drove on her own inner autopilot toward Oregon. After a thousand scenic twists and turns that she was also blind to, she mowed across the Klamath River bridge. Finally something broke her trance—maybe the silly, gilded, life-size bears posing on the bridge approach like lions in front of a library. Whatever it was, she swerved onto the gravel shoulder and the big Lincoln whipped around like a hippo *en pointe* and headed south.

What was she going to do now? The building inspector would tell somebody, who'd tell somebody else, and it'd be all over town that she'd sicced him on that woman. Even if Hansen kept quiet, that woman had chopped her own property down like some kind of performance art for gawdsake and then strolled over to Margaret's SUV while Margaret sat frozen there, too mad to think. Tassy'd nailed her with half the town listening and watching—rubbed her nose in it. Now they were laughing at her. Now the fence was a much bigger eyesore and the yard was completely trashed.

Like Margaret's reputation. Face it: A Realtor lived on reputation, community status, integrity. Lose that and watch the FOR SALE BY OWNER signs sprout and the RE/MAX jackals swarm in from the county seat. That woman had hurt her dignity, her honesty, and, yes, her livelihood. Now Margaret would have to tough it out with the city council or the chamber of commerce or the goddamn, *goddamn!* beautification committee.

So far her campaign had not been personal—simply an effort at civic improvement, a part of her public-spirited plan for the town. She didn't want a fight; she hated unpleasantness and everything else that was negative. But that woman didn't have to smash that fence, didn't have to do it with a screaming chain saw that brought the whole town out, didn't have to dump the blame on her. That woman had humiliated Margaret maliciously and unfairly.

Now it was personal.

~

While Margaret rode US 101 south like a slender Valkyrie, DayGlo Dave and Bill the Fixer started loading fence debris into Bill's pickup.

Dave whispered, "Hey! Linc said we gotta be quiet."

Bill was used to Dave's worries about things. "I know that, don't I?" he said mildly. "But if we have to pussyfoot around we'll still be here when Tassy gets back."

Dave looked doubtful. "Where she go?"

"Linc took her over to the B an' B."

Dave stared at the restored Vickie just up the hill. "You think they're . . ." He stopped and thought some. "You think they're maybe . . . ?"

Bill said, "Maybe got something going? Now, how would I know?" That seemed to bother Dave more than it ought to, so he added, "Probly not."

Dave thought a bit more, then nodded and resumed muscling used fencing into the pickup bed.

Listening inside a parlor window, Linc satisfied himself that the men were quiet enough. Tassy was in the kitchen sucking numbly on a Steelhead ale, so Linc streaked up the stairs with a second bottle and got to work. He filled the huge tub in the bridal suite bath, wrestled with the spa controls, rustled up some kind of bubble stuff Ellen'd bought for guests, and dosed the water generously. The bubbles were pretty aggressive. Had he used too much? He placed the full ale bottle on the inner ledge of the big tub, batted away the foam that was already rising to hide it, and grabbed a white terry robe from the back of the door.

The logo stopped him. Ellen had designed a leaping gray whale motif with "San Andreas B&B" underneath in some kind of Celtic lettering, and Dottie Franklyn had stitched it on the robe's terry breast with her computerized sewing machine. Both women had been so proud of their work.

Yeah, well.

Linc shook his head, then laid out the robe and two giant towels. Those bubbles were going to be trouble but he hadn't time for them now. Back to the kitchen.

Tassy was now extracting splinters from her legs and dotting wounds with the antiseptic he'd found for her. Linc thought about offering help, then stopped when he realized he'd have to handle her long thighs, though that shouldn't be a problem for a couple of middle-aged neighbor acquaintances, should it? But it was, so he didn't.

Instead, he made lame conversation. "Good thing the fence was cedar: Redwood splinters fester."

"I can't reach one in the back of my leg." Tassy stood and held out Ellen's tweezers. He squatted and looked at the job site. An ugly little sliver was buried toward the inner side of her right thigh, up near the hem of her shorts. If he pulled the flesh around it into a mound, it might pop its tip out. He inserted four fingers between her legs, then pinched them gently toward his thumb. The splinter head did emerge as planned and he trapped it with the tweezers and worked it free. He inspected the culprit, forgetting that he was still holding Tassy's warm thigh.

"Want some antiseptic?" She reached a cotton swab down behind her and Linc took it. He dabbed at the tiny wound. After ten or twelve dabs Tassy looked over her shoulder. "I think it's sterile by now, don't you?"

Linc stood up quickly enough to crack his knees. "Looks good," he offered inanely. "Now, come on upstairs."

Tassy stared at him a moment; then an *Okay, I'll bite* sort of look crossed her face and she followed him wordlessly.

In the bridal suite bath he showed her the robe and towels and rescued the ale from the bubbles again. Tassy smiled at the frothy cumulus. "You sure there's a tub under there?"

Linc only nodded, retreating toward the door. "Throw your clothes out in the bedroom."

"Why?"

"I'll put them in the washer. You'll want clean to go home in." He closed the door behind him.

Tassy stripped off her filthy shirt, dropped her shorts and panties, and unhooked her bra at the back, wincing at the aches in her arms. Tossing the lot out the door, she closed it and fumbled into the giant tub, trusting her feet to find it down there someplace.

The water was hot and it pounded where she dearly needed pounding. She'd finished her first ale but here was a brand-new one awaiting her pleasure. She'd have to fend off invasive suds, but that was fun in a dumb kind of way. All in all, she could go with this.

The thermostat kept the water hot, the jets kneaded away the kinks, and even the bubbles persisted long after bubbles were meant to decay. With the soothing massage and two bottles of ale, she was half-asleep when Linc tapped on the door.

"C'min."

He walked in, saw her still in the tub, and dropped his eyes.

Tassy snorted. "There's lots of bubbles left, if that's your problem."

"No." But his tone was just slightly defensive.

Tassy studied him. "Linc, what would you do if I stood up right now?"

"Hand you a towel." His casual tone was a shade too casual.

"Okay." She put her feet down and stood up, haphazardly draped in persistent bubbles. Keeping his eyes strictly on hers, Linc unfolded a great fuzzy towel and held it out to her. She took it, trying not to smile at his evident struggle to keep his eyes on her face.

"Your stuff's in the dryer; robe's there." He turned like a dignified butler, retreated to the hall, and closed the door behind him.

She stepped out and toweled herself dry. What was the deal here? He offered his Jacuzzi, made a production of giant towels and robes and bubbles, pumped ale into her. The robe was skimpy on her; one size did not, in fact, fit all. Admittedly, she'd been out of circulation for twenty-five years, but she didn't think the basics had changed, and Linc's response to her was nothing if not basic.

Out in the hall, Linc wondered why he was shaking. He wasn't some horny teenager. He'd seen provocative female skin—hell, he'd once hung out with cinema superstars who made allure their profession. Must have been the light. The ceiling downlights modeled rich slippery curves and made little rainbows in the bubbles clinging to them like props in a peekaboo strip act. That was all: a fleeting impression, a fleeting erotic image.

But all the way down to the kitchen the fleeting image wouldn't flee. Linc stirred a rich stew he'd unfrozen and nuked, bustled with flatware and paper napkins, rummaged for clean bowls—Should he stick plates under them? He guessed so. Glasses for the ale? Too formal—all the while trying to blink Tassy's lush body off his retinas.

It didn't help when she walked in wearing the too-short terry robe and scrubbing her hair with the second towel. Her high-arched feet were bare and the long legs above them were too tan for May. She must live in those skimpy shorts of hers. She studied the table, glanced at the stew in its bowls on the counter, took in the gleaming appliances and the work areas lit by pin spots. "Quite a setting," she said.

Linc thought about pulling her chair out, then decided to just wave at it. "Sit. I thought you could eat something." He brought the big bowls to the table, set them on their plates, and sat down.

Tassy sank into her seat with the gingerly moves of a candidate starting a job interview. Linc made an *eat, eat* gesture and she fumbled for a soup spoon without looking down. He started on his own bowl.

They spooned thick stew awhile. "Good," Tassy said. "You cook it?"

"You're joking, of course. Ellen made the stew and froze it on November sixteenth of last year."

"She dated her zip bags?"

Linc shook his head. "I did." He thought a moment, smiling. "It's funny: Ellen's compulsiveness stopped at the freezer. Left to herself, she'd just stuff something in and then tell its age by how frosty it looked or how gray the meat was." He lifted his spoon again, but paused because Tassy was sitting there smiling. "What?"

"You were smiling. I've seen you speak of Ellen before, but never smiling."

Linc considered this seriously. "That's certainly worth some thought."

Time for a subject change. "When a girl gets talked into a Jacuzzi complete with bubble bath she starts to think. And when she ends up in a robe at a dinner"—she waved around the softly lit room—"with everything but candlelight and music, she keeps on thinking."

Linc made it halfway through a shrug, then quit, leaving his shoulders at an uncomfortable angle.

She went on, "I get signals from all this, and from you. So what's up?"

His shoulders dropped. To tell God's truth, Linc just didn't know.

God's truth was, oh yes he did. What's up was Tassy: howling through her fence like a banshee, gunning for Margaret like the street was the O.K. Corral, trembling as she struggled to manage the tweezers, sprawled in the tub with her nipples just floating. And now calm again—not suspicious, not accusing, just watching him with that big, warm smile. Could he tell her all that? Hell, he could barely tell himself.

Instead, he puffed his cheeks and blew a fat sigh. "I don't know what the story is. The Jacuzzi was a trick to get you away from your house."

Tassy's smile faded.

"While Dave and Bill cleaned up your yard. The wood's at Dave's place if you want it for fires."

Flatly: "I don't have a fireplace."

"Right; well." Looking at the floor, Linc noticed her bare toes wiggling and the sleek tan shank of one crossed leg swinging up and down. He made himself focus on her face again. "I made dinner so we could talk about your house."

Her face went stiff. "What about it?"

Linc suddenly sensed he could lose her, keep his damn poker face and his thoughts to himself and watch her walk out, robe and all. He had to try, at least try: "To answer your question first, when you stood up in the tub you completely blew my circuits. Half an hour later I'm still seeing everything through an image of you with the suds running off you."

Her face softened again and her smile returned.

"I've realized that I'm looking for excuses to see you, talk to you. Maybe my part in your house business is one of those excuses." When she started to speak, he added, "Not completely, but part." He scooped up stew but didn't eat it. "Ellen's been gone seven months now. I think that's . . ."

"Are you worried about the 'rebound' thing?"

"No. Yes. I don't know. Jeez! I haven't done this for twenty-five years!"

"Me either."

The implications of that reply stopped him dead. He blinked stupidly. Then, almost desperately, "Just let me sort this out, okay? But don't go away—please."

Tassy nodded slowly, then said, "Either eat that bite or put the spoon down." He ate it sheepishly. "Now. What'd you get me over here to sell me?"

"The usual: peace and quiet. You let Dave fix what's left of your fence. Bill says Dave can realign stuff and add a top cap—a new gate, whatever—make it all pretty. Then I see to it that you're not hassled about your paint color."

Tassy thought a bit. "And you are going to pay for this like you paid for the fence—and the cleanup too, I'll bet."

Linc shrugged. "Put it in perspective. Would your income let you spend a dollar to get rid of a nuisance?"

"Yeah, but that's about the limit."

"Suppose your income was a hundred times as big as, well, whatever it is. Would the nuisance then be worth a hundred bucks?"

"Sure, it'd be lunch money—" She broke off. "You really are loaded, aren't you?"

Linc winced. "I didn't bring this up to brag."

"Sorry. Bad taste and all. I'm okay with a three-foot fence, but what about that Realtor?"

"I'll give her the rosewood wall treatment."

Tassy's face said, *Huh?*

"Picture it: The law office takes up three floors of a huge building, the secretaries whisper, the Persian carpets are a century old.

Before I give Margaret legal advice, I lead her into a conference room with a table you could play hockey on and polished rosewood walls twelve feet high."

Tassy still looked puzzled.

"With portraits of the founding partners in big whiskers. The advice I give her may be crap but it comes with rosewood paneling."

"And portraits."

"Works every time."

"Where's that office?"

Linc tapped his forehead.

"Now you *are* bragging."

He looked around the kitchen as if he'd forgotten what it was for. "There's still a few things I do well."

The dryer buzzed. Tassy stood up and followed the sound into the laundry. While Linc watched through the doorway, she pulled her clothes out of the dryer and placed them on top. After staring at the small pile, she slowly stripped the robe and let it drop, then dressed—with neither haste nor provocation, but in the open doorway nonetheless.

She picked up the robe, returned to the kitchen, and handed it to him. "I'll think about your offer."

He wanted to tell her that wasn't his only offer—not even the important one—but his courage failed him again. Linc said, "Your Nikes are on the front porch."

10

The morning after the San Andreas chain saw massacre Tassy went instinctively to the gallery, as if going home to mother. Sitting at Orson Wellesley's breakfast table, she reported on the hot tub and dinner. "He says he'll fix the fence and the city council too. What do you think?"

Orson started dabbing his chin with a napkin—a major project due to the size of the chin. "Linc can pull it off—but is that really the point?"

"It should settle things. Finally."

"What's settling, dear, is the house."

Tassy raised her arms to say, *What can I do?*

"All right, listen to Orson for once."

Orson explained the ruse of replacing a house by pulling a permit to restore it instead, while promising to remove only a few unsavable bits.

"But how can I get a new-construction loan for a restoration?"

"My dear friend Archie will lend a hand, and he's a biggie at Lost Coast Bank."

"Norman Stihl said he could fix the bluff."

"Then he's the man for you."

Tassy sighed at the prospect. "I'm afraid that's what *he* thinks."

Orson lifted understanding eyebrows. "Ah! Speaking of which, did you get laid last night?"

Tassy could only blink. Village gossip flew on the wind, but this was ridiculous.

"Evidently not. Don't let Linc wander off, darling. Behind that glum face there's quite a man coming back out. Trust cupid here."

Tassy flashed on a pink, naked Orson up on one foot, with tiny wings and a bow and arrow. Orson did not deign to notice her chuckle.

Over at the Good Vibrations latte parlor, Sharon Morning Sky tidied the celery snacks, bran muffins, and jelly donuts arrayed to tempt her varied clientele, while her assistant buffed the counter with a cleaning cloth.

Sharon's thick black hair fell straight to her sacrum and her brown, chiseled face resembled the portraits sold to tourists in Taos; but the hair was dyed and ironed, the skin bronzed in a salon at the county seat, and the name long changed from Van Gelden. Sharon Morning Sky was not of the Narowa or any other tribe, though she fervently believed that her identity must lie somewhere in that area.

Moving to the gleaming steel machines that she deplored philosophically but required for her living, Sharon built a rich concoction in an oversize cup and served it to Norman Stihl at his regular table, by the window. Norman didn't notice her much anymore, though there'd been a time not long ago. . . . And maybe there would be again. How many beds were there in a village this size?

As she approached, the big man clicked off a tiny cell phone. "That was Tassy Morgan." At her raised eyebrow, he added, "She wants me to rebuild her bluff; redo her house." Norman had no reason to explain this to Sharon but he wished to broadcast his big new job to the latte parlor's three other patrons.

She sat down across from him. "Can you make it work?"

"Have to reengineer the whole property—excavate most of the land."

"The whole . . . ?"

"Right in from the ocean."

She laid a hand on his. "Well, you're the guy to do it."

He looked at the hand, then covered it with his free one. His smile seemed genuine.

She patted his hand in turn, so that all four were piled up on the table. Then she laughed, withdrew hers, and stood up. Norman's smile broadened and she took a deep breath. She hadn't all that much chest, but what she had, she'd wave at him. "See ya," she said, and then head-flipped her long silky hair, which waved with far greater effect.

~

As it happened, Sharon's assistant *was* Narowa—or mainly, though her appearance placed her only in the vast tan gene pool of Hispanic Asian Pacific Native African folks who were benignly repopulating the West Coast. After helping Sharon close up she drove to her second job, dealing drinks at the casino. She'd taken this job to get close to Erik Halvorsen and she was talking to him now, for all the good it did her. Erik was friendly and nice as could be, but he didn't seem to see her as female, even in this silly cocktail waitress getup. She consoled herself, thinking he never looked at anyone else she knew either, so maybe he didn't like girls. Anyway, he was a nice guy and also her boss, so it didn't hurt to talk with him—trade a little gossip.

His interest seemed to perk up when she told him what she'd overheard about Norman's proposed surgery on the town's seaside bluff, but he didn't comment and after a while she picked up her drink tray again and went back to work.

Erik decided to consult Grandmother Halvorsen. Grandmother was easy to find because she took her dinners in the casino restaurant, ex officio, of course. Erik walked down the aisle dividing slots from blackjack, passed the Jim Thorpe Sports Bar with its eight hi-def video screens, passed the virtuous gamers in their separate smoke-free enclosure, passed the cheap and popular buffet, passed the men's room with its actual fresh cloth towels stacked beside each sink, and entered the restaurant foyer through doors that suddenly silenced the jingling casino.

The restaurant was everything that the Beach House seafood shack might have been but wasn't: spacious and tasteful, with ocean view windows that would still delight after dark because the lights of San Andreas—now just winking on—would pick out the coast and harbor to the south. Erik nodded at the waitstaff, who responded with more warmth than just the courtesy owed a boss, as he made his way to the best table, by the gas log fireplace.

Grandmother was dismantling a rancher's cut of rare roast beef. He kissed her forehead, sat down opposite, and after minimal pleasantries, disclosed what he had learned. When he'd finished he waited while she methodically whittled the pink plank in front of her.

Finally, "Do you see what it means, Grandmother?"

It was unwise to imply that Grandmother might not see the implications of a situation—any situation—so she just cut and chewed, cut and chewed until the silence stretched long enough to convey her disapproval. When she had finished her meat and launched into Yorkshire pudding—strangely shaped because it'd been baked in a popover tin—she said, "Fully permitted construction means a proper construction site, fenced to prevent accidents. That would close the beach access trail."

"At least for this season. Maybe by next year we can close it for good."

"By next year, we'll own it."

Erik stole a french fry. "How's that coming?"

Grandmother sighed. "It's not. Parks and Rec won't talk, and if I twist *their* arms, there's the coastal commission and the board of supervisors after them."

"Can you do it?"

Maybe it was the pinot noir or maybe she was finally getting

tired, but for once, Grandmother unbent enough to confide in someone. "You know what, Erik? This time maybe I can't. I know a stall
when I smell one and right now I smell three in a row. I'm going to
have to go downtown."

Erik asked, "Will that help?"

She cleared her throat and pulled her regular face back on. "Glass
of wine?"

"I'm supposed to be on duty." He rose and pecked her forehead
again, then left her to her pinot noir and dessert.

~

Everything in Tassy's nature made her want to jump up and
dance. Perched on a tall draftsman's stool in her studio, she watched
the nearly June sunset, enriched this evening with intermittent bands
of fog between harbor and horizon. The highest clouds blazed pink
below a hard blue sky, the fog bank edges shimmered red and mauve
and even greenish, and the orange sun disk swelled and flattened as
it flirted with the ocean.

How could a sight so corny, so 1920s-hand-tinted-postcardy,
make her want to laugh and weep at once? Yes, it was excessive; yes,
God was showing off—why not? Why was affirmation so uncool?
With all the petty squabbling going on around here, it felt so good to
recall what San Andreas really was about. It was about the sun painting fog banks and the ancient, indifferent sea.

She opened her phone on its second ring.

"Hello, Mom, it's Dana."

The first contact in months and her daughter talked as if they
spoke daily, but Tassy still felt a lift of love and hope. "Yes, dear, I still
recognize your voice. How are you?"

She could hear a dismissive head shake in Dana's tone. "Listen,
I've got a kind of a thing here, y'know, to work out?"

Clearly, Dana had inherited her mother's dazzling gift for small talk. Tassy answered wryly, "What kind of a thing is 'a kind of a thing,' dear?'"

"What?" Dana did better with straightforward sentences. "Oh, just a—well, here's the thing: I'm getting married."

Tassy clamped down a violent urge to shift into full mother mode. The situation was bound to be more complex than it seemed. She settled on a careful, "Wonderful! Tell me about the groom."

"Oh, you don't know him."

"No, dear, but I'd like to." Tassy's voice was warm but not, she hoped, pleading.

"Anyway, the wedding's next week."

Tassy was shocked into incautious humor. "Are you eloping?"

"Of course not! I've been killing myself—me and the wedding planner—for six freaking months."

Six months. A small pause, then, "I hadn't heard." She couldn't hide all the hurt.

The phone was silent a moment, then Dana said anxiously, "I guess I should've said something, but well, it's just . . . Dad's just . . ."

"I'm not sure I understand." But she was only too afraid that she did.

She could hear a deep breath, then, "Here's the thing, Mother. Dad'd like you to, well, maybe give this one a miss. I know you're my mother and I want you to know I really appreciate that. I *really* do." A long pause that Tassy made no effort to fill. Finally, Dana resumed. "But, well, Dad's got a few little, well . . . *issues*."

"Issues?" People didn't have problems anymore, just issues, as if life were a political campaign.

"Just a few—about some of his friends. You know, the old ones."

"The ones who knew me too."

"There you go. You know how it is." Dana's tone shifted to indulgent exasperation. "Well, he just insists on inviting them—he says it's because they've known him, well, the longest, I guess—and, so, there's just . . . issues."

"So it would be easier on you and your father . . ."

Her daughter jumped on it gratefully. "Yuh, that's it, yuh, right—hey, not easier on *me*, but, well, yeah, I guess when it's easier on Dad he makes it easier on me." Another dead pause. "Well, something like that. I dunno."

Tassy felt hit on the head with a hammer. The silence went on so long that Dana said, "Mom?"

She searched desperately for some reply, some way to negotiate out of this, but at bottom she knew she was wasting her time. Finally, for lack of anything better she said, "Meanwhile, how *have* you been?"

"Well, *you* know, same old same old." Dana sounded awkward, but quickly rescued herself. "Oh, I forgot: The registry's at Neiman Marcus."

Tassy could just manage, "Ah."

"You can order online, get it shipped; we're the Morgan-Stanley wedding—isn't that a kick? *Morgan-Stanley?* I mean, it's just a coincidence, of course."

More autopilot humor, "Aw, tough luck."

"What?" A silence for processing. "Okay, whatever. Gotta run. Thanks for understanding, Mom."

"Good-bye, love."

The sun sagged into the horizon, drowned in the ocean, and left the red-rimmed fog banks behind. These faded to gray and then black, along with the rest of the day, leaving the harbor lights and the long, dark sweep of coastline. Tassy watched the show until only those intermittent twinkles remained. Why was sunset so melancholy—so much like a daily death?

She'd sealed the remains of her former life in a rickety mausoleum and mentally walked away, never returning to leave flowers or remember her dead. Now the weak structure had crumbled like mud bricks in a flood and released the old ghosts to torment her.

She remembered when her husband, Larry, had reverted to "Lawrence" and enforced the change strictly, remembered when he started wearing hand-tailored suits and how she'd gaped at their prices. She recalled when her Subaru had been suddenly swapped for a Range Rover—he'd presented it as a loving surprise, but she knew he disapproved of her unassuming mommy wagon. Had she finally failed to conceal her boredom with arcane financial instruments, or had Lawrence grown tired of talking about them? Maybe both.

Her mildly bohemian friendships had faded with time and distance and her husband's evident lack of interest. He'd had so little leisure to socialize anyway that it seemed unfair to subject him to people he didn't understand or care for. Those mutual friends he'd invited to the wedding would be from his working world only. That they'd once known Tassy as well was an accident.

She thought about Dana, a plump, passive girl who'd become a solid young woman until she'd starved her body into submission. Her daughter's ferocious diet had been the only vocation she'd pursued with passion or even much interest, and her fashionable boniness was her one source of pride.

During her adolescence, the posters and music in her bedroom had halfheartedly followed the fads her friends followed. She hadn't even liked horses.

Maybe that was it: Aside from the comforts of money, her daughter didn't much care about anything. Growing up, she'd been obedient, even affectionate in an absent sort of way. But then she'd reached the age at which daughters turned into friends—or some did—and Tassy wasn't good at friends, wasn't good at making them or keeping them, so Dana was now just a relative, like a second cousin or something.

In her time Tassy'd earned her keep as a uterus, nanny, and

housekeeper when they couldn't quite yet afford a live-in. But then Dana'd left for college, the new house was far too big to take care of, and Larry's income—sorry, Lawrence's compensation package—had ballooned with the times and José and Maria were trifling expenses.

Tassy might have survived indefinitely, painting in her "playroom," as Lawrence called it, and handling the loneliness that was, after all, nothing new. But skilled socializing was a growing part of her job description and she simply hadn't the gift for it. She had no small talk and no instinct for safe conversation, so it was no coincidence that those were the only talents that her replacement, Lindsay, did have, beside youth and rubber boobs, of course.

She guessed it was the politeness that had finally destroyed her. If she and Lawrence had fought, had hurled accusations and vases, had wept and got drunk and tried to make up and then fractured again, then at least the passion of the breakup would have mirrored an opposite passion in the marriage. But the sheer emotional emptiness of the process made her wonder what the hell she'd been doing for twenty-five years. What had she been thinking? Why had she fallen in love with Larry to begin with—or had she, really? Now she honestly couldn't remember.

When the civilities had run their course, the revised and updated Lawrence hadn't even discarded her. He'd simply moved on, as if from one house to a better one, leaving a busted sofa behind. Hell, he hadn't even bothered to set her out on the sidewalk. As for Dana, her daughter had, as always, glided down the path of least resistance.

Though the divorce had been destructive enough, Tassy had crawled out of its ruins and was painfully assembling a new life from personal resources that were bruised but not broken. But Dana's vague fadeout from her mother's life had damaged Tassy. To lose a daughter to death would be agonizing but comprehensible. To lose her to distance and indifference was shattering.

She realized that Beowulf was sitting there watching her. "Wallowing in self-pity, right?" Beowulf grinned. "But you don't care, do you? You just don't judge." She got down off the high stool and into a catcher's crouch. "C'mere, Wolfie!" Was it her imagination or did the dog respond more enthusiastically than usual? Arms hugging his big chest, nose buried in his sweet-smelling ruff, she snorted and mentally shook herself. Better to rebuild the cheap tomb and seal the ghosts in again. Besides, she'd made better friends here.

~

Standing on Tassy's front stoop, Norman Stihl revved up to resume his campaign. He'd prepared it with a couple of scribbled project plans for an excuse and a bottle of chardonnay for persuasion. The wine ought to impress Tassy, because Bess at the market said it was good and it'd set him back eight bucks. A bourbon man himself, Norman saw wine ignorance as a guy thing of some importance.

He rang and in due course was admitted. "Hey, Tassy, you tied up? Oh, hi, Wolfie."

11

*U*p the street, Linc sat in a New England rocker at the kitchen table. The chair was civilized by a seat pad and lit by a lamp bright enough to read by. Tonight he'd fallen back on a fat science fiction saga from the stash in his room after failing to find anything in the parlor bookcases.

Typically, the shelves in B and B's and summer rentals offered *Reader's Digest Condensed Books*, paperbacks yellowed enough to trigger asthma, ancient economics texts, and, if you were lucky, a hardbound Pearl S. Buck novel with a $2.95 price on its front jacket flap. But like everything else in this B and B, Ellen had designed and assembled the book inventory from scratch to match a hypothetical profile of guests who would pay hundreds of dollars a night for a suite but bring nothing to read in it. The result was a bountiful library that appeared to have grown over twenty years of eclectic but upscale collecting, though it had been less than two months old when the B and B was shuttered by Ellen's death.

The best laid schemes. Hmh. If he reopened the joint he'd rename it Gang Aft Agley.

He wouldn't reopen; he'd known that, though he'd avoided confronting the implications. Now, without warning, the implications were getting right in his face.

What *would* he do? He was fifty-one, healthy, unencumbered, and just rich enough: not a billionaire, so he lacked both the power conferred by staggering wealth and the moral imperative to use it well—not that big CEOs and financial twisters seemed unduly oppressed by moral imperatives.

On the other hand, he had vastly more income than he needed. He could live anywhere on earth he chose. He could party with the people who party and sleep with the women who sleep with rich men, even if they're over fifty—*especially* if they're over fifty. For fun, he could produce boutique movies—it had worked for the Weinsteins—or follow the ski season or play venture capitalist or pretend to be a Montana rancher. . . .

But the operative words there were *fun*, *play*, *pretend*, and that wasn't Linc's style. He'd gone with the B and B idea because it was something to occupy him. He couldn't care less about inn keeping, but he *had* cared about Ellen and hoped that getting her launched could preoccupy him, at least for a while. Then *a while* had turned out to be just six weeks.

He wouldn't go back to the entertainment business; by now he'd be Rip van Winkle in Hollywood, and he was fed up with that whole life anyway.

There were other kinds of law to practice. Yeah.

The Law is the true embodiment
Of everything that's excellent.

He'd never believed that, of course. The law was a game—half chess, half Dungeons and Dragons—whose tendrils of statutes and case law were tangled as tightly as Celtic line mazes and just as intriguing to follow. But like a great initial in the Book of Kells, the law had become a stand-alone work of art, so gorgeous, so self-complete that it had lost its connection to the sentence it was charged with beginning.

The Law is the true embodiment
Of everything irrelevant.

Well, not really, but that's how he felt about it now.

Quite a coincidence that Tassy knew Gilbert and Sullivan. How many people still liked them these days? He cast about for some excuse to go see her but couldn't think of one, and he lacked the courage to simply get up and go. Disgusted with his cowardice, Linc tried to sink into his space opera.

~

Tassy'd seemed kinda strange when she opened her door, but Norman had offered his drawings—okay, still the same scribbles— and she'd invited him in to sit at her kitchen table. He'd allowed as how the couch might be better on account of . . . on account of the good reading light over there. Her expression changed from strange to thoughtful, but she just kept standing there; so to make some kind of talk, he'd waved the wine bottle and said he brought a little toast to the new construction job.

The thinking expression went on awhile longer, then Tassy looked at the bottle, looked Norman in the eye, then thanked him and said what a nice idea. She took the bottle to her little kitchen area and Norman watched her cycling hips and buns. She didn't ex- aggerate that swivel, didn't have to, but studying her was just plain art appreciation.

When they were side by side on the rump-sprung couch with Wolfie on Tassy's far side, she spread the drawings across her near thigh, which was perfect. In pointing out different features of his plan, Norman could pat her leg through the paper; and by keeping his wineglass on the floor between them, he could sort of brush her bare calf as he picked the glass up and set it down. Apologizing for mislaying his Kmart reading glasses, he shifted up against her so that his bird's-eye view of the drawings was half-blocked by the swell of her right-hand boob, which was also great by him, except the layout wasn't quite right for grazing it with his forearm as he tapped here and there on the sketch.

After maybe ten minutes of this, he checked her face, in profile, and saw she was wearing a funny little smile—almost smug. T'hell was that all about?

She turned her head toward him. "How much are you looking at?"

The whole damn package, but he was pretty sure she meant the job. He sidestepped the answer with a small confession to show the client he was on her side: "Truth is, buying a factory-built'd give you more for your money."

"Then . . ."

"But that'd be new construction." He shrugged regretfully into her arm and shoulder.

Tassy sighed. "I get it." The bottom sheet of paper whispered on her shorts as she drew it out to place on top. She tapped it. "How about the bluff job?"

"Depends on what's underneath." Norman pushed even closer, peering down as if he disremembered what was on his sketch.

She sucked breath in through her teeth. "I can't finance this open-ended."

Norman pretended to think while reaching down for his wine, his knuckles stroking warm skin in both directions. "Tell you what: I'll quote you a fixed price, no matter what we find."

"That's good of you, Norman."

He refilled the glasses. "Well, what the hell, I like you. I think we'll fit right together." He toasted her with a gesture and they both drained their wine.

That smile on her slowly grew and her eyes shone. Excepting a few little crinkles around them, she looked half her age in that soft light. She studied his right hand, still resting on the drawing on her thigh as if he'd absentmindedly mislaid it.

When she looked up again the smile had opened up into an actual grin. "I'll tell you something, Norman: Your offer's made me feel good. . . ."

"The house?"

She shook her head. "No, not the house." Tassy patted his hand, displaced it from her thigh, and stood up. "On a night when I really, *really* needed to feel good."

"Always glad to help out." He couldn't figure this *at all*.

She handed back the sketches. "So what do you need to get started?"

One thing he could figure: The way she was walking toward the door, she wasn't about to sit back down and get cozy. Strike two, but he kept his disappointment inside. If you knew how to quit before things got awkward, you might get another chance to score. He stood up and walked to the door. "Well, give me a day or two to work it out."

"I thought you had it worked out."

He gave her that rueful, self-mocking look like George Clooney did so well. "I thought I did too."

Her smile and nod said she knew what he meant. To hide it, she bent and patted the dog at her feet.

12

*B*eing mainly boilerplate, the house rehab paperwork took only two days to draw up: plan printouts, an application for permits, and a pair of proposals, one for the bank and one for the town council or beautification committee or whatever they were when they next met.

The proposal would be buttressed—literally—by a design from a licensed soils engineer to stabilize the bluff for the foreseeable future. In the small, cozy world of the Redwood Coast, the power of a soils engineer to foresee the geological future was proportional to the size of his fee. The same was true of his loyalty: Once he'd been bought for Tassy's project, he would never admit to her neighbors that strengthening her piece of bluff could very well weaken theirs. Norman Stihl nourished a link with one such local expert, to their longtime mutual profit.

~

Returning to the site of the project, he explained the documents to Tassy at length, fanning them across the big drafting table in her studio. She'd led him out there despite his hopeful suggestion that they review the plans as before, on the couch. The late-afternoon sun blasting through the big windows was counter-romantic, but Norman was ready to rise above this handicap. Standing beside Tassy, he gradually managed to snug his left side up against her right. When Tassy shifted away, he re-snugged, until finally she was at the far side of the table edge and still inching leftward. She tried pushing back toward the middle, which was just what he wanted, of course.

Abruptly she tossed her reading glasses onto the plans and turned to face him.

Norman gave her his best Clooney grin. "Any questions?"

Tassy looked at him as if deciding what to say, then took a big breath. "Norman, I'm going to be straight with you. Will you do the same with me?"

"I'm always straight with my clients." Up to a point, of course.

"No, I mean about us."

So there was an *us*! He couldn't figure how to play this yet, but the right answer here was obvious. "Okay, complete honesty."

"From the way you glom on to me, I get the impression you think I'm attractive."

Great: An answer he wouldn't have to fake. He said fervently, "Oh, I do. Do I ever!"

"Why?"

Jeez, was this a trick question? "Well, who really knows—?"

She shook her head. "No, I just mean physically."

Women didn't ask shit like that, did they? "Physically?"

"You have to admit you're a pretty physical guy."

A compliment; that felt good, but he knew enough to keep to the party line. "You're a lot more than just physical."

"But let's stick to that. Why is my body attractive?"

What the hell did you do with a conversation like this? Desperately, "Yeah, well, it sure is, Tassy."

"But *why?*"

Norman rose up on mental tiptoes. "Well . . ." How to say it nicely? "You're, ah, *shapely*." Was she ever: legs, boobs, butt.

"You mean my legs, boobs, and butt."

Jesus Christ! Was she reading his mind? "That and . . . *stuff,* yeah." But women didn't want to be just tits and ass; he knew that. Hastily, "Don't forget your hair; don't forget your face."

She waved at the brutal sunshine. "In this light? I'm a roadmap."

"Just shows you're grown-up." He didn't plan that one; it popped out.

"That's kind."

"No it's not." The words kept on coming. "You're just . . . just sexy all over."

After a long moment she nodded. "Okay, thank you." She reached out and took his hand. "Now I'll be just as honest with you. I think you're attractive—*very* attractive."

Three cherries!! The quarters clattered out of the slot machine.

She was still looking him square in the eye. "But I'm not attracted to you."

Now, just a damn minute! "I don't . . ."

"You're a big, virile guy and a pretty nice one too, I think."

Norman was lost, dead lost. "Well . . ."

"But the chemistry isn't there, and without the right chemistry . . ."

"What the hell is chemistry?" He couldn't keep the squeak out of his voice.

Tassy sighed and let his hand drop. "Norman, if I knew that, I could write a sex manual, but whatever it is, we don't have it. We're just not in the cards." She tidied the papers on the table. "But we're starting a big project—going to be together almost every day. I can't take that on if you're going to chase me around the sawhorses."

He said stiffly, "I don't force myself on people."

"I know you don't; I can tell. And you're grown-up enough to understand how I can think you're very attractive but not be attracted to you."

No, he couldn't understand that, not all. If he was attractive, she should be attracted—hell, they *all* were. He must of screwed up somehow.

Without seeming to, she'd been walking him into the living room. She opened the front door and offered her hand. "Can we shake on the deal?" By now he was out on the step.

After a pause Norman stuck out his own hand.

"The *whole* deal?"

He nodded numbly and shook on it.

She gave him a friendly smile. "I know you'll keep your promise." Tassy let go of his hand and closed the door.

Hell if he would! She wanted to play hard to get, well he could play hard too, and a job this size'd give him ten months to do it. Think of it as a challenge, yeah. More fun than a quick roll in the hay, right?

Wrong. T'hell was he thinking? The woman said no, loud and clear, and he wasn't about to force anyone. Besides, there was Margaret, and Margaret seemed like—well, more eager lately.

A bit snug in the crotch, Norman tugged at his twill work pants. He wondered if Margaret was home yet.

~

Inside, Tassy studied the drawings and the two proposals, line by line, word by word, as the sun set behind her. Turning away from her drawing table, she watched the wavering, half-squashed fireball disappear and the clouds sing their daily chorus. In her time as a moneyed wife, she'd visited half the sunsets in *Condé Nast Traveler* magazine, but not a one surpassed this. This was it, no doubt about it; San Andreas was the place for her. And with Norman's plans and a construction loan, she could make it work. But only if she put it the right way to the town council, and God knew they were unpredictable. Her proposal had to be bombproof.

And, say, guess who knew both the legal stuff and the council?

That one-man bomb squad Linc Ellis, that's who. Tassy gathered up her paperwork and went looking for him.

He wasn't hard to find. She followed the music through Linc's parlor, across his big kitchen, and into his overstuffed bedroom. The mighty speakers were pouring forth a Beethoven piano concerto; she knew that much but not which one. Oh: It was the second—said so right there on the cover of the score he was reading.

From the quick pace of the music, she figured this must be the last movement, so she waited till the end, then rapped on the doorframe.

Linc looked up and smiled. "Howdy."

"Hi, counselor. Got a minute to look at some stuff?"

"Sure."

She started back toward the kitchen and, as he followed her, laid out her plans and proposals on the table. "I'm ready to take my rehab plans to the city."

"I thought we were fixing the fence."

She grinned at him. "Orson showed me how to get a rehab permit and Norman Stihl knows how to finesse a new house out of it."

"He do some plans for you?"

Tassy nodded happily.

Linc stood on the opposite side of the table. "Well, that's good; that's very good."

"And I thought you might look this stuff over—see if he's dotted and crossed everything."

For a moment, Linc just studied her, then he said, "Tassy, I can't do that."

She felt her cheerful look fade.

"I'm counsel for the city."

"I didn't mean officially."

"Even informally, I can't advise clients on opposite sides. It's unethical." He spoke slowly, as if to a slow learner.

She resented his tone. "I'm not a client, Linc; I'm a friend."

"Just the same, I can't do it." He aimed his hand at her paper-work and made small push-away gestures in the air, saying impatiently, "This puts me in a bad position."

"Puts *you*?" Tight-ass son of a bitch! She abruptly grabbed her paperwork and snatched it out of the splash of downlight on the table. "I think I know just where it puts both of us. Sorry to bother you." Tassy turned and stomped out through the parlor and the front door.

Linc followed her. "Tassy . . ."

She held up a hand like a cop stopping traffic. "See you at the council meeting, *counselor*." Tassy marched off down the street.

Linc called after her, "But that's not for another two weeks."

"Good!" She crossed to her place, swept through the ruined gate, entered her house, and closed the door with a decisive *clack* that didn't quite qualify as a slam.

Linc walked back toward the kitchen. What did she expect? Honestly! He stalked through the kitchen, into his bedroom, and over to his CD player, where Beethoven waited with the perfect patience of digital media. Honestly! He popped the disk and stowed it. Was conflict of interest such a hard concept? How could she even think of it? He wandered out of the improvised bedroom. Did she have a clue what would happen if the council found out he'd advised her on a matter before them? Oh, Margaret would jump right on that one.

By now, Linc was back in the parlor, pacing.

Margaret and Dottie and Jack on one side; Tassy and Orson on the other. He stopped pacing to stare out the newly repaired parlor window, just as the lights behind Tassy's front windows went out.

For what seemed a long time his head felt completely empty, not with the familiar numbness of grief but as if waiting for some secret process to complete and reveal itself.

Then it did. It should have been obvious that logic told him one thing and feelings said the opposite and feelings were winning the argument. When he came right down to it, when he really faced himself, he knew which side he wanted to be on; ethics be damned. He would stand with Tassy.

Okay, deal with it. What did it mean? First, he'd have to resign as city attorney, hand in his badge. They could find somebody else. . . .

Bad plan. If he quit he'd lose control of the legal situation—hell, he'd have to quit the council too, or at least recuse himself re: Tassy's application.

Now he was out on the front porch.

But if he stayed on and kept quiet, he'd be unethical, plain and simple. He paced back and forth in front of the gleaming teak porch swing.

But if he couldn't run interference, they'd keep nitpicking her to death. Her paperwork would have to be nit-less, so perfect they'd have no choice but to give her permission. Uh-huh, and who knew how to make her paperwork perfect?

Linc was on his front walk, still dodging and weaving around his dilemma. And so, addressing the asphalt, then the three-quarter moon, then the paving again, waving his arms vaguely and tracing an uneven path, he argued himself down the street and across to his neighbor's front door.

Tassy opened it to his knock. "What?"

"I changed my mind. Can I come in?"

She studied him a moment, then swung the door wide.

Linc pulled up suddenly. "Um . . . no." He turned and sprinted back up the hill. Tassy watched him all the way back up onto his porch and through his front door.

This time, her own door truly did slam. Furious, she stalked into her studio and stood at a big window, hoping the harbor lights would soothe her.

Three minutes later she was starting to calm herself when she heard another knock. Furious all over again, she stomped back to yank open the door.

"*What?*"

Linc held up a fat, messy three-ring binder. "Town codes and ordinances," he said, wheezing slightly.

Sigh. "You could have said something. . . . Oh, never mind." She led the way back to the studio and switched on the big work lights. "How come you changed your mind?"

Linc looked her in the eye. He opened and closed his mouth slightly, paused, repeated the movements, repeated again.

"Don't you know—or won't you say?"

"Partly both—at least, so far." He shook his head. "Listen, do me this favor: Go over your stuff with me, and afterward, I'll try to tell you."

Tassy shot him a speculative look, then laid her paperwork out on the worktable. She rolled up two drafting stools, sat down on one, and offered the other. Linc sat beside her.

~

By eleven p.m. the city binder was even messier, the papers were covered with notes, and Linc had filled four pages of a legal pad. Two emptied bottles of sauvignon blanc were now starting to dull the old knife-sharp legal mind, but the old knife-sharp legal mind was essentially finished anyway, and while still working, it belonged to a killer contract attorney who'd given this one his all. Talk about bombproof. Tassy's application was now a freaking missile silo—yes!

Linc set down his empty glass, leaned back on his drafting stool, and remembered, just barely in time, that it was backless. Tassy chuckled as he windmilled his arms and wound up more or less standing. She'd done her fair share of work on the wine. She stood up too, threaded her arms inside Linc's, and hugged him. "Thanks, Linc," she murmured. "Thanks."

Ellen wasn't—hadn't been—the hugging type, and even her subtler shows of affection had now been gone these many months. He hadn't realized how good it felt.

And Tassy was big enough to give an industrial hug. Her hands between his shoulder blades pressed him to her. When she shifted off center to lay her cheek on his, her big breast pushed hard on his rib cage and her thighs straddled one of his.

She leaned her head back to look at his eyes. Then she kissed him. It wasn't a friendly smooch or a familiar smack on the mouth, but it wasn't aggressive and probing either. It was a connecting kind of a kiss that let feelings flow back and forth as if their mouths were a soft communications port—hear the romantic geek, jeez!—and it went on and on while she stood pressed against him with her lips moving just softly and her nose offset enough to breathe.

Not that he was remembering to breathe. He was sensing her palms on his back and her breast at his ribs and her long thighs clasping his, and his own palms that had slid down to bracket her lush behind.

Not to mention his equipment waking up for the first time in— wow! Its message was unmistakable. He leaned back, breathing hard now, maybe from lack of oxygen or maybe just because she made him breathe hard. They looked at each other, both smiling, then Tassy nodded very slightly toward the front of the house. That's where the couch was, maybe even the bedroom. He nodded back calmly, though his brain and parts south bellowed YES!

They moved together into the great room, laughing because they couldn't decide whether to walk arm in arm or stay locked together as if doing a tango. In the middle of the room, Tassy stopped and looked at the couch, saw Beowulf flaked on the center cushion, then looked at Linc with an almost strange expression. Then, walking backward, she pulled him into the bedroom.

They sat on the bed together and Tassy switched on the bed

table lamp. She studied the warm light on his face, then her eyes narrowed and she brushed her fingers down her own cheek. She shifted the lamp to the floor and then nodded, satisfied.

He wasn't sure of the next move—hell, of course he was! Only he didn't know quite . . .

She solved it by taking off her shirt, first the sleeve buttons, then the front buttons, one, two, three, four, five—this was agony! She pulled off the shirt and set it on the bed table. Reaching both hands behind her to unhook her bra, she arched her back, which didn't exactly reduce the effect.

She saw his expression and grinned. "Gee, Grandma, what big eyes you have." In fact his eyeballs were drying because he didn't want to blink.

Her own eyes lit up and her face acquired the radiant look of someone who'd found a precious possession after thinking it long-since lost. Her bra hooks yielded as slowly as the shirt buttons: one, and then two, and then three; then she hooked her thumbs under the straps and, still slowly, pulled the bra off. The straps left indentations in her shoulders.

He felt like a twelve-year-old opening *Playboy*. His mouth was dry and his shorts were truly painful.

Still watching him, she straightened her back and inflated her lungs. "Acceptable?"

When Linc whispered, "*Sweet Jesus God*," Tassy's grin turned downright triumphant. She reached out and took his right wrist and pulled his hand . . .

Then she stopped. She dropped his arm, stared into space, and started flexing fingers, as if counting.

"Oh, Linc, we *can't*!" She looked absolutely stricken.

"We . . . ?"

"I mean *I* can't. I'm probably—well, it's corny, but I guess you'd have to say *fertile*."

Linc sorted desperately through his male grab bag of disconnected facts and ignorant assumptions about female processes. She said she was forty—what? Maybe pushing fifty. How *hard* was she pushing? Wasn't all that supposed to be over by now? "You mean you haven't . . . ?"

She shook her head.

"You mean you're still . . . ?"

She nodded.

He stood up, relieved that at least there was suddenly room in his pants again. "I don't know much about it. I guess Ellen stopped early or something." Poor Ellen's innards had always been troublesome; it was why they hadn't had children. He sat down again. "Well, no, no, of course we can't." She offered a hand and he took it. "I'm out of my depth here, but what about birth control?"

"I gave it up long ago." She snorted. "No need. Well, and it always had side effects." She tried smiling. "Sort of kills the old spontaneity, doesn't it?"

He smiled back. "Yeah, and me the crazy impulsive type."

He embraced her and they swung their legs up on the bed to lie down, and then remained quiet awhile. Finally Tassy said, "You could still sleep here. I do wear a T-shirt."

Linc sat up, erupting with laughter.

"What's wrong?"

"How do you think I'd respond to a T-shirt now that I know what's under it?" He stood up and his smile turned rueful. "So, I'll just take my three-ring binder and go home. You can console yourself with Beowulf." He stopped dead, then, "Well, *that* was a stupid thing to say!"

Tassy's laugh was a full-scale honk. "Poor Beowulf: He can't console anyone now." At Linc's puzzled look, she mimed snipping scissors with two fingers and Linc winced.

They went back to the studio for the paperwork. She didn't trouble to round up her breasts again, and Linc could hardly force himself out the front door.

13

*U*nable to sleep and then some, Linc worked much of the night on Tassy's application. Norman Stihl had included the soils engineer's report and obtained extra blank copies of each form to use as worksheets. Fast work all around; Norman was really hustling the project, which, given his proposed job fee, wasn't a stunning surprise.

Linc was a very good writer, as the best lawyers often are, so after tweaking the language on the fill-in forms, he created a rehab proposal that didn't *quite* exclude replacement and a construction loan proposal that didn't *quite* include the word *rehab*.

He was feeling the lack of sleep by now, so he wandered out through the parlor and opened the big front door. Pacific dawn wasn't as gaudy as sunset, but the sky was pink, the surf—as always, inside the breakwater—was gentle, and the breeze was warm. He took several deep breaths, then went off to start coffee in the kitchen, leaving the front door open.

Forty minutes later he figured Tassy might be up, so he gathered the paperwork, trotted happily through the parlor, bounded out the door, and rebounded off Orson Wellesley, who wasn't displaced an inch by the impact.

"We're frightfully perky this morning."

"I'm sorry, Orson. Come in, will you?" Linc led him into the kitchen and poured him a mug of coffee.

Orson sipped and looked pained. "I hope you're starting an asphalt business; otherwise you should be shot. Allow me." He bustled about, spurning the jar of instant, digging out the coffee beans and grinder—both relics of Ellen, of course—clucking at the lack of springwater, and loading a paper filter with expert care.

As boiling water dripped through his project, Orson hungrily surveyed the gleaming appliances and long slate counters. "Ah me, dream on, Orson." His eye lit on the plans. "Doing some remodeling?"

"No, ah, just old papers. Need to file them." Linc swept up the papers and stuffed them in a random drawer, which, being already stuffed with flatware, resisted their intrusion. He forced the drawer half-shut, then gave up.

Orson watched this performance impassively. "Ah," he said.

"Well," said Linc just a bit too briskly, "what's up?"

"I came for a bit of advice." When Linc made a hand sign for *stop*, Orson added, "Not legal advice; business."

"You're not talking to John D. Trump here."

Orson's look implied, *Tell me another one.* "Good manners prevent me from comment, dear boy, but you realize that news of your assets precedes you." He shook his big head. "Anyway, you know all the big studios."

Linc nodded.

"And I know that the executives are always moving."

Another nod.

"When they move, how do they decorate their new offices?"

"Mainly use their own decorators."

"Not good. I was thinking Tassy's personal work would be perfect for upscale offices."

"Come to think of it, yeah. But the industry's maybe not a good bet."

"Any suggestions?"

Linc pondered, then, "I do know one guy—decorates a lot of

hospitals, hotels, corporate headquarters and the like. He did my law firm just before I left." He grinned at the memory. "Twelve-foot rosewood walls." When Orson looked puzzled, Linc added, "He bought antique portraits of gents with big whiskers and hung them up so they looked like the founders. Anyway, name's Jeremy Burgin."

Orson smacked his forehead. "Shoot me now! I should have remembered him. But he's based in the Bay Area."

"He works all over the state. I could give him a call."

"No, I will. Jerry and I go w-a-a-ay back. But I'll use you for a reference. What was your law firm's name?"

Linc opened his wallet and extracted a business card.

Orson took it. "Dear boy, you retired some time ago. Why do you cherish their business cards?"

Linc looked sheepish.

"Never mind." He grinned happily. "We may just get your lady some major sales."

My lady? Was the stupid town already gossiping or was Orson just hyperacute? And was she his lady? Well, maybe she was, at that. Linc felt faintly surprised that he hoped it was true.

Orson poured a second mug and leaned forward. "Now, let's talk about those plans you've stuffed into your silverware drawer." When Linc started to waffle Orson said, "I talked to Tassy this morning. Orson's Free Breakfast Club opened early today."

Linc blanched, at least mentally. "She wasn't supposed—"

Orson waved it off. "Yes, yes, conflict of interest, et cetera. We're coconspirators, comrade." Linc puffed out his cheeks and Orson continued, "Next council meeting's two weeks off and we need some preemptive strikes—*proactive*, as our beloved mayor would put it."

Like it or not, Orson had dealt himself in, so Linc filled his own cup and listened. Linc's role was to pay a soils engineer— not Norman's—to report that the bluff face could be stabilized with minimal disturbance and no, repeat *no*, excavation on the property.

Orson would work on Jack Millhouse and also launch Tassy on a pair of specially commissioned paintings. By the time Orson had laid it all out, Linc wondered how a fellow master strategist had wound up owning an art gallery.

At length, Orson rinsed out his mug, waved bye-bye with the business card, and sailed out. Since Linc's wallet was still on the table, he explored it with two fingers and pulled out more business cards. He stared at them blankly. Why did he have those cards? Was he keeping some unconscious connection to his old work? He thought about tossing them in the trash, but by the time he'd stood up and wandered over to the rank of recycling cans, he'd somehow slipped the cards absently back in his billfold and forgotten them.

~

Margaret Nam was also up early. Rolling into the driveway beside Norman Stihl's dramatic cliff-hanger house south of town, she took a moment to watch the waves smashing rocks below, while harbor seals sunned and honked, indifferent to the Wagnerian drama surrounding them.

Like many in these benign parts, Norman seldom locked his door, and Margaret silently let herself into the foyer. She slipped out of her pumps, carried them to the bedroom, and found him on his side in bed snoring at the wall, as predicted. For some odd reason, she thought he looked sweet that way.

With her usual quiet efficiency, she started removing her clothes. She unwound and folded her trademark scarf—ultrafine cashmere on this brisk morning—of robin's egg blue. The skirt really needed a hanger but the back of a chair would do, with her jacket over it and creamy silk blouse folded on top, just so. Thong and bra on the chair seat and shoes precisely aligned on the floor. She thought about her pearl necklace and ear studs, then decided they might help spice her surprise visit.

Limber and sleek as an ocelot, Margaret tiptoed to Norman's bed and inserted herself behind him. He mumbled incoherently, then carried on snoring. Snuggling against his back and butt, she reached an arm over and started tickling his hard belly, lower and lower, teasing with her fingertips and scraping his skin lightly with her wristwatch band.

In due course he woke up. "Whoa! What? Margaret? Hoo!" Though still half-asleep, Norman rose to the occasion.

Sometime later she emerged from the bathroom, radiantly naked this morning and clean both top and bottom. The sex had been better than ever, even though the man's morning mouth could wilt a philodendron. Fortunately, she had found and used Norman's mouthwash.

Anyway, his expression made up for it. Norman watched as she moved about, dressing. Margaret knew what he thought of her body, so she played to him, pausing halfway into her bra before slipping the lace down over her nipples and undulating slowly into her silk blouse. She posed for a moment, all prim and severe from her perfect hair to her shirttails; all wanton bare promise from there to her manicured toes. She was proud of her Brazilian wax job, which she'd driven all the way down to Santa Rosa to obtain. She put on her underwear gracefully—a neat trick in itself—then finished with skirt and shoes. Margaret couldn't resist adding a small stripper's flourish with the scarf—she was feeling that good!

She said, "I'll make some coffee; you go ahead and shower—oh, and shave, will you, or no good-bye kiss. *Brush your teeth too.*" She flashed him a sunny smile and clicked out on her business heels. Yes indeed, the sex had been good enough to repeat this experiment, and now it was time for agenda item two.

The house was small enough to hear the electric razor and then the shower, so she would know how much time she had. Nipping into his workroom, she scanned the mess. Did the man ever file anything? Shaking her head, she started sifting papers on his worktable.

The razor had quit and the shower begun before she found it: a bright green presentation folder with Tassy's address visible behind the cover window. The cover sheet, on the letterhead of Cummins Associates, Geologists and Soils Engineers, solemnly avowed that the enclosed plan would stabilize Tassy's property and provide a replacement foundation for her house. It was signed by Ansel Cummins. Pay dirt! Looking around, she spotted Norman's all-purpose copier-scanner-printer-fax and switched it on. Working on the flat glass plate, she copied the report.

Too intent to hear that the shower had quit, she was almost caught in the act. Norman was starting out of the bedroom in his usual twill pants and flannel shirt as she stuffed the copies into her portfolio briefcase and tossed the proposal back on the desk. She barely had time to see that it didn't slip off the pile before streaking back into the living room.

Norman appeared, grinning smugly. "Where's that coffee?"

She should have remembered that; damn! "Uh . . . oh, I guess I couldn't find it." When Norman glanced at the prominent coffee-maker and coffee can on the counter, she added hastily, "Anyway, I can't stay."

He looked puzzled. "Then what'd you come over for?"

She bathed him in a slow, shy smile. "Now, what do you think, Norman?" Margaret gave him the promised kiss, putting her back into the job. He was still grinning foolishly when she waggled her fingers at him and slipped out the door.

Enthroned in her SUV, Margaret thought about Norman. He really was a sweet man beneath all his draft beer manners, and sex this morning had felt like more than the usual tennis game. What would her father say if she got serious about Norman Stihl? She slapped her hand on her mouth and giggled behind her fingers. Great sex, successful espionage, and the thought of shocking her father were enough to make her whole day right there!

Inside, Norman made coffee himself and toasted this unexpectedly fine morning with OJ drunk straight from a half-gallon carton. Funny thing, though: Margaret was usually cool about sex. It wasn't like her to drive down to his place at six a.m. just to get laid.

~

Orson waited until after the lunch rush—though the coffee shop was lucky to fill its booths even at noon—before strolling in for a one-on-one with Jack Millhouse. The mayor was at the counter with the waitress.

Orson and the waitress smiled at each other. "An omelet for me, darling, and the usual chardonnay; and you like Reubens, don't you, Jack? I'll buy both of us lunch."

The mayor looked gratified by the offer and flattered that Orson remembered his preference. He added a Coke to the order and the two men established themselves in an unobtrusive booth.

They made small talk until their lunches arrived, then Orson said, "Tassy Morgan's fence is quite a mess."

"Don't remind me." Millhouse leaned in and almost whispered, "I've been avoiding Margaret for days."

Orson nodded sagely. "As one businessman to another, Jack, I confess I'm worried." He knew that Jack didn't like worried; worried was bad.

"About what?" Millhouse asked.

"June is here and the tourists are coming, but we can't seem to solve this ridiculous problem."

The mayor grumbled around his Reuben, "'Ridiculous' is right."

Orson sighed regretfully. "Knowing Tassy as I do, she's quite capable of leaving that fence wrecked indefinitely."

Millhouse muttered vaguely, "I guess there's some litter ordinance. . . ."

Orson pressed on to point two. "Then there's that bluff she's sitting on: It's collapsing."

Tassy's bluff, thankfully, was not Jack's problem. "Well, I'm sorry about that. . . ."

"And that bluff includes the path down to the beach."

The path *was* Jack's problem. The stunning beach at the bottom of that path was all San Andreas could offer its hoped-for hordes of tourists. "Oboy! As if we didn't have enough trouble."

Orson held his glass to the light and studied it as if the future were visible there. "What would you say to a plan that would solve both problems?"

Millhouse brightened. "Kill two birds with one stone, eh?"

"Well put, Jack; you have a gift for the apt phrase."

Looking pleased at the compliment, Millhouse made a *'t'aint nothin'* gesture. "What is it?"

"Hm?"

"Your plan: two birds, one stone."

"Ah! You know how we, quote, *rehab*, unquote, houses around here, wink wink nudge nudge?"

"Wink? What? Oh, oh sure! We did that with our house."

"And got a beautiful, *brand-new* house out of it."

"My wife designed most of it. Drove me nuts for ten months."

"I think I could talk Tassy into *rehabbing* that ugly shack of hers, and stabilizing the bluff to do it."

"Is that practical?"

"Norman's Stihl's already got plans."

Millhouse chewed on that, then looked suspicious. "Before she even asked?"

Orson said smoothly, "Well, you know Norman: always hustling. For all I know, it was his idea to begin with." The big man tried hiding behind his wineglass.

After another lengthy pause for processing, Jack grinned. "Well! Sounds like a great idea. Think she'll do it?"

"I can guarantee it—*if* the city lets her."

"Why 'if'? The *county* cuts the permits."

"But *we* pass on design, colors, trim, *fences*—that kind of thing."

The mayor nodded as his brain caught up.

Orson continued, "And you may have noticed some little, well, *issues* developing there."

Millhouse looked pained. "I wish those things didn't happen."

"But don't forget, Jack: Three to two carries it. With Linc and me, *you* can win the day."

"I guess I can, can't I?" But the tone carried a politician's conviction.

Orson picked up on it. "I won't even talk to Tassy if you won't guarantee it'll pass. *I need your promise, Jack.*"

"Well . . ."

Orson Wellesley fixed him with a certain stare, a stare he rarely had need for in these laid-back parts. Orson came from Very Old Northeast WASP money, money that always got its way because it always *had* got its way and always *would* get its way. "Do you *promise* to vote with Linc and me?"

Visibly cowed by The Stare, Millhouse said faintly, "I promise; I definitely promise."

Orson pledged him with the last of his wine. "Stout fellow."

14

During the following days Tassy's plans flew below the San Andrean radar; but Orson and Linc and Tassy herself spoke to just a few people, who spoke to just a few more.

Beyond which Tassy started loading her own ammo by creating the two new paintings. She gave the very large one to Orson and carried the smaller one over to the Hair Place to accept Jimi's offer of a free wash and cut.

In the cheerful jumble of the shop she luxuriated in the first professional wash since her divorce. There were no other customers, so Jimi took her sweet time. Tassy lay back with her neck in the sink cutout and her long, thick hair cascading into the deep bowl. "I could fall asleep like this, Jimi."

A few minutes later she asked, "How'd you come to be doing this here?"

"Honey, I could write a book. Luther keeps saying, go ahead, do it." Luther was Jimi's third husband. Tassy learned that her first was the owner of a Napa Valley vineyard and the second a Marin County builder of upscale tracts. The death of the first and divorce from the second had left her extremely well fixed, and she'd moved up here just to get the hell out. But managing her North Coast properties bored her and hair was her one true art; so here she was, doing the same damn thing as when her first husband-to-be had spotted her through her Mill Valley shop window twenty long years ago.

Jimi was the kind of woman Tassy warmed to, and the stylist seemed to return the compliment. "And how did Luther come in?" she yelled over the dryer.

"Well, there's another long story."

"You should write that book."

Jimi just shook her head, then said, "That's enough; don't want you too dry. Migawd, I don't see a lot of real color your shade, especially at our age. Don't want to cut it short. Well, I'll just nag at it a little here and there."

'Here and there' took nearly an hour. When Tassy let herself look in the mirror she saw her own hair apparently unaltered but somehow looking as if she wore it that way on purpose, rather than letting it do what it liked. It was beautiful. Discounting a little erosion, *she* was beautiful. She surveyed the floor around the chair and saw maybe three dozen scissor snips' worth of hair. But each had been perfectly selected. Each was the inevitable snip, *le snip juste.*

"Oh, Jimi! I can't . . ."

"I told you, compliments of the house."

Tassy nodded, smiling. "I knew you'd say that, so I came prepared." She picked up the wrapped painting from the seat by the door and gave it to Jimi. It was a sunset view of the harbor beyond the bluff-top houses, as seen from Linc's front porch.

Jimi's delight was genuine. "Oh, I love it! I'll hang it right in here." She studied the watercolor. "Must be your own street. There's the summer rentals and your place and . . ." She cocked her head at the image. "It's your place, all right, but it's nicer—sort of idealized." She added meaningfully, "Pastel colors and no fence."

"That's how it'll look when it's rehabbed."

Jimi studied Tassy shrewdly, then broke out a broad grin. "Do tell. Well, I'll show all my customers."

Tassy grinned back. "I'll need to borrow it for the council meeting."

"I'll bring it myself." As Tassy got out of the chair, Jimi added, "You come back now, kiddo; I'll tell you all about Luther."

~

Walking happily home, Tassy detoured up Bill and Dave's street. Dave wasn't on his cinder block, but the howl next door said that Bill the Fixer was at work. When he spotted her he grinned, killed the saw, and stopped carving a Roosevelt elk. Bill explained he'd have to garnish it with young deer antlers faked to resemble elks' because the sculpture was only half as big as an actual elk. What the hell, Tassy thought; unlike totem poles and Paul Bunyans, Roosevelt elk were both local and real. Tourists might well be delayed by a whole herd crossing US 101. She admired the sculpture with a warmth Bill could feel.

He repeated his joke about sculpting a nude and Tassy repeated her offer. He didn't blush this time, but just looked at her steadily; then they both laughed and nodded together. She told him she wouldn't be fixing the fence and confided her plans for the house. Bill was enthusiastic. She said she had to get it through the city council and Bill allowed as how he might show up and lend moral support. Dave'd come too, he was sure. Tassy grinned and waved and continued on home.

That evening, Bill claimed his usual stool at the Beach House bar and ordered his usual Wild Turkey, rocks. Other regulars showed up predictably, and by and by, Bill was talking about the hassles the town had put Tassy through and her generous plan to make everything right. Bill had a certain gravitas—though he would have scoffed at a word like that—and when he uttered a rare opinion, his buddies listened respectfully.

~

The next day Orson Wellesley rolled into the Good Vibrations latte parlor, ordered a double mocha special and two wannabe Krispy

Kreme donuts, and kissed Sharon Morning Sky on the cheek. "Darling, you look so right here—a classic Indian maid."

Sharon snorted and said, "Not technically," but looked pleased at the compliment. "What's that?"

"Well, you know, I've been studying that wall." He waved at a large surface painted a rich Etruscan red ochre and blank except for a taped-up menu. "What would you think of this?" Stripping the paper off Tassy's second, larger new painting, he held it in place on the dark surface. It dominated the room.

Sharon gasped. One of Tassy's nonrepresentational works, the painting didn't show anything plainly, but managed to suggest a glade in a forest of venerable redwoods, splashed with sun and suffused in a mystic glow—a cathedral envisioned by the original people, the Old Ones who understood it and worshiped in it before white men came to chop it all down.

"I'm trying not to cry," Sharon whispered.

"It belongs right there, doesn't it?"

Sharon could only nod.

"Why don't we let it live here, then? With a little tag naming the artist and the price."

Sharon was still nodding.

Orson sighed dramatically. "With a three thousand dollar price tag, I'm afraid you'll keep it a long, *long* time."

"Oh, Orson, I love you."

"I know, darling; everyone does." He rolled out again.

~

Shortly before the cutoff date for agenda items, Linc officially delivered Tassy's plans and proposal to Mayor Millhouse—a set for each council member. Linc explained that Tassy'd asked him to drop them off since he was headed that way. He did not explain why he was headed that way or volunteer the information that he was coming back from the county seat, where he'd paid for the copying.

Tassy's application was supported by a new engineering plan, this one from a rival of the firm Norman favored. It proposed to restore the existing bluff face by reinforcing it with unobtrusive components and minimal disruption. Its cover letter was addressed to Tassy, who had bought the proposal—with a hefty surcharge for the rush job—with money supplied her by Linc.

"How's it look to you, Linc?"

Linc kept a straight face. "Very good, Jack; I might have written it myself."

"We gotta get it through, Linc; put all this behind us."

"Glad you feel that way, Mr. Mayor."

Millhouse held up the stack of paperwork. "I'll see everyone gets one."

So Linc kept three for Tassy, himself, and Orson. Millhouse took three more for himself, Dottie Franklyn, and Margaret Nam.

~

That night, Linc and Tassy ate at the casino restaurant. The excellent menu had entrées to satisfy carnivore Linc and salads to satisfy Tassy's conscience, though by the end of the main course Linc's baked potato had somehow teleported to her plate, along with several soup spoons of sour cream, butter, chives, and more butter.

She had seen the dessert tray on the way in, as the restaurant intended, and now entertained thoughts of a sweet—oh, not one of those gooey delights, but maybe a chaste scoop of sherbet. To first give her entrée some processing time, she made the long march to the restroom out in the foyer. On the way back she passed a magnificent Indian woman in her—what, seventies?—eating alone at a table by the fire. When their eyes met they exchanged the cheerful smiles that were customary in these rural parts, and Tassy moved on.

Approaching her table from the side, she saw Linc before he noticed her. He was doing his piano thing, this time right on the tablecloth. As she watched his complicated fingering she realized that something was new: Linc was playing with both hands, the left hand roaming the invisible keyboard quite independently. He executed a tricky little cross-hand maneuver, then whipped his hands into his lap as she walked into view.

She sat down. "What were you playing?"

He didn't say anything for a moment, then seemed to make up his mind. "*The Beethoven Second.*"

Grinning, Tassy swiveled to look at surrounding diners. "Where's your orchestra?"

"Ever try to play kettledrums under a table?"

Their waiter rolled up the dessert trolley. Tassy was so distracted by Linc's piano playing that she ordered a Bavarian chocolate delight.

"So you played 'just a little' and 'a long time ago,' but you can remember and perform a Beethoven concerto. I think you better come clean."

"Well . . . the thing is, I did study—a lot, like fourteen years, including two at Juilliard."

"And?"

Linc only shrugged, but made the mistake of looking into Tassy's eyes. He saw sympathy there and a kind of patience uncommon with her. The silence threatened to last indefinitely. Finally, he muttered, "I felt I had to be the best, nothing less; and even at twenty, I realized I was not going to get there. So I stopped trying so hard, and after a while it more or less dwindled away."

"You became a lawyer instead of a pianist? That doesn't add up."

"I told you: It's where the money was." He snorted. "At twenty, money seemed important."

Tassy grinned to break the tension. "I'm here to report it still is, unless you happen to have some." She let the subject go then, because to her, Linc's attitude was incomprehensible. She knew she wasn't the world's absolute greatest painter, but she was very good indeed, and that was plenty.

Free-associating from this, she said, "I'm going away tomorrow." Linc's look of alarm was so sudden that she couldn't help feeling good about it; but she added at once, "Just a few days. Drive up the coast into Oregon. Do some sketching and painting." His quick relief made her feel even better. "I need to think about the kind of work I'm doing." She covered his hand on the table with hers. "You ought to do the same, Linc."

Linc said, "I'll miss you a lot."

She nodded.

"But then, I miss you here at home too."

"That one's a bitch, isn't it?" Tassy smiled but her tone was uncertain.

Later, when he'd driven her to her door, Linc asked casually, "Going to call it a night?"

She looked at him. God, she was in her late forties. How much chance was there she'd get pregnant? Well, still some kind of chance, and then what the hell would she do? She saw Linc's hope-against-hope expression and felt like a lust-addled kid again. But the grown-up finally prevailed, dammit. "I'm afraid so."

He looked so forlorn that she twisted toward him enough to kiss him long and thoroughly. She got out then, but just before closing the passenger door, she added, "For tonight, anyway."

As she watched him drive away she couldn't suppress a perverse kind of glee. Lust-addled! How about that?!

15

After seeing Tassy off the next day, Linc trekked down to the Walgreens at the county seat because he didn't want to go through the San Andreas market checkout with a pack of damn condoms.

The number and range of products bewildered him. How could things change so much in twenty-five years? Clearly, prophylactic technology had undergone feverish R & D, and, imagining test labs, Linc couldn't help smiling. He weighed types, features, lubricants—even colors. Did ribs make some kind of difference, and if so, as latitude, longitude, or spirals? He obviously lacked the receptive equipment to find out.

Finally he settled on what seemed a sensible type—if you could call such things sensible—and picked a large box of individual foil packets. At least that hadn't changed: You could still walk around with a rubber in your wallet in the forlorn hope you might score.

He wandered the aisles awhile, looking for other products to surround and deemphasize his intimate purchase, then decided he was being childish and headed toward checkout. Speaking of childish, was that girl the only clerk on? She didn't look more than thirteen. He winced as his solitary box rode majestically down the black belt to the register, but she scanned and bagged it without even looking. Linc paid cash; it was quicker.

~

By this time, Tassy was somewhere north of the Rogue River, painting seascapes just for herself. She'd found a vacation hotel off US 101, halfway between Notmuch and Nowhere, with ocean views, a restaurant, and almost-affordable room rates. The other guests enjoyed finding an artist sketching on the bluffs and beach, and the little resort was happy to let her lay her big board on a glass patio table, where she created large watercolors from her field drawings.

The experiment was delivering more than she'd dared hope for, as her paintings ventured deeper and deeper into the personal mode, where she really wanted to work. Each one picked ideas from the previous one and ran with them; and by the third day, her big watercolors were starting to stir up butterflies in her gut. Finally, finally, she was going someplace that was absolutely hers, and she was going there so fast it was scary. She wanted to shriek out loud, except for that kid who was sweeping the patio around her.

Still, no one had ever bought one of these paintings, except Linc.

Linc had been so gray and bland at first, but every time she saw him, he unfolded another petal. If he made it to full bloom he'd be really something. He was obviously attracted to her, but that couldn't account for all the time and effort and money he'd put in on her house thing. He was simply a very rare bird: a naturally generous man.

Generous with attention too. When she talked he really listened—really absorbed what she said. She thought of the big F.U. on her house wall, her bottle smashing his window, the fence she'd butchered just after he'd paid for it. Nothing she did put him off; he accepted her. In her life that was a novel reaction.

But come to think of it, more and more people seemed to like her these days. Was it because she'd somehow normalized her behavior or because she was slowly ceasing to fret about it? Maybe Beowulf had a good effect on her. He did exactly what he pleased and when he pleased, and everyone in town liked him for it. She'd left the studio door open for him and asked Linc to check on his food and water. She hoped he was okay.

As she worked paint and water with even more than her usual energy, she thought about Linc's attraction to her. It was certainly mutual. After several minutes without conscious thought she decided she might just take herself to a gynecologist down at the county seat. At her age!

~

On the day Tassy left, Linc had strolled into the front parlor and over to a pair of pocket doors on his right. Beyond was the smaller, "family" parlor. He slid the doors open and studied the room, now empty except for heavy curtains and a giant antique Persian rug. After a few minutes' thought, he slid the doors closed, then climbed the staircase and walked through the two big B and B suites facing the harbor. They were getting dusty; well, rooms did that, didn't they? He studied the wide front windows. If he pulled off what Ellen had referred to as "window treatments," there'd be a lot of light in here, not to mention a view as good as Tassy's, and even higher.

Thinking of nothing special, he ambled into the hall and down to the door at the very end, then entered the master suite, where he and Ellen had slept. It was as big as the front ones, with the same extravagant bath and huge closets. A recently cut archway with French doors revealed a cheerful room beyond it that had once housed a housekeeper-cook, with its own back door to the kitchen staircase. So much planning, so much work. Now he lived in the breakfast room.

Linc had long since cleared Ellen's dresser top and vanity, as well as her stuff in the bathroom; but her drawers and her closet were just as she'd left them. He pulled open a dresser drawer, revealing neat piles of bras, hose, and panties, and then touched the top layer with his fingertips. To his relief, he found they were no longer talismans; their connection to Ellen had faded away. After a long moment of thought, he keyed his cell phone with his right hand, his left still touching the underwear.

"Hi, Dave, it's Linc. . . . Listen, you know all those empty boxes they put out behind the market? Could you give me a whole bunch, and a day's worth of your time? . . . Today if you can. . . . Great—oh, I almost forgot: Does the county seat have a Goodwill store? . . . Okay, the hospital thrift shop works."

So the hospital where Ellen arrived already dead would get a big posthumous donation. There was some kind of irony lurking in there, but he wouldn't bother to tease it out. As he started down the back stairs, Linc put in a call to Mayflower Moving and Storage in Los Angeles.

~

By midweek Grandmother Halvorsen had finally lost patience with the stonewalling, so she invaded the county seat. Her progress was slow because everyone knew her—or had at least heard of her. The welcoming cries and hugs were from folks who loved and revered her; the other clerks and officials respected both her reputation for intelligence and her power in her tribe. Either way, the ceremonies were time consuming.

Grandmother was a consummate bureaucrat, and she worked her slow way through both county and federal offices like a tree root cracking a boulder. By the end of the day she had hit the County Office of Records, the Parks and Recreation Department, and the county rep for the Bureau of Indian Affairs. The California Coastal Commission had no local presence, but old friends supplied information and Internet links. (Erik could take care of that. Grandmother disliked computers, and, retiring along with the twentieth century, had almost contrived to avoid them.)

Her final call was on Carl Semson, chairman of the county board of supervisors. In private life Carl was president of North Coast Resource Management LLC, which managed resources by cutting them down, especially old-growth trees on private lots too small to be governed by harvesting rules. In private life, Grandmother despised him, but she was here on public business.

"Three million dollars for that beach, Carl," she repeated with her best public face on, "and no more maintenance costs for the county."

Behind his desk, Semson eased his turquoise belt buckle. It had been one of those lunches. "Aw, Clara, you know we haven't spent a dime on upkeep there for years."

"You will if San Andreas gets fired up about it."

"And you'll see that they do." Semson was a seasoned politician, as his seven terms attested.

Grandmother didn't say yea or nay. Instead, she seemed to change the subject. "The old coast road's back to gravel again, and a big piece fell into the sea. How do your constituents feel about *that?*" The oceanfront estates south of San Andreas were owned by big campaign contributors.

Semson sighed. He knew where she was headed.

"Three million would plug that hole in the road—course, it would still be gravel. . . ." She let the thought trail off.

They sat silent awhile, as if out-waiting each other, then Semson sighed again and hauled his bulk off his executive chair. "Clara, you *know* I'll go the distance to keep our friendship"—Grandmother *knew* he despised her right back—"so, I'll bring it up with the board. How would that be?"

That would be worse than useless, but Grandmother knew this exchange was over. She thanked Semson with the same sincerity he'd lavished on her and beat a strategic retreat.

So the day's results were dispiriting. Despite all the hugs and glad-handing, despite all the protestations of support, the county was not about to sell that beach; and without that beach, the luxury resort would be just another hotel next to another casino. In short, the Indians were screwed again. Rolling home in her Mercury Grand Marquis, she peered through the top of her steering wheel with a sour, defeated expression.

It wasn't until she reached the stand of somber redwood giants flanking the road south of the casino that she thought of Plan B. Was it the Ancient Ones calling another ancient? Grandmother snorted; no, it was simply Plan B.

She considered it as she drove through the gloom of the grove. The beach had just one access route. Pinch that off and the beach would be closed. How would the county feel about maintaining expensive property they couldn't get to? She wrinkled her nose at this crude approach, but sometimes there was nothing to do but shake the tree and see what fell out of it.

At just that moment Grandmother drove through a great shaft of sunlight piercing the high tree canopy. Clearly, the redwoods approved of Plan B.

~

Throughout the week, Jimi managed to work Tassy's painting into most of her customer conversations. Old Mrs. Lagan still groused that Jimi made her hair fall out, but she forgave the woman who was, after all, the only hairstylist in town. Mrs. Lagan just *loved* Tassy's bright, traditional seascape. Jimi explained that it showed her house after rehabbing, and Mrs. Lagan strongly approved of the new color scheme. The tidy riot of front yard rhododendrons was especially gratifying, and she tottered off to enlist the garden club.

Angela was already back on station, shuttling between manicure jobs and the tiny infant in the back room. Jimi thought she looked tired as hell, but then what did you expect? The baby girl sure wasn't tired, and that was the important thing.

Angela had told her husband about the rehab project. Norman Stihl hired crews on a by-the-job basis, and this could mean lots of work. Her husband would spread it around the saloon and general store that were all that remained of the hamlet three miles up the old county road.

~

Tassy had been gone several days when Linc stood in the owner's bedroom of the B and B and planned his attack. The furniture was okay: a cherry king bed with matching bed tables and dressers, a bentwood cane-seated rocker with side table, and a wardrobe that was redundant, given the two gaping walk-in closets, but handy for extra blankets and pillows. So far so good.

Linc had returned from a visit to Kmart, the classiest store of its kind in the county, which was understandable because the county harbored ninety thousand rustic souls in a space the size of Connecticut. Over the next two hours, he changed the bed linens, replaced the curtains with simpler ones of a rich, dark color, and did the same with the matching bedspread and pillow covers, discarding the flouncy little bed skirt thing. He removed all the plants, which were terminal anyway, and brought from the kitchen the only green thing he'd managed to nurture; he wasn't sure what it was. The lamps were all right as they were, though he wasn't thrilled with the curly fluorescent bulbs. Well, no one said it was easy being green, and the amber lampshades took most of the curse off.

He took down the reproductions from eighteenth-century botanical atlases, which belonged in a Hilton hotel. In their place he hung Tassy's paintings, borrowed from Orson's ample supply. His friend had chosen the least touristy, most individual scenes.

Lastly, he seeded strategic candlesticks on the tables and dressers—it'd taken an hour to unearth the dumb things downstairs and another hour to find polish and clean them—and fitted Martha Stewart tapers, noting smugly that their colors harmonized with everything else in the room. Say what you would about Martha Stewart; her home furnishings and accessories had done wonders for blue-collar taste. Too bad she'd abandoned the proletariat. Methodical as ever, he placed a matchbook on every table. Damned hard to find them now that smoking was banned everywhere.

That was it. He didn't know when he would need the bedroom, but whenever he did, it was ready. Linc went off to attack the bathroom.

Later, after bouncing down the front stairs, he crossed the main parlor and slid the pocket doors open to look in on his treasure. The family parlor now held a piano—a nine-foot concert grand.

16

The rare city council meetings that were legal were held Mondays at three because the merchants were mostly closed on Monday, and at three p.m. the seniors who dominated the audience were mostly awake, more or less. As usual, the folding chairs in the shabby town hall supported these and the prosperous retirees and other refugees who had moved to the village from elsewhere. Today, however, they were leavened by people who rarely showed up, such as Norman Stihl, Bill the Fixer, DayGlo Dave, Jimi the hair genius, and half the inmates of the trailer park known as the Geezer Bin. Bill's drinking pals were on hand and Jimi had recruited some customers. Old Mrs. Lagan had marshaled the fragile ranks of the garden club. Angela's husband had rounded up dudes from the bar on the old county road. Orson had brought Sharon Morning Sky, who was now Tassy's biggest fan, and warned her to be ready for action.

Tassy herself showed up, breathless, as the meeting was called to order. She'd returned from her painting safari less than an hour before, with barely time to unload and wash up.

Council member Margaret Nam bitterly noted the big cheering section rounded up by the Morgan woman. Was there no justice? Margaret had worked 24-7 for *years* to win the town's acceptance and respect—thought up endless projects to improve San Andreas, help it prosper. Through steady application she'd made herself the town's leading citizen. What had Morgan done? *Not one damn thing*, but she still had the town on her side. Well, Margaret wasn't through yet, not by a long shot.

Mayor and Council Chair Millhouse finished routine busy-work and then announced the only important matter. The audience seemed to sense the difference too, for now they were standing, gossiping, wandering, as if on a seventh inning stretch. Then Millhouse banged his beloved gavel and the hall settled into its butt-numbing chairs. Nobody noticed as Grandmother Halvorsen entered and claimed a seat at the back.

Margaret watched the mayor carefully. She could tell when he was uncertain, which was most of the time, but today he seemed extra shaky. She noticed he took a deep breath before saying, too offhandedly, "Last item is Tassy Morgan's rehab project. Everybody review the plans?" Margaret's council colleagues muttered assent and Dottie Franklyn held up her packet of paperwork, though Margaret knew she hadn't bothered to look at it. Orson made a motion to accept the application, Linc seconded, and the mayor called for discussion.

Jimi had brought Tassy's painting and during the pause Orson had set it on a tripod on the stage beside the council's long table. Now he pointed at it and said, "Seems fine to me. It improves her house beautifully and preserves the look of the street." Murmurs of assent here and there in the audience.

Linc added, "Nice color scheme too: pastel blue with white trim." More audience approval, this time louder and more general.

The mayor said, "Dottie?"

Dottie flashed a quick look at Margaret. Knowing Dottie would vote with her, Margaret hadn't bothered to include her ally in her plan, so she just kept her pleasant poker face. Dottie was reduced to equivocating, "I can't see anything wrong right away."

Millhouse turned to her. "How about you, Margaret?"

She kept her professional smile secure while inwardly girding for

battle. "I certainly think this would be a wonderful improvement."
Margaret sought and found Tassy three rows back in the house. Smiling broadly at her, she continued, "And I want to specially thank Ms.
Morgan for her care in conforming to the city's beautification guide-
lines." More noise from the Morgan cheering section and even a light
applause patter.

She adjusted her scarf while allowing this approval to ebb, and
then she put on a puzzled expression. "I can't help feeling concerned
about just one thing."

Millhouse got that constricted look of his. "What's that,
Margaret?"

In her most reasonable tone, "The engineering plan. It calls for
very rough treatment of a very fragile environment."

Linc spoke up from the other side of the mayor. "In what way
'rough'?"

Margaret tapped the stack of papers in front of her. "This excavation. It'll gut the whole property."

Fat Wellesley piped up, "Which excavation would that be?"

"Well, the engineering plan calls for . . ." Margaret pulled the
folder out of the stack of documents. "Calls for . . ." Opening it to
the cover sheet, she suddenly realized it was not from the firm whose
pages she had in her briefcase. Impossible! What kind of shifty . . . ?
"Just a minute." She turned pages, skimming. There wasn't a fucking
word about any excavation!

The rage didn't quite reach her face. "I may have mistaken a few
technical details."

Orson nodded. "There's no excavation whatever," he said to the
audience. "Plus a minimum of surface disruption and a treatment
that blends with the rest of the bluff." More noise from the Morgan
claque.

Speed-reading the engineers' document, Margaret could only
nod assent. Like a competing gymnast after an early slip, she focused

ferociously. Glancing up, she spotted Norman in the audience. He looked as puzzled as she felt.

Millhouse said hastily, "Well then, are we ready to vote?"

Margaret took a deep, cleansing breath. She said calmly, "Mr. Chairman, I'd like to clarify a point of procedure."

Millhouse's look decayed from wary to anxious, as well it might. "All right, Margaret."

"It occurs to me that one of our members lives right across the street. I think Linc ought to—what's the word?—*recuse* himself because he has an interest in the outcome." Without him, of course, the council would stall, two to two.

Linc said, "I think the plan's fine."

Enthusiastically, "Oh, I do too!" Then her sweetest tone, "But however you feel about it, you do have a vested interest."

Orson spoke up again from the far end of the table. "You know, I'm having second thoughts myself."

He was?

"I wonder if we should be deciding this at all?"

Something going on here!

Fat Orson continued, "Linc, you're our legal expert. Doesn't this decision really belong to the beautification committee instead of the council?"

So that was it; the son of a bitch Linc wasn't on that committee. Who was? Sharon Morning Sky. Margaret swept the audience and spotted her, sure enough, right on the center aisle.

Orson called out, "Is Sharon Morning Sky here?" Sharon jumped up. Of course, she'd been primed. Orson said, "All right, I move the council meeting be closed and the beautification committee be convened in its place."

Linc sighed. "No-no-no-no. We still have a motion under discussion." He leaned in toward Millhouse and talked him through a complicated sequence out of *Robert's Rules of Order*.

The process finished with Millhouse saying, "Council meeting's adjourned; beautification committee meeting's open."

Linc stood up and offered his seat at the table. "Come on up, Sharon."

In the bustle of seating Sharon and the general chat from the audience, Margaret's vicious expression went unnoticed. She'd suspended policing her face to aim every last atom of attention at launching her next assault. While the new committee slogged through the mechanics of reopening the discussion, Margaret armed her doomsday device. Sifting the stack before her, she asked innocently, "Where's the coastal commission paperwork?"

There was silence for a moment. She'd blindsided them on that one, all right. The public, professional Margaret flowed back and her face was again beautiful.

Finally Orson said, "I don't think we're ready for that."

"Why not?"

"Let's not bother the commission with a project that's still hypothetical." The audience murmured approval.

Margaret addressed them directly. "That's exactly when they *should* get involved: We should get their approval before Ms. Morgan spends a lot of time and money."

Orson said, "Time is of the essence here, Margaret."

Margaret said sympathetically, "I want to see this wonderful project as much as anyone here." She swept a smile like a lighthouse beam across the audience. "But I deal with these problems professionally and I know how they work." Margaret was going to take that bitch down! "It's much safer to apply now. In fact I move that the committee postpone the application pending receipt of coastal commission approval." *Come on, Dottie, come on!*

Maybe telepathy worked. Dottie Franklyn piped up, "I second."

Sharon didn't know what to say. After an awkward silence, the mayor called for the vote.

Margaret and Dottie voted yes; Wellesley and Sharon voted no. Millhouse stood frozen in the center, as if time had stopped just for him.

Finally, Margaret asked ever so gently, "Mr. Mayor, what's your vote on this?"

"Well, in the light of . . . in the interests of . . ." He waved vaguely around the hall. "I think . . ." His look moved to Margaret and locked. She stared at him, as mesmerizing as a cobra. "I think . . . I think I'll have to vote yes. Motion's carried. Tassy's application's, rejected. . . ." He finally managed to break eye contact with Margaret. "*Postponed*, I mean—but only for now, okay? Only for now."

And long before the commission's response, the bluff would crumble and—oh dear!—destroy that poor woman's home. It took more than Margaret's usual discipline to keep the grin off her face.

The room buzzed with talk. Surveying the crowd, Margaret saw that her move had raised more than a few tempers. She thought briefly of the elections, now five months away, then dismissed that worry. They'd get over it. To make sure that Tassy got the point, she sent her a *win some, lose some* smile. You bitch, don't even *try* to get cute with me.

With nothing else to do, the committee adjourned and people began clearing out.

Norman Stihl caught Tassy outside the old hall. She didn't look so good—well, no wonder. "Hey."

Though she didn't seem overjoyed to see him, Tassy said, "Hey, Norman."

So now what? "Uh, looks like our job's pushed back a little." When Tassy nodded silently he added, "Stuff like this happens." He put a hand on her arm. "We'll get there."

"One way or another." That was a funny answer, but at least she didn't push his hand off.

There didn't seem any way to bring it up gracefully, so he just said, "Someplace, we lost our big hole in the ground." He hoped he was keeping it light. "Where'd it go?"

Tassy watched him a moment, then said, "I worried about what it would do to the bluff, so I got another design."

"From who?"

"Benson and Jones; you know them?"

"Well, sure, they're good, I guess. How'd you hear about them?"

Tassy shrugged. "Asked around."

Shit, Benson and Jones were *too* good to argue with. Adios forty thousand bucks. Well *shit*! He tried to cover his irritation. "A whole brand-new plan. Surprised the hell out of me."

"It seemed to surprise Margaret Nam too." She studied his face so intently that Norman got the idea: Tassy thought he'd showed Margaret the plans.

"Yeah, uh . . ."

Before he could get his brain back in gear, Tassy did pull her arm away. "So we'll just put this away for a while. See you, Norman." She turned and walked off.

He was thinking so hard he forgot to watch her butt. How *did* Margaret know?

Right on cue, the lady in question clicked down the meeting hall steps in her tidy dress pumps. She stopped and waited when Norman called her.

"Hi, Norman. I'd like to talk but I'm overdue at the office."

"Margaret, it seems like you did all you could to kill that rehab proposal. How come?"

"I did no such thing. I just want everything done right."

She started to turn but Norman took her arm. "Did you think about me losing all that work?"

"Don't be silly; it's only postponed a bit."

"You know better than that. That bluff'll never hold up until we get permission."

"Why, that's not what you told me. You said the bluff was okay for a while. I remember perfectly."

Shit; he had, hadn't he? He tried another angle. "That stuff about excavating. How'd you know about that proposal?"

Margaret gave him her biggest professional smile. "We'll have to talk later; I'm *way* overdue."

There was no way to keep her without making a scene, so he watched her climb into her white tank and drive off.

~

Tassy trudged over to her street along the bluff, turned uphill, and made her way home very slowly. When she reached the remains of her gate and lifted her eyes from the sidewalk she found a large and venerable sedan parked there, and a short, wide woman making her way back from the bluff face to the sidewalk. Hm, if she'd gone to the front door, what was she doing around at the side?

Smiling, she joined Tassy at the gate. "We saw each other at the casino a few nights back. I'm Clara Halvorsen."

What now? "Nice to meet you, Ms. . . . ."

The old woman squeezed Tassy's arm reassuringly. "Tassy—can I call you that? I'm chair of the Narowa Tribal Council."

Tassy could only reply, "Ohh-kay?"

"I was at the meeting. I've been following this situation."

Warning bells sounded. "Why would you follow this situation?"

"You could say it's part of my job." She looked Tassy up and down and then said, "I think I may have some ideas for you. Tell you what: Come have dinner with me at the casino." When Tassy hesitated, Ms. Halvorsen added, "I'd say the treat's on me, but they feed me for free." She sent Tassy an open, friendly grin.

The grin did it. "All right, thanks," Tassy said.

The old lady strode back to her car. She called, "Seven o'clock," as if it were an instruction, got in, and drove briskly away. All Tassy could think of was that Ms. Halvorsen was one spry old tribal chair.

And tooling home in her aging land yacht, Grandmother chalked up yet another win for that open, friendly, long-practiced grin.

~

Recalling the old woman's neat business suit, Tassy chose a dress—one of two—for dinner. As she assembled herself to go out she wished Linc could come with her to figure out what was up. She drove to the casino, growing more worried by the minute.

But Grandmother Halvorsen put her at ease. During dinner she made conversation with the skill of a professional who'd spent half her career at public functions. She had urged the sixteen-ounce rib eye on her guest, and Tassy, who felt tense and abstracted, had easily had her arm twisted. Now they were slowly relaxing into beef and potatoes and many soft rolls paved with butter. Tassy smiled inwardly as she noticed that Grandmother, too, avoided the cooked vegetables.

As they waited for dessert Grandmother sipped her shiraz. "I've seen at least one of your works."

Tassy's huge barking laugh filled the room.

"What is it, dear?" Grandmother seemed to like that big laugh.

"I've never heard them called 'works' before." She lifted a pinky finger. "So refined."

"They deserve it. The one in the Good Vibrations place is quite fine."

"Thank you; that's one of my personal paintings. The buyers all prefer scenics."

"Depends on the buyer," said Grandmother. "I have plans for these restaurant walls—oh, but that's for another time." She set down her wineglass. "Now, let's talk about your project."

Tassy held up her hands. "I really don't know if I have one anymore."

"You didn't think of the coastal commission?"

"Well . . ."

Grandmother said, "Margaret Nam certainly thought of them."

"Mm, didn't she, though?"

"It's pretty clear she's not on your side."

An exasperated shrug. "Though I've never understood why."

Grandmother shrugged too. "Some human motives are explainable and others not. You just have to tell the two types apart and then waste no time on the ones you can't figure."

Tassy asked, "What'll the commission do?"

"Review your petition."

"How long will that take?"

"Six months to a year."

Tassy felt close to panic. "My house'll never last that long."

"I heard that. I'm sorry. But as I told you, I'm an old hand at this. I might be able to expedite things."

Grandmother hauled a briefcase onto her lap and deployed her harvest from county seat offices. "You have a path beside your house and down your bluff."

"Sure. Not too many people use it, though I did see Erik Halvorsen—is he . . . ?"

"My grandson, yes. Now: Because that path provides the only beach access, the coastal commission can exercise 'prescriptive rights' to it—even on your property and without your consent."

"And that's going to help me?"

"The fine print says the path must have been used *without bona fide attempts by the owner to prevent or halt such use.*"

"I still . . ."

"So all you have to do is *prevent or halt such use*—close that path."

"Why?"

"Closing the path will close the beach, and that will make the commission very, very nervous. Beach access is political dynamite—much more sensitive than the details of a bluff face."

Tassy's look said she still didn't get it, so Grandmother continued patiently, "Reopening that path would be a long and expensive process—if they could even do it. If you agree to grant beach access, they'll suddenly see their way clear to approve your project."

"That's political horse trading. I don't know how to do that."

Grandmother bathed Tassy in a Cheshire cat smile.

Tassy said, "But *you* do."

Grandmother nodded. "Been at it for many years."

Tassy stared at her, frowning. "Why? What's in it for you?"

Grandmother leaned forward. "This is all confidential. The rancheria is discussing certain . . . *arrangements* with the Bureau of Indian Affairs and the county parks and recreation people. It's in our best interest to close that beach, at least through the end of the summer season."

Tassy looked skeptical. "After that you don't care if it's open?"

Grandmother hesitated, then said, "Yes, that's one way of putting it."

Tassy heard warning bells in her head. Just how *else* might Tribal Chair Halvorsen put it? Trying to think the way Linc did, Tassy said only, "What would I have to do—besides submit my proposal?"

Grandmother raised her hands. "Not much; just ever so slightly adjust your fence." She handed Tassy the page of relevant county codes. While Tassy was reading it, Grandmother saw the waitress approaching. "Oh look, here comes dessert!"

Later, in her office, Grandmother briefed Erik Halvorsen, who had trouble with her logic. "If she gets her permission and saves her bluff, the beach path will reopen again when they're done."

"Grandson, I looked at that bluff today. Even if I shorten the approval process by nine months, she's still going to lose her house. That beach path will stay closed forever."

"Then why pretend to help her? Why not just wait nine months?"

Grandmother felt both pleased and annoyed. Maybe her grandson could think, after all. "Nine months is long after this year's tourist season. We want the path closed *now*."

Erik pushed his luck. "But if the only path is closed, how could *we* get to it?"

Grandmother shrugged. "Buy up the pier if we have to—make an end run around."

"Can we afford to buy the whole pier?"

Grandmother looked at him and sighed.

~

When he got home from the bar at the Beach House, Norman Stihl strolled into his office to drop off the mail he'd just opened. He turned on the light and his eye lit on the bright green binder on top of his towering pile: his engineering proposal for Tassy's job.

Norman filed things by date; the older the paper, the deeper it was in the pile. Real simple, but it worked. He hadn't looked at that proposal in—what?—more'n two weeks, so what was it doing on top? He wasn't Sherlock Holmes or anything, but it didn't take a rocket scientist to figure Margaret's sudden early morning sex drive. He didn't know which was worse: finding out that she'd conned him or finding out that her extra warmth wasn't real. *Norman you're so sexy I just had to come get laid before breakfast by the way I couldn't find the coffeemaker see ya.*

Well, shit.

~

While Grandmother talked to her grandson, Tassy drove home and then walked down to Orson's gallery. She found him and Linc in the kitchen in back, staring glumly into their glasses. Laying out Ms. Halvorsen's papers, she reprised her dinner conversation.

Orson lightened from dour to doubtful. "Think it'll work?"

"Tribal chair, huh?" Linc thought a moment. "Her idea's good enough; is *she* good enough to finesse it?" He stood up and pulled out his cell phone. "What time is it, not yet nine? Let me call a friend of mine in town, Don Fedderman. He's a guy I have lunch with once in a while." He walked out into the night, punching keys.

"You know what he's done for you?" Orson asked Tassy.

"I think so."

Orson shook his big head. "Today's meeting blew his cover. Anyone could see he was on your side. His promising civic career has gone bye-bye."

"Oh no!"

Orson covered her hand with his own. "Not to worry, sweetie; I don't think he gives a good goddamn." He smiled. "Besides, trading the council for you is a great deal."

"Is that how he sees it?"

"Well, not quite that crudely, but more or less."

Linc returned, pocketing his phone. "Tribal Chair Clara Halvorsen makes heap big medicine. Used to work for the BIA. Knows everyone." He sat down and poured one more inch of bourbon. "I'd say she could do it if she really wanted to."

Orson echoed, "*Could?*"

"Mm. Fedderman says she's trying to get the beach away from the county—been working on it for months. So far, she's been stonewalled."

Orson nodded. "So closing Tassy's path would make the beach useless to the county—"

Tassy cut in, "But it would reopen as soon as we fixed the bluff."

Linc stared into his bourbon. "Yeah. That part doesn't compute."

~

Tassy and Linc walked home arm in arm beneath the stars of high summer. With the lights of the county seat thirty miles distant—and the local street lamp project stalled because Margaret insisted on ornamental cast iron the town couldn't afford—the black sky opened to the Milky Way and let 'er rip. Under the breathtaking show in the balmy air, they ambled along, just glad of the night, glad to be out in it, together.

Spying the snaggly remnant of her fence ahead, Tassy allowed as how Dave might get started on fixing it.

"I'll pick that up," Linc said.

"You can't keep doing that; it's too big a burden."

"Aw, c'mon. . . ."

"A burden on *me*. I can't go on piling up obligations."

They strolled a moment in silence, then Linc said slowly, "There's no obligation—but that's not for me to say, is it?" They went on a few paces. "How about this? Candy and flowers are corny and picking out jewelry's simply beyond me; so what do you say to a nice, romantic fence?"

They stopped and she turned to him. "Is that how you think of it, as if you were courting me?"

"No *as if* about it. Are you okay with that?"

She kept quiet all the way to the remains of her gate, where they stopped uncertainly. "I'm exhausted," she said.

"Too exhausted to come have a glass of wine?"

She nodded.

"Got something to show you."

Tassy studied his eager expression but was just too shot to make anything of it. "Linc, it's been a terrible day."

His eagerness faded. "I know." He wrapped his arms around her and kissed her deeply but, in some odd way, carefully. Then they separated and he started to turn uphill.

"Linc."

He turned back.

"I'm okay with courting."

They both said good night. Going inside, she thought, Well, that does it. I don't care if I break out in hives or foam at the mouth. I'm scoring some contraceptives.

17

The very next morning, Tassy rode down to the county seat in Dave's truck.

Dave thought it seemed like he was seeing her more than average these days. He knew it was just work and all, but anyway, it felt good. She had some kind of doctor's appointment, so he dropped her off on Carson Street and went on to the lumberyard. He had to remember to buy her a bubble level too, though he couldn't figure why she wanted it.

When he picked her up again to drive home, she looked sort of down—well, worried, more like. She hardly talked, but that was okay. Dave found talking hard going, even with someone he liked as much as Tassy.

Five miles south of home, they topped a rise on US 101 and Three Mile Beach spread out before them, a long, shallow arc of sunlit sand and driftwood and the rolling combers that never reached the shore inside the town's breakwater. The endless beach hosted one car and two pickups, their beds filled with free firewood. The car's occupants were down at the intertidal level, digging the best razor clams in the world.

The freeway dipped to just a few feet above beach level, then swooped up again toward the sentinel redwoods. At a pull-off next to a slope cut for grading, a horizontal white pipe stuck out of the cut face, gushing water like an open tap. A man and a woman were out of their pickup, filling plastic jugs with this perfect springwater. Tassy thought if the world ever discovered all this it'd be paradise lost for sure. She was so lucky just to be here, though it was hard to be cheerful about that right now.

Tassy's appointment with the gynecologist had not gone well. There were all kinds of options for birth control now, from the venerable Pill to a small stick sewn into your arm, for gawdsake. They were effective for women of childbearing age, but the trouble began as you approached the undiscovered country beyond it. Birth control didn't work as reliably when you were still fertile but increasingly unpredictable; and if you'd had side effects like hers, those could grow even worse as menopause loomed. Overall, it was really not a good bet.

Tassy thanked Dave for the ride and entered her house. Beowulf's fallout was now all over the great room: fine tufts of near-white undercoat from his seemingly endless supply. Every day now, she brushed him with the curry rake until the front yard looked like a milkweed field after a pod explosion; but his fur was no thinner and his shedding no less exuberant. Still, his greeting—he was actually romping by now—more than made up for it.

After the hugging and petting ritual, she retrieved some pliers from the anything drawer in her kitchen, unfastened Beowulf's collar, and replaced his old name tag with a new one, purchased downtown, that listed her cell phone. Not that it mattered, since everyone in San Andreas knew the gray dog who went everywhere unmolested, and not because she owned him now. Nobody "owned" Beowulf. The new tag was just her gesture of responsibility. Maybe love too; yeah.

In the bedroom she set her new bubble level next to the baseboard and aimed it at the harbor. Sure enough, the room was more than a full bubble off level. Sighing, she went to shower. Her bathroom had been cheap to begin with and sixty years in the salt spray belt hadn't helped. Overall, the depressing effect was of rust and mild mildew. She finished as quickly as possible, toweled off, dressed in a fresh denim shirt and crisp shorts, and wiggled her feet into sandals.

She'd have to tell Linc the bad news about birth control—discuss it sooner or later. Hey, Linc, we're good for a lip-lock and maybe some groping, but that's it, dude; that's all she wrote. Might be less painful to just call it off.

She didn't have to tell him right now, but Tassy somehow found herself through her front gate and walking uphill toward the B and B. As she approached she could hear Linc's music, as usual, floating out into the road. It seemed louder than normal today.

When she climbed the front steps she was struck by the sound, a piano piece that might have been Bach, only Bach as if he'd been French or Italian: rigorous and yet delicate, with a humor that didn't quite cover the sadness beneath. Tassy moved to the open porch window, where the music seemed to be coming from.

It was Linc with his back to her, playing a huge black piano, a piano she hadn't seen before. As she stood outside the open window, the piece shifted briefly to minor, then returned to the major for a final, quiet restatement. Linc let the last notes die away gently, and Tassy felt tears leaking out of her eyes and rolling down her cheeks. The elegant pathos in the music somehow articulated what she felt about her cursed female systems and her rusty bath fixtures and her home that was passing away after a long illness.

"What was that?" she asked.

Linc turned and smiled. "Scarlatti, K. 502 in C major." He noticed her tears and jumped up as fast as the piano bench permitted. "Tassy, what's wrong?"

She shook her head and walked into the main parlor as Linc rushed through the pocket door archway. He embraced her. "What is it, baby?" With one arm still around her, he led her into what must now be the music room.

Tassy shook her head again, scrubbing her cheeks with the heels of her hands. "It's enormous. When did you get it?"

"Oh, it's been in storage a long time. It's a Steinway D series." He sat down. "Can you believe it? This county has a piano tuner." Linc ripped a three-octave scale that included an awful lot of black keys. "Perfect."

Tassy sat on the far left corner of the bench. "Play the Scarlatti again, would you?"

Linc looked at her quietly, then did so. When he finished this time she was smiling. He said, "It's an easy one. Good thing too; I'm so-o-o rusty." He pulled a yellow-covered folio out from behind the Scarlatti score.

"Who's C-zerny?" she asked.

"Pronounced *Cherny*. He composed piano exercises." Linc opened the book at random to a double page exploding with notes apparently inked with a shotgun.

Tassy goggled. "*Jay*-zus!"

"That's what I say when I practice it now. Been away much too long."

She rubbed her finger on the black front lip of the keyboard, then sheepishly wiped the spot with her shirttail.

Linc looked at her, still quietly. "Want some supper?"

"You mean *here*?"

"Come back in—ah—maybe three hours. I'll surprise you."

"You've learned to cook?"

He shook his head. "Drive."

~

Supper turned out to be a cold party tray: vegetable munchies, meat and cheese wraps, and a half ton of glorious shrimp. Linc supplied cocktail sauce, mayo, and very cold sauvignon blanc.

"That was perfect," said Tassy, pleased to be stuffed with more protein and fiber than starch, though excessively stuffed, to be sure. "How did you happen to have it?"

"I didn't but Costco did. That's why I needed three hours." Linc pushed away from the kitchen table. "Let's carry our glasses out on the porch." He picked up the second wine bottle.

They sat down on the teak swing in time to catch the sunset. Linc said, "Just a few days to midsummer." The sun went through its nightly horizon routine, then left the high clouds to complete their own performance, while swallows swooped in the twilight to vacuum up flying insects. As the sky darkened, a bat took over the insect patrol. Tassy still missed the night sounds of her native Midwest, but by way of compensation, bugs were fairly scarce out here—which was great for her, if not for the swallows and bats—and the gentle surf made dependable white noise. They rocked and sipped for some time, Linc with his arm around her shoulders.

When the stars were out and the wine was gone, Linc said, "Come upstairs, Tassy." He stood up and held out his hand.

Well, there went the ball game. A shame to ruin a night like this, but Linc would have to be told. "Linc," she said, shaking her head.

"I just want to show you something."

Resigned, she took his hand and they mounted the sweeping front staircase. Was he planning Jacuzzi à deux? But they kept on to the end of the hall, where Linc paused to open a door. He switched on some lights, small bulbs in wall sconces.

It was a bedroom and very nice, too, but it only confirmed her first fears. "Oh, Linc . . ."

He went, "Shh," then drew her to the near-side bed table, opened its drawer, pulled out a box, and presented it to her with ceremony.

She squinted to read in the faint amber light: some kind of drugstore package . . . it was condoms! Her eyes filled up for a second time that day and she threw her long arms around him.

Linc lit a few candles and Tassy snickered because that was so corny, but their light was romantic and their effect enhanced by the effort he'd made to provide them. He removed the bedspread, folding it neatly, and turned down the bedcovers. Then he opened the box of condoms, cursing the plastic wrap, and placed a packet on the bed table. He thought a moment, then tore open one edge of the foil.

While Linc was systematically waxing romantic, Tassy studied the bedroom. She was surprised to find four of her paintings hung up, and the sight of them more than made up for the plodding way he was ramping up lovemaking.

Paced by Tassy this time, they undressed each other with rather less care, flinging clothing and underwear as they stumbled about, getting naked. Once in the big bed, Linc started to pull up the sheet but Tassy stopped him.

She was warmed by their leisurely explorations, seeing as both were practically shaking with lust. Linc was clearly controlling himself with some effort. Finally she murmured, "I think it's time for that raincoat."

He fumbled the condom out of its foil, a latex drumhead with a thick tan rim. After a moment's study, he placed it and started to roll it down.

"Ow!"

"What's the matter?"

"It won't unroll; it just pinches."

"Let me look. Dummy, you put it on upside down."

"How could I? It only opens at one end."

"I mean it's flipped over. You can't roll it down because the sides are inside instead of outside."

"What?"

"Here, let me do it." Tassy turned the condom over and rubbed it open and slowly down while Linc groaned audibly.

She said, "Patience; I've almost got it."

"Patience my ass; I'm gonna screw something."

Tassy's huge laugh filled the bedroom. Oops, shouldn't kill the mood, but it didn't seem to dampen Linc down. How long could a fifty-year-old man keep going?

Quite a while, it turned out, and he brought her down slowly, deliciously afterward. Then they lay side by side on their backs and just smiled.

After a while, Linc surveyed the deflated condom and attendant mess. "Yuck!"

Being a woman, she was blasé about genital inconveniences. "You don't like those things, do you?"

"Never tried one before."

"Why am I not surprised?" And they both snorted with laughter.

Linc climbed out of bed, comically holding himself and the condom. "Did we get it on?" At another bark of Tassy laughter, he said with dignity, "Well, obviously *we* did, but I was referring to *it*." He nodded down at his protective hands.

As he shuffled off to the bathroom she muttered, "Beats me. I was too busy to notice."

When he returned, tidied up, she studied his body. Okay, not an Olympic swimmer, but not flabby either. How did he do that without working out and would he please tell her the secret?

She took a turn in the bathroom to clean up and process some wine. Unfamiliar with the layout, she first turned on the lights, squinting until she adjusted.

When she was finished, she stood up and found herself confronting herself in a mirror. She took a tough, careful inventory. Though she couldn't escape time and gravity, she guessed she was holding up—well, the top half, anyway. She sucked in her stomach, then whooshed her breath out and relaxed. She was what she was, and to hell with it.

She turned out the light and walked back to the bedroom. As she strolled toward the bed, she couldn't resist swinging side to side just a little. Linc's expression said clearer than words that whatever time had done to her body, he was definitely all for it.

She got into bed and climbed on top of him, bracing herself on her elbows so her long hair tickled his ears and neck and her nipples ruffled his chest hair. For some reason, she thought, *Poor Larry; poor, poor Larry*, and grinned like a madwoman.

"What?"

Instead of answering, she relaxed until her weight was on him and her mouth brushed his ear. She kissed the ear. After a minute or two she kissed it again and murmured, "Counselor, you're getting lumpy in the middle."

"Mm, wonder why. Can you reach those packets?"

"How many left?"

"Nineteen, I think."

"Should hold us—well, I mean, should hold *you*."

"Until morning," he drawled, and they giggled like kids.

Eventually—who knew what time it was?—Linc staggered up, snuffed the candles, pinching each wick with wet fingers and then wiping the fingers with a tissue—then turned out the wall lights, then came back to bed. She reflected that he hadn't troubled to gather, sort, fold, and stack all their clothing. By God, she'd fried the man's brain! Tassy wriggled comfortably close to him and drifted off, most redundantly satisfied.

18

*L*inc woke up to the astonishing feel of a large, warm softness more or less wrapped around him. The softness was stirring and so was he, so he fumbled for the condom box, knocked it to the floor, nearly joined it in trying to retrieve it, fumbled again for a packet, tore off its end with his teeth.

By this time Tassy was helping, between chuckles, so he just said, "Aw, hell," and gave her the latex drumhead. They reprised all their earlier progressions, from prefatory farce through prolonged and delicious play, to a completion that left them both gasping.

Tassy said feebly, "How many times is that now?"

Linc wheezed melodramatically, "I dunno; count the damn packets."

"I think I forgot how to count," Tassy said and collapsed on him.

The only trouble with Tassy's breasts was that he couldn't look at them and feel them against his chest simultaneously. Granted, this would be true of all breasts, but with most others this drawback would be less obvious.

He free-associated from breasts to Ellen's body and then to Ellen generally. Something was different this morning; something inside him had shifted. His sorrow remained and possibly always would, but its source had somehow been moved to the past, like a document archived when a legal matter concluded. Tassy was *now*—very much now, in fact, with her tongue in his ear—and that felt entirely proper and comfortable, not to say damp. It was not as if he'd satisfied some specified grieving requirement, but rather that life had changed around him and was asking for new responses—maybe a whole new strategy.

Without warning, a wonderful strategy popped up fully formed, a strategy with tactics already in place, a plan with multiple parts, all detailed, all requiring synchronization. During his career he'd excelled at these strategies, and suddenly the Napoleon of entertainment law was back in command. As Tassy wandered off to the bath and then down to forage for coffee, he lay there envisioning lines of action.

After breakfast on leftover Costco buffet, Linc drafted and printed a letter for Tassy, kissed her long enough to consider dragging her back upstairs, and reluctantly released her.

Tassy opened Linc's front door to find Beowulf camped in front of it.

"Oh, baby, I'm sorry; I just forgot." After their usual reunion ritual she beckoned to Linc and led both of them back to the kitchen. "I'm going to be here, off and on now, and you can stay right here too." To Linc: "Can't he?"

Linc considered it. He'd thought about adopting some kind of dog. Aristocratic Beowulf was hardly the mutt he'd envisioned, and the dog put out more fluff than a cottonwood grove, but otherwise, he couldn't see any downside. "Sure," he said. "I'll pick up dog chow and stuff at the grocery."

That earned him another steamy embrace and then Tassy went out again, trailed by Beowulf, to supervise DayGlo Dave.

Dave had arrived at Tassy's at eight a.m. in his truck full of lumber and tools. He'd knocked but she hadn't answered, though her little car was out front as usual. No problem; she had an outside electrical outlet to use and he knew what to do with the fence.

He found the surveyor's button planted in the front sidewalk and eyeballed a line toward the harbor. Sure enough, the near side of the neighboring house was right on that line.

Dave worked at his slow, steady pace and by noon he'd extended the front fence to its new corner on the property line. It was at this point that Tassy came out of Linc's house and jogged downhill toward him. She looked extra bouncy today. He watched as she approached him, all sparkly and smiling, and when she saw the look on his face she gave him a great big hug. She said, "Hey, Dave!" and skipped into the house, trailed by Beowulf.

Dave made himself go back to work. After he settled down from the great big hug he figured out she must've been up there since before he got here at eight a.m. He didn't really like to think about that, so he didn't.

Once inside, Tassy checked the level in the bedroom. It now looked to be almost two bubbles off. Had it been that bad last night? How did you measure fractions of bubbles? She transferred the level to the ocean-side studio floor: two bubbles and then some. Opening the door to the deck, she reached out as far as she could and set down the level. Even viewing at such an acute angle, it wasn't hard to see that the bubble was at the very end of its travel through its glass tube. The deck was now too tilted to measure. Did she really have three months left? She reluctantly locked the sliding door. From now on, Beowulf would have to come in through the front.

～

An hour later Linc sat at the game table in the main parlor—for some reason he now felt comfortable here—with a pencil and two yellow legal pads, one for notes and one for outlines, identifying first steps. A visit to Bill the Fixer, a consultation at the Seaside Café, and a second call to Lawyer Fedderman downtown. The master plan called for legal work that Linc couldn't—well, shouldn't—do. Then another call to—whom, Tribal Chair Halvorsen? Right. Linc made a note to phone the casino.

When the brainstorm had passed, he copied his outline, threw out his rough notes, stashed all his working materials, and unholstered his mobile phone.

Later, Linc strolled over to Bill the Fixer's house, on undesignated row. Bill was taking a time-out from carving—a waterfall sculpture was giving him fits—and he was happy to walk back with Linc.

Now they stood in the bridal suite bath, contemplating the giant Jacuzzi. "Pulling it's no problem," Bill said. "Them fiberglass tubs are light; it's unhooking all the plumbing takes time." He stood there meditating and Linc had the sense to let him alone.

After five silent minutes Bill started sketching right on the wallpaper with a wide, flat pencil, explaining that it was okay because he was going to knock the wall down anyway. The new bath had been tucked in a corner of the big bedroom and enclosed by an L of two walls. Bill would replace these with shorter ones to turn the toilet and vanity into a half bath. Outside the new walls, where the Jacuzzi now stood, he'd install kitchen cabinets and a counter. Bill allowed as how he and Dave could do the job pretty quick and Linc offered to pay double for speed. With the rate he proposed, Bill walked away a very happy man, to set up the job with Dave.

~

By the end of the afternoon the fence lacked only the new gate, which Dave would build and install the next day. As he was loading his pickup, Tassy ambled out the door, smiled cheerfully, and held up a plastic NO TRESPASSING sign fresh from the hardware shelf at the market. Dave promised to post it and Tassy headed off toward the art gallery, clothing boutique, latte parlor, and tchotchke palace that made up much of tourist row. At each place she left her signed letter, written and printed by Linc, below her own letterhead in the Bookman Old Style font he'd suggested. She delivered the last copy to Mayor Millhouse personally at the coffee shop. The critical paragraph read:

Due to the instability of my bluff and my inabil-
ity to repair it without permission from the California Coastal Commission, potential liability issues
have forced me to close my property to all pedes-
trian traffic. A "No Trespassing" sign has been
posted and will be strictly enforced.

Millhouse looked up from the letter. "But there's a path right
through there."

"What path?" innocent Tassy replied, as instructed by Linc.

"The one right next to your house."

"There's no path there; never was."

By now the mayor's face was almost a cartoon of stress. "Sure
there was—*is*."

"Jack, you might want to check with your legal counsel; find out
what qualifies as a *path*."

"But it's the only way to get to the beach."

"Exactly. The beach is now closed."

Desperately, "How—?

"Indefinitely." She smiled at him ruefully. "If we'd been able to
start on the rehab, we'd have fixed the bluff first and this wouldn't
have happened and San Andreas could offer the tourists the best
beach in the county." She sighed sympathetically. "I think it's called
the Law of Unintended Consequences."

"I'll ask Linc about it."

"Oh, that law won't be on the books. See you, Jack." Tassy
walked out, just slightly exaggerating that rolling stroll she had.

Within minutes, the phones of the town power players were
threatening to choke on the traffic as everyone tried to call everyone else, all at the same time. Since Good Vibrations had closed for
the day, Sharon Morning Sky invited the two overlapping commit-
tees—in effect, the town council plus herself—to meet in the latte

parlor. Good soul that she was, she served coffees and tea all around and, unlike the mayor, didn't charge for them.

After a short free-for-all of shouted questions that no one could answer, they agreed to wait for Linc to show up. When he did, he listened as gravely as if this were all news to him, and then pointed out three deadly facts: a) no public path existed unless and until the town could prove it; b) they could prove it only to the California Coastal Commission because no other agency was empowered to designate private land for public beach access; and c) the commission wouldn't even *look* at their problem until long after tourist season.

"Could we—could we get an injunction?" The mayor was practically gargling by now. "You know: Keep it open until the commission rules?"

Linc said, "Possibly."

"Hey . . ."

"But she's closing her property to *avoid liability for injuries* on her bluff. If we force her to open it, *we* would be liable instead."

This produced a protracted debate, which at length resolved into the reluctant consensus that the town was screwed.

In the glum silence produced by this, Orson spoke up. "Margaret, you did everything you could to delay that rehab job. You want to tell us all why?"

Margaret's calm face resembled a cloud with heat lightning flickering faintly. Finally she answered with perfect control, "I just wanted things done properly."

"Nothing against Tassy personally?"

Her control slipped a bit. "Of course not; that's nonsense!" She surveyed the other faces and saw that they didn't buy it. She stood up abruptly. "Well," she said, forgetting it was now six o'clock, "some of us still have a business to run."

After Margaret stalked out, the group dissolved quickly. Orson rolled off and Linc walked away with the mayor.

While Sharon cleaned up, Dottie Franklyn lingered to send up a trial balloon. "Do you think Margaret *was* being spiteful?"

Sharon paused and regarded her steadily. "What do *you* think?"

Even to Dottie, her meaning was clear.

At the coffee shop, Linc procured a takeout menu and asked to have phone orders delivered. When Millhouse declined to offer that service, Linc offered a one hundred percent surcharge, pointed out that his house was a one-minute walk, and guaranteed generous tips. Since the mayor paid only minimum wage, either the busboy or the dishwasher would be tickled to death with this chore.

Distracted by civic stresses, the mayor gave in and agreed. "So, Linc," he said not very steadily, "what's your take on all this?"

Linc studied him gravely. "This whole business has been shabby, vindictive, and petty—also completely unnecessary. And now, because you failed to control things, Tassy Morgan's going to lose her home."

"Not necessarily."

"That bluff won't last three more months without fixing. You think the commission will rule before then?"

"Well, of course, I can't speak—"

"Yes, you *can* speak, Jack—or at least you *could*. But you didn't, not until push came to shove, and then you let Margaret shove you."

"It's really her fault," Jack said petulantly.

At this point Linc practically lost it; but he calmed himself with the thought that elections were near and perhaps the mayor's days were numbered. When he had recaptured his self-control he said, "We still on for takeout delivery?"

"Oh, sure," Millhouse said absently. After all, business was business.

19

Tassy and Linc didn't spend every night together, for reasons that neither could fully explain, though they discussed it and both admitted the obvious: They'd been blindsided by feelings strong enough to be frightening. Tassy was scarred by rejection and Linc had been shattered by loss, and so both were excessively self-protective. Each could also acknowledge a half-guilty pleasure in full independence after a quarter century of marital compromises. But as for deeper pressures and fears, their most earnest efforts at self-exploration did not turn those up.

They more or less alternated, with Tassy sleeping one night at home and the next one with Linc. Beowulf accepted the arrangement with his usual sangfroid. During the day Tassy painted while Linc battled Czerny and monitored Bill and Dave upstairs. When Tassy asked about that, Linc shrugged and said that he'd decided to turn the B and B back into a residence, doing one room at a time.

On their evenings together she'd walk over to watch the sunset and eat in Linc's dining room, to which Linc had become reconciled. She was surprised at the café food, but Linc didn't say what he was paying to get it and—give Millhouse credit—the menu was varied and the cooking was good.

The lovemaking was better, though they never mastered the condom procedure and their efforts were, so to speak, slipshod at best and at worst they were downright negligent. It was lucky they saw the humor in it; luckier still that, for them at least, humor could not kill romance.

Tassy's biggest concern was her house, as the bedroom bubble crept slowly uphill. It was like an hour hand, its movement invisible but its progress inexorable. She could still paint by shimming up her big work board, but she had to reverse her bedding so she could sleep with her head uphill. That way, Beowulf no longer threatened to roll down on her.

~

As part of his master strategy, Linc once again huddled with Bill the Fixer, who sent him in turn to Jimi at the Hair Place. The shop was empty of customers and Angela was nursing the baby at the manicure station. When Linc strolled in she started to cover the baby's face, but he walked over to them, eased the blanket away, and studied the small critter chowing down at its swelling pink pillow.

"Forgive me, but I'm just a man. Boy or girl?"

Angela smiled. "Pamela Anne."

"Beautiful," Linc said. "Both of you." The sad truth was that Angela was one of those local dairy farm daughters, shiny and plump at sixteen but turning doughy by thirty.

He grinned at Jimi. "Got a slot for a walk-in?"

"Got the whole Grand Canyon. Have a seat."

After a suitable ration of small talk, Linc said, "Does this town have a historian?"

Jimi snipped around Linc's right ear. "Like, official? No. Lemme think. . . . Years ago we had a little museum in the town hall, but it went when they tore out the wall to make the auditorium. Now, where'd all that junk go?" She snip-snipped away for several seconds. "I know! Old Mrs. Lagan had it in her garage. If I know her, she still does."

"Good."

"Why do you ask?"

"Oh, just curious." He looked in the mirror. "Still my own hair, but now it looks like I take care of it."

Jimi snorted. "Funny, that's just what Tassy told me." She grinned at him.

Linc grinned back but said nothing. He paid and, on the way out, gave Angela's tiny bundle a pat.

"Hey, Linc!" Jimi called after him. He paused in the open shop door. She was still grinning. "Welcome back."

When he'd gone, Jimi thought about Linc and that last grin of his. "Well, well, well," she said. "Well, well, *well*." If she was right—and she usually was—things were starting to look up for Tassy, and that was excellent news.

~

In due course, Tribal Chair Clara Halvorsen and Assistant Casino Manager Erik Halvorsen faced Mr. Lincoln Ellis across the polished redwood table in the casino's conference room.

Linc began by noting the tribe's failure to get control of the beach. "Of course, you have to have that beach for your resort."

Erik sat up. How did you—?

Grandmother chopped the air with the edge of her hand. "Continue."

"But if you can't control the beach, you might be able to close public access to it."

Grandmother raised an eyebrow.

"Suppose, for example, you owned Ms. Morgan's property."

Grandmother's second eyebrow joined its partner.

"That way, you would also own the only beach path."

"That's true," Grandmother admitted.

"And since her property's also ancestral tribal land, you could then transfer it from the city of San Andreas to the sovereign Narowa Nation."

Grandmother nodded. "Why should we keep the path closed?"

"If the county had to maintain a beach they couldn't reach for a town that couldn't use it, they might change their minds about selling it to you."

Erik spoke up. "Would Tassy sell her property?"

"Yes, to the Lost Coast Charitable Trust."

"I never heard of it," Erik said.

Grandmother said, "Something tells me it's newly incorporated."

Linc ignored this. "And the trust, in turn, would give it to the tribe."

Grandmother stared at him awhile, then, "And why would this trust want to do that?"

"So that the town could use the beach again. Under your control, with an engineered access path, the beach would be safe and protected." Linc rolled smoothly on. "Now, suppose the tribe and the town built a new tourist attraction *together* on that lot: an interpretive center for the beach and its village, plus a museum for the town. All those resort guests would be treated to the charms of San Andreas on their way to Native culture and a suntan with genuine Narowa mai tais."

Grandmother smiled slightly. "Anything more?"

"Yes, one: The trust would underwrite the building cost."

They locked eyes a long time, and then Grandmother nodded. "I'll talk to the Bureau of Indian Affairs." She pushed herself to her feet and the men stood too.

Linc said, "Don Fedderman will handle matters for the trust. I'd appreciate your keeping my name out of it."

As he turned to leave, Grandmother said, "Just one more question."

Linc turned back.

"Why doesn't the trust simply give the lot to the town? Why include the Narowa?"

Link smiled briefly. "First, because the town is obviously not competent to manage it."

"And secondly?"

Linc stared at nothing for a while, then looked at her, smiling. "Because I feel like it."

When Linc had left, Erik said, "That man is smooth."

The old lady nodded absently. "Rich too, apparently."

"Is this a good deal for us?"

Grandmother shrugged. "Cheaper than buying the pier, I guess. It doesn't happen often, but sometimes the salmon jump into your net." Outside, she maintained a magisterial calm; inside, she was jubilant.

~

Half an hour before sunset, Linc returned home to find Tassy pacing around his kitchen, too agitated to stop for a kiss. "I'm going, Linc, I'm going."

He felt that sudden clutch again. "Going where? How long?"

She shook her head impatiently. "My bedroom's two bubbles off."

What the hell? "Is that like two bricks short of a load?"

"Jesus, Linc, get serious. My house is going—falling over!" Tassy stomped around the table. "I can't paint anymore, I can't sleep, I don't think I can live there!" She started muttering, "Sonsabitches, sonsa*bitches*!"

Linc poured a prescription chardonnay, wrapped her fist around it, and sat her down. He stood behind her and rubbed her shoulders while she gulped the wine; then she leaned her head back on his belt buckle.

Quieter now, Tassy said wearily, "I guess I knew it was coming."

"I confess I did too." He came around the chair and pulled her upright. "Come upstairs, Tassy."

She tried to wave him off. "Hey, sex with you cures almost everything, but not right now."

"No sex. Just come up."

Instead of heading for the big front staircase, Linc opened a door off the kitchen and led her by the hand up the back stairs and into a cheerful, empty room. She could see the bedroom—their bedroom now—through closed French doors on the opposite wall.

He spread open his arms. "This is yours—you know, to get away, be private; your own space. You pick the furniture—bring some of your own or we could buy new, or maybe do both."

She stood still a long time and then said to the room at large, "You want me to move in."

"Yes, but don't decide yet." Recapturing her hand, he led her through the French doors and the bedroom, down the main hall, and into the bridal suite.

But it wasn't the bridal suite anymore. The furniture was gone, the big, bare windows poured sunset into the room, and the light bounced off matte white walls and the gleaming oak floor. The bridal bathroom was gone as well. Linc showed her the toilet and vanity enclosed by new walls and door and then led her to the twelve running feet of kitchen-height, counter-topped cabinets where the Jacuzzi had sat. At one end there were two—count them—two stainless laundry sinks side by side, each with a high-arcing spigot and temperature mixing controls. "This whole side's for storage and cleanup," he said. Twelve feet of wall cabinets hung above the long counter.

"And now, the pièce de résistance," Linc said, and threw the wall switch. Soft, diffuse daylight flooded the room through milky panels under the ten-foot ceiling. "Those aren't standard fluorescents. They're called 'sunlight.' Guaranteed ninety percent accurate. The store guy said they shoot films with them now." Linc didn't reveal that the tubes cost ten times the price of standard fluorescents.

Tassy wandered from counter to windows to bathroom to sinks. "It's . . . it's . . ."

"It's your studio."

Pausing at the sinks, she stood in the cheerful fake sunshine, expressionless, motionless, except for the fingers of both hands, which curled and uncurled and curled up again. When she turned to him, Linc saw hurricane warnings.

She started quietly enough: "You son of a bitch, you did it again."

Linc took her arms. "Stop! Don't break the windows, don't get the chain saw—not yet. Listen to me first, I *beg* you." He slid his hands down her arms and reached for her hands. She tried to yank free but he trapped her in fingers now pumped on Czerny.

For a minute he simply looked at her. Then he sighed and began, "When I woke up our first morning together, I knew instantly, absolutely that I wanted you, not as a lover, not as a companion, not as a roommate—well, all those things rolled into one: as my *wife*. I instantly knew that I loved you and always would. I wanted you forever."

"There is no forever."

"Hear me out. So I cooked up a campaign to get you to marry me."

"How impulsive—how romantic!"

Linc snorted. "The impulsive part was falling in love—*bang*—just like that! The whole thing simply dropped into place. I planned the studio conversion that day, that very same day, while you were repairing your fence. I did it because I love you, Tassy."

She started pacing. "So you love me. How do you love me? Let me count the ways. First you paid to paint my house for me—a service I didn't ask for and a color I didn't like. Then you organized a fence for me." Linc opened his mouth, but she held up a hand. "Oh, you asked that time, but you also paid for it."

"You let me."

"Bad judgment, but I did. Then you cleared away the mess after I cut the fence in half—again, you didn't ask and again you paid."

"Well . . ."

"Then you talked me into repairing the fence and paid for that too."

"Well . . ."

"Then you got this place all ready to move me in—did a huge remodel—without bothering to find out if I wanted to, let alone what I might want in a studio. What are Dave and Bill doing? I asked; what's going on upstairs? Oh, just some minor remodeling; don't worry your pretty head."

"That's overstating . . ."

"*Now* is not the time to say you love me. The time was before you maneuvered me into this."

Tassy was marching around and around the big room, striding faster with each circuit. "Here's how it goes. You say, 'Tassy, I love you and want to marry you,' and I say, 'I'm pretty sure I love you too, Linc,' and you say, 'So, you want to set a date?' and I say, 'Um, I don't know if I'm ready yet. Tell you what, though, let's hook up— try things out.' Then we *discuss* whether to make this studio and you *consult* me about how to do it."

"I was only trying—"

"They'll put that on your fucking tombstone, Linc: 'He Was Only Trying to Help.'" Tassy stopped her circling at the door and went through it.

"Where're you going?"

"Back to the tiltin' Hilton; where do you think?"

"Don't . . ."

Tassy marched back, right up in his face. "Don't you ever say *don't* to me again!" She turned, took two steps, turned back again.

"And come to think of it, I'm *not* pretty sure I love you. Right now, I'm pretty sure I do *not*!"

Linc stood frozen in the happy white light while Tassy thudded down the carpeted front stairs and clacked across the hardwood parlor floor. A pause while dog toenails clicked along behind her, and then the outer door slammed.

20

After a long, blank interval, Linc wandered back down to the kitchen, cursing the vacuum in his head and wondering how Hollywood's fastest counterpuncher had lost the ability to change tactics on the fly. A Jack Daniel's would hit the spot right now, yes sir. In fact, there might be *several* spots to aim for.

Eureka! happened halfway through the Jack and soda and made the other half unnecessary. Linc believed you could negotiate anything, everything; and he'd grown better than wealthy believing that—well, and also by choosing the ground, tweaking the rules, dealing from strength. Okay, people labeled some things "nonnegotiable" (though that'd never stopped him), but he hadn't truly registered that some things weren't just nonnegotiable, they were outside the very concept of negotiation—things like charging tigers and babies toddling into traffic and loving Tassy. These things required a different mind-set.

No! Not a mind-set at all. Mind—his mind—was precisely the problem here. These things required instinct, assuming he had any. Linc paced the kitchen until slowly, imperceptibly, a memory coalesced again: waking with Tassy beside him and feeling an instant, perfect understanding of what he wanted. He still felt it and it was still perfect. If that wasn't instinct, what was? Linc headed through the parlor, grabbed a heavy jacket, and strode out the front door.

It was dark now. He walked up to Tassy's door and knocked. No answer. No lights anywhere. He knocked again. Still nothing. He waited, then knocked one more time. Nothing. He almost started pounding on the door—almost—but his newly awakened instinct told him this was not the moment for a peremptory summons. He started thinking, remembered he was through thinking, and stepped off the front stoop. Creeping along the side of the house, he tried the windows: crank-out casements, impossible to open.

Moving cautiously, he approached the lip of Tassy's bluff. He could inch forward enough to just barely see the ocean side of her house, with its huge windows and sliding glass door to the deck.

Sliding glass door!

How to reach it? He'd have to climb partway down the beach access path, then cut sideways across the treacherous bluff face to the deck. Stepping over the lowered back fence, he did that, stumbling on stones and kicking frightening divots of dirt downhill.

Right! With his back braced against a deck support, Linc squinted up at the ghostly outlines of more supports staggering uphill. Lurching from one upright to the next, he could work high enough up the bluff face to grab the deck railing, pull himself up, and climb over. As he moved, the ground crumbled under his shoes and tumbled away in the darkness, and one of the smaller supports pulled off in his hand and almost sent him pitching backward toward the beach below. He caught himself, launched a final effort, and frantically embraced the base of a deck post.

Okay. He breathed some. Okay. Now, how to pull himself over the railing? Linc grabbed a lower deck rail, but it bowed alarmingly toward him, too rotten to bear any weight. He considered a moment, then pushed one end of the rail inward instead and it came away from the post. It was indeed so rotten that it made no noise tearing loose, and he was able to detach the other end by just twisting the board in his hands. He laid it quietly on the deck planks and pushed it inward.

Using the post for leverage, he managed to haul himself up and through the gap left by the railing. He was on the deck, lying on his belly, winded.

After a moment he got to his knees and then his feet. Something groaned beneath him like a troll waking under a bridge. Oh jeez! This deck was unsafe; Tassy'd said so. He took a step toward the sliding door, twelve feet away.

Another sound below, this time like a giant chicken bone snapping. Linc froze. Instinct wasn't cutting it; time to resume thinking. Okay, the closer to the house the safer, right? He could walk it in maybe five steps. Step one.

Another noisy protest.

Or crawl; crawl was good. In slow motion he sank into a crouch, leaned forward until his palms touched the deck, and slowly, slowly shifted weight onto them. Left knee down, touching, taking weight; right knee following. Another creaking noise, but shorter. Was shorter a good sign? Left knee, right knee, left knee, right knee, Linc shuffled forward toward the glass door, three fearful inches at a time. It took forever.

Still in slow motion, he stood erect and tried the door. Damn! Why would it be locked? To keep people in, of course. The deck was so hazardous not even Beowulf could use it now. Sighing, he knocked. And knocked and knocked and called out and knocked some more and then overrode his early caution and pounded. Then he stopped and listened to the deck's continuing complaints and the scuttling-rat noises of bluff bits tumbling downhill.

He thought about retracing his shuffle and sank onto his haunches, then imagined wriggling backward through the open rail section and trying, blind, to find a purchase on the bluff below. He shifted until he was sitting with his back against the door.

Now what? Reason and instinct had both failed him. His grand design had driven Tassy away instead of reeling her in—well, jee-*zus*, what was she, some kind of fish? Is that how he thought of someone he loved so deeply? All he could do was manipulate people. Pathetic. As more, much more, in the same vein trudged through Linc's mind, he was gradually captured by the inertia he hadn't felt since, well, since Tassy—the pathological stasis that resembled deep depression, except he couldn't feel enough to feel depressed.

~

San Andreas was a three-by-three-block tic-tac-toe grid, not counting the micro shopping center next to the freeway. Stomping up her street and easily paced by Beowulf, Tassy had quickly reached an outer grid corner, where she'd stopped and looked out to sea. There'd be a storm before morning, and the clouds already assembling made the sunset even gaudier than usual—all pinks and mauves and ambers swirling above an equally riotous ocean. It looked the way she felt, and yet the sight of all this turmoil started smoothing down her anger. After a few minutes to absorb it, she had turned inland.

Jimi was locking up the Hair Place when Tassy passed, while her manicurist headed for a rust-bucket pickup, lugging a vast plastic baby caddy that must have cost more than she earned in a week. Jimi waved, and when Tassy waved back, Angela, too, wagged a friendly arm. Tassy and Beowulf kept going.

She and the dog covered the town together: across and then up Bay Street past the trailer park that people called the Geezer Bin. So many of those old folks had turned out for her proposal hearing. Down the next street over, past the ghostly totem poles and red-wood Narowas in Bill the Fixer's yard and the bulk of the old Dodge Charger in Dave's. Across and up again, past Dottie Franklyn's pretty curio shop, past the funky latte parlor, where her big painting held pride of place, past dear Orson's gallery, now dark for the night, past the warm windows of the coffee shop, where Jack Millhouse's last customers were finishing. Left turn onto her own street above the beach and then a second circuit.

As she walked the tiny village Tassy realized how much she'd come to belong here—how many people she liked and how many, Margaret notwithstanding, liked her back. She threaded through the village again with Beowulf. He knew everyone in town and yet he'd chosen her. He liked her too.

Something here had liberated her. She was painting what she really wanted to. Orson had reported that a San Francisco decorator loved the photos he'd e-mailed, and old Mrs. Halvorsen had mentioned the restaurant walls. Imagine, after all these years!

And Linc, the manipulating, infuriating son of a bitch. Who said he loved her. Did he? It took her two streets to decide that yes, he did. He most definitely did. Tassy started another circuit.

Did she love him? That didn't take two streets; she loved him back, oh yes, she did, though he was still a manipulating, infuriating son of a bitch.

She could cure him of that.

Wow! She'd really changed. Imagine thinking she could "cure" her former husband of *anything*. Tassy was actually smiling when she unlocked her front door and went in.

Beowulf woofed at something, what? Some passing seagull, maybe. Who knew what set him off half the time? Tassy shushed him and they went to bed together as usual. The rain was already pattering on the roof.

~

She got up again at dawn, partly because the rain was louder now and partly because her canted bedroom sent queasy signals into her sleep and left her waking early, cross, and tired. She made coffee, wondering where Beowulf had got to, and carried a full mug into her studio.

The dog was lying against the sliding door . . . and someone was lying outside it on her deck! A man, from the size of him, not moving, soaked. A drunk, a homeless guy, some druggie? She moved quietly up to one side of the door, where she could make out the man's features.

It was Linc! On his side, eyes closed, water streaming off his face and puddling on the deck. Linc and the dog lay back to back, with only the glass between them. Beowulf got up and stretched.

Her instinct was to slide the door open and grab him, save him from the deck and all that rain. But then she checked herself. What was Linc doing? How long had he lain there?

She walked uphill to her worktable and stood with her back to it, sipping coffee and watching the motionless form on her deck. Tassy trusted her brain to do its own quirky work in its own good time, so she studied the lightening sky and the storm passing off and the dim, hopeful gulls wheeling over the harbor.

When she finally popped the latch pin in the base of the door and slid it open, Linc rolled forward out of the way, then back as a loud creak sent a warning. He fell backward through the opening and lay half in, half out.

"What do you think you're doing?"

"Can I come in first?"

"Can you stand up?"

"Who knows?" Hand over hand, Linc hauled himself up the frame of the opened door. "Yes, I can."

"Doesn't look like it to me. Here." She grabbed his sopping arm none too gently, hauled him over to one of the drafting stools, and turned him around. "Sit."

Linc sat. "I couldn't get in, then I couldn't get out—well, off."

"You were going to wake me up before dawn?"

"It was last night."

"Last . . ." Tassy thought about that as she slid the door shut, then held out her mug. "Here. I'll get more."

He grasped the handle as if each finger took special attention. "Oh God I'm stiff."

"Probably caught cold." But it was she who sniffed. "Sit there while I get more coffee."

Tassy strode away, leaving Linc to listen to the weather. He'd been in it all night long.

In her pocket-size kitchen she found a terry dish towel. As she poured another mug of coffee she stacked up all her beefs with Linc—all his manipulations, his smooth dominating—and then she placed beside the stack the image of Linc soaking all night on her deck, trying to get to her, waiting for her. Yeah, she could cure him.

Tassy brought in the towel and second mug and exchanged it for her own, waiting patiently while Linc operated his fingers. While she scrubbed his head dry, he thanked her, sipped, then said, "I listened to the waves last night. You know, 'Begin, and cease, and then again begin'?"

She opened her mouth to say, *What—?*

He waved it off. "Not important." Another sip of coffee and a deep breath. "I came to say I'm sorry, but I don't know how to make you feel I mean it."

She looked at him a moment, then asked, "Sorry for exactly *what*? You tell me."

"For managing, negotiating—I guess for treating you like a business deal instead of the person I love."

They sat there staring at each other on the two high stools, Tassy calm and blank as Buddha, Linc looking more miserable than even a night on a cold, soaking deck should make him. After what seemed a long time he said slowly, "I'm sorry, Tassy; forgive me."

Tassy nodded. She'd wanted him to say that. It was the one last thing she'd been waiting for.

Linc drained his mug and set it on the drawing table. "Tassy, would you like to stay at my place awhile and use the studio?"

"Thank you, Linc, I would."

"Dave and Bill can modify it to suit—"

"Stop. The studio's perfect." She took his hand. "That's part of what pissed me off: How could you know my mind so perfectly? It's scary. Whee! Your hand is wet and cold. You must be freezing."

Linc took her other hand and drew her up off her stool. "Yeah. I could use some help with that."

21

Over the next few days, Tassy, Linc, and Dave and Bill moved her into the B and B, leaving her own house empty. During that time, Margaret Nam grew increasingly uneasy. Reactions at the public meeting had warned her of trouble, and Dottie Franklyn had later confirmed it.

"Why *did* you kill that application?" Dottie asked on the phone. Margaret was halfway into a lengthy self-justification before realizing that this was just dim *Dottie*, for God's sake! She broke off.

"Margaret?"

"I don't have to explain to you," she said stiffly.

But for once, Dottie was not suitably abashed. "You don't have to explain to *anyone*; everyone already knows." She hung up.

Later, when Margaret entered the Hair Place for her weekly nail appointment, talk stopped abruptly. Nobody looked at her but Jimi, and Jimi's level stare announced where *she* stood.

"Are you busy?" Margaret asked Angela, though the manicure chair was unoccupied.

"No," Angela said, "but I have to check on the baby. Be just a minute." She disappeared into the back, leaving Margaret to seat herself. Margaret put her left arm on the manicure table where she could look at her watch without seeming to, and after exactly one minute had passed, she got up and walked out without speaking.

The last straw was Norman Stihl. Since he hadn't called her for several days, she broke her long-standing policy and called him. "Hi, Norman, where've you been?"

"Uh, busy, I guess."

"Are you working a job now?"

"*No, Margaret, I'm not.*" Norman wasn't a subtle man but even for him the sarcastic tone was extreme.

She'd have to take care of this. "Why not come by for supper?"

A pause, then, "Well, maybe a drink. Around six?"

"I thought eight." She would get him to stay for supper and eventually bed. Bed never failed with Norman.

Reluctantly, "Eight's okay, then."

Margaret closed up her phone almost cheerfully. She knew she could handle Norman, and that put everyone else in perspective. Small towns loved these trivial tiffs, and towns didn't get smaller than San Andreas. In a day or two folks would find something else to deplore. And after all, she'd only done it for their sake, hadn't she? At election time she'd remind them of all she had given the town.

~

Norman was twenty minutes late, which was not a good sign at all. Margaret poured him his usual bourbon and a glass of white wine for herself. Then they moved out of the kitchen and into her stylish living room. Margaret sat on the couch and patted the seat beside her.

Norman didn't obey. Instead, he drank off his whiskey in two slugs while he stared down at her from his six-foot-three-inch height. Then he banged down his glass and said, "Why did you screw me, Margaret?

Careful! "What do you mean by—?"

"You killed the Tassy Morgan job. That was *my* job."

"I did not."

Norman started pacing. "I coulda pulled—jeez—near a year's income out of that job. What did I do to you?"

Her most reasonable tone: "It wasn't you, Norman."

"Come on! The engineering study?"

That again.

He yanked a folded green binder out of a hip pocket. "Uh-huh, yeah, this one. You came to my house to get it."

"I did no such—"

"Like, a week before that meeting!"

"No."

"You really think I'm a dumbass, don't you? Wake ol' Norman out of a dead sleep and fuck his brains out. By the time I showered and got my head straight, you had this proposal."

"What makes you—?"

"Don't give me that shit. At the meeting you thought they had *my* engineering report. Why, Margaret?"

She wasn't handling this well. "I don't know. I . . ."

Norman wagged the green binder at her. "Because you read it!"

Margaret was *not* about to take more of this. She jumped up. "All right, I read it!"

That stopped him briefly and he calmed down a little. "You planned that whole routine you went through at the meeting. Why?"

This was much worse than she'd thought. She would have to concede him some explanation. "Oh, Norman, it wasn't you. It wasn't you at all."

"Who else could it be?"

"Her."

"Her. Her." His look shifted from puzzled to incredulous. "You mean *Tassy?*"

"She embarrassed me."

"She . . . ? How did she . . . ? Oh, screw it, I don't care."

"It's important!"

"Enough to make her lose her house? Make her property worthless? You know how much she'll lose?"

"Oh, she'll get approval."

"That house won't hang on long enough. It's six percent off level now."

Margaret shrugged.

"I was mad when I thought you were after me. But ruining Tassy because she *embarrassed* you?"

"She really did worse than that."

He shook his big shaggy head. "Yeah, I'm sure." Norman walked to the door. "You know, Margaret, you got something wrong somewhere—some kinda switch that's, like, I don't know, not turned on. You're scary."

Margaret watched as he closed the door behind him. It was just a misunderstanding. He'd get over it.

By the time she got into the kitchen she was shaking all over. She wanted to throw her glass in the sink, but that wouldn't solve anything and her crystal was too expensive to sacrifice. She refilled the glass instead.

Margaret leaned against the counter and thought. At her petite height the Corian lip dug into her back but she was thinking too fiercely to notice. Maybe he wouldn't get over this one. Damn it! Every time she squared off with that woman, she lost. Why was that? She'd even won at the meeting but then she lost the whole town. Now she might lose Norman too. So the big bitch's house would fall down in—what—six months? A year? Who could tell? Norman'd said it was six percent off level. How long would six percent take—?

Margaret suddenly stopped and the focus that served her so well kicked in. Six percent. Already six percent. She looked at her watch: nearly nine o'clock, but she had John Hansen's cell phone number. With the hours he worked, he might be in bed, but never mind; she'd wake him up. It was time for an urgent call—an *emergency* call—to the county building inspector.

~

At precisely 12:00:00 the next day, Inspector Hansen showed up from the county building office and knocked on Ms. Morgan's door. When there was no answer, he walked around to the side and made several measurements with his laser level, which was accurate to 0.01 percent. The deck was a full 9.23 percent off and the house foundation was 7.08.

No doubt about it. Sighing, he filled out a bright red cardboard square and affixed it to the front door. It read:

UNSAFE

DO NOT ENTER OR OCCUPY

(THIS PLACARD IS NOT A DEMOLITION ORDER)

This structure has been inspected, found to be seriously damaged, and found unsafe to occupy, as described below.

On the lines provided he'd written, "excessive building foundation shift and risk from collapsing bluff."

This house was giving him no end of grief. A lot of folks were unhappy about all this and he didn't need that. Hansen wanted to work with people; he didn't want to be seen as a cop. Spread thin as he was, he could never uphold building codes if folks started seeing him as an enemy instead of collaborating with him. Margaret kept siccing him on this shack and technically, she was right both times. But he was getting damn tired of jumping when she said jump.

After a moment's thought, he drove off to find DayGlo Dave or Bill the Fixer, who were old acquaintances. It wouldn't hurt to tell one or both that the idea of red-tagging Ms. Morgan's house had come straight from Margaret Nam.

~

Tassy'd been oddly vague since breakfast. Linc watched as she wandered down to her front porch, collected yesterday's mail, did something or other with her door, and then wandered back. She sat beside him on the porch swing and gave him a big red card.

"That's a red tag," Linc said.

Tassy nodded. "What does it mean, exactly?"

Linc glared at the card. "I could give you the gist but I'd better check the details." He got up to consult his online resources. As he walked into the house, Tassy opened a piece of mail, still in that vague, abstracted way. Linc wondered what was up. Normally, she'd be building to hurricane strength by now, but instead she just sat there.

After a few minutes at his computer, Linc returned to the front porch to find Tassy just as he'd left her, now holding a thick sheet of letterhead.

Linc sat down. "You really have only two choices: Correct the listed defects or walk away from the property."

"I can't fix a thing without a loan."

"Mm." He tapped the sheet of letterhead and asked, "Whatcha got?" though he knew perfectly well it was from the trust.

She gave Linc the letter. Don Fedderman's prose was clunky, even for legalese.

Linc knew he was stuck. This was the moment for the new, honest, nonmanipulative Linc to tell the whole truth about his foundation. But something odd was going on with Tassy—something weird—and he couldn't predict her reactions right now.

Instead, he just said brightly, "How about that? Somebody untied you just before the train ran over you. Let's see: 'comparable market value'—very nice. Check out this part: 'We will accept it in any condition.' You're off the hook, kid. The timing's too good to be true." Keeping up this farce was making him feel like a perfect shit.

"It isn't coincidence."

Uh-oh.

"Ms. Halvorsen was hinting at something—though I don't think it was this."

Linc said too heartily, "Well, this is more than a hint." He waved the sheet. "How about I draft you a gracious letter of acceptance?" When she only nodded Linc eyed Tassy narrowly. "Listen, maybe you love the place . . ."

"No I don't. It's a dump, except for the view. Yes, write the letter, please." She pointed at the numbers in paragraph two. "That's many hundreds of thousands of bucks. My problems ought to be solved."

Linc put an arm around her. "*Ought* to be? What is it, Tassy?"

They rocked gently while she stared out to sea, then, "This morning I had an informative pee. I'm pregnant."

Inside, Linc froze solid, but he carefully kept the swing moving. Finally, he ventured, "Aha."

Five or six more swings, then Tassy asked, "'Aha' what?"

In the midst of his shock, Linc knew that his answer could make him or break him with Tassy—though he didn't know what kind of reply would do which. He'd just have to feel his way, and for God's sake, keep at least *this* subject honest!

Finally he said, "I can tell you what's running around in my head, all mixed together. I think, a baby; your baby; our baby. Then I think, you're too old to have a baby—what if something . . . ? We're too old to have children. When the kid got out of college I'd be seventy-three and you'd be, what, pushing seventy?"

Tassy nodded.

"Then I think, a baby. I like babies, like children. I've always wanted them. But then I think, you're the one who has to have it or not have it—either way, that's a decision too huge for a male to even *comprehend*. When you weigh your choices, I don't want to pile my needs on one side of the scale. But then I think, I don't want to leave all the burden on you. Above all, whichever—I mean *whatever* happens, I don't want to lose you." A long silence. "Am I making sense at all?"

Another long pause, then she said softly, "You did it again: You're thinking exactly what I am—all the way. I just don't know what to do yet."

"How do you think it happened?" At Tassy's look, he added, "I know how *it* happens, but we took . . . precautions."

Tassy roused enough to sneer.

Linc shifted topics quickly. "How long have you—*we*—got?"

A shrug. "A month, maybe. I'll have to read up on it." She huffed out a shuddery sigh, like the ones that often end weeping jags, and stood up. "I'd better put this back on the door." She stared at the big red card. "I can't go inside my own house anymore—but then there's no reason to, is there?"

Tassy walked down the road again, still wandering, still in a fog.

assy and Linc spent the rest of the day with a quiet, reciprocal tenderness, as if each was helping the other convalesce. They didn't say much, but took care to touch often and sent frequent, tentative smiles.

They both had chef salads for dinner, which was delayed an hour while they churned through endless Internet articles on drinking while pregnant. They finally concluded that half a glass of white wine would be safe, subject to an obstetrician's opinion. That reminded them that the situation might not last long enough to require an obstetrician, and the thought evaporated what little ease they'd regained.

Later they showered and Linc put his palm on her soapy belly, which, of course, was no rounder than usual yet, but the gesture recaptured their earlier ease and they smiled again.

Then they turned out the lights, got into bed, wrapped up warmly in each other, and held on. Tassy actually went to sleep, but Linc stared into the dark until circulation loss forced him to extract himself. He brushed her lips lightly, then lay back beside her.

～

By the following day the latest news of Margaret's vendetta was all over town and support was draining away from her. Dottie Franklyn had already reregistered in the Tassy party and others were falling in line. Sharon Morning Sky was quite militant and recruited several latte addicts.

Linc called on old Mrs. Lagan with a bottle of Harveys Bristol Cream sherry. The old lady was ecstatic that someone inquired after the town memorabilia and brought sherry, and when Linc floated balloons about a possible museum, she almost cashed in her very tall stack of chips—she was that thrilled—and required a couple more snorts to recover.

He steered the conversation to the current brouhaha and old Mrs. Lagan confided that the garden club was disgusted with Margaret Nam. This was bad news for Margaret because the club members were of an age to cash in their own chips, and their very pricey properties would hit the market sooner rather than later. Linc drove home carefully, leaving a half-empty bottle and taking with him a healthy respect for old Mrs. Lagan's capacity.

At the Seaside Café, Jack Millhouse opined that enough was enough and he would put an end to this nonsense. Orson Wellesley, who was enduring the pot roast special, congratulated the mayor on his newfound spine and otherwise kept his own counsel.

At the B and B things went on as before. Tassy furnished and fussed with her new sitting room and organized her walk-in closet—a five-minute job, with her near-nonexistent wardrobe. She had switched her address to a post office box, not yet ready to decide whether her move was other than temporary.

But everyone knew she was living with Linc, and even DayGlo Dave could no longer deny the obvious. He was crushed, of course, but then all life for Dave was a slow-motion downhill ooze, and he absorbed this blow as stolidly as he'd taken all the others and would go on taking them.

Linc hammered away at Czerny exercises, leavened by sprightly Scarlatti and soothing Schubert. Every night dinner arrived from the Seaside Café because they had worn out both the casino and the Beach House.

Neither Tassy nor Linc brought up the baby, and the trivial chatter they traded showed they were avoiding the subject. One night they resumed making love, overcoming lame jokes about relief from the tyranny of condoms. At first Linc was so tender and tentative that Tassy had to point out that, whatever she was, it wasn't sick or frail. They slept in each other's arms again.

~

Linc woke up in the false glow before dawn. What was that? Just a few early birds and the endless, persistent surf.

There! A short, loud, wood-on-wood groan. Linc got up but could see nothing from this side of the house, so he groped for his pants and some loafers.

He was buttoning his shirt when Tassy woke up. "What's the matter?"

"Probably nothing." But another groan belied him.

Tassy yelled, "Oh Jesus, I know what that is!"

She was out of bed and streaking for the door when Linc shouted, "Put clothes on!" When she looked disgusted he added, "It's cold." Tassy swarmed into shirt, jeans, and sandals, then raced down the hall to the stairs.

Linc pounded after her. She was outside by the time he hit the parlor. Thinking fast, he grabbed coats from the tree in the hall and followed her out the door, off the porch, across the road, and down to Tassy's front yard. They both jumped the new low fence and ran to the uphill side of the house.

Nothing happened. The beginning of dawn showed an outline of timbers supporting her deck. Linc draped Tassy's jacket around her and put on his own.

He said, "Well . . ."

A major support post suddenly, literally lost its footing and dangled free under the deck. The deck shuddered and croaked as it canted downward. There was now enough daylight to see that the bluff was crumbling—no longer in dribbles of rock and sand, but in bigger and bigger pieces. Tassy started forward but Linc held her fast. "We better stay clear," he said.

Within minutes the deck sagged so far that it finally ripped loose from the house and clattered and crashed to the beach. This seemed to encourage the bluff to shed larger and larger sections, until half the studio projected beyond the receding edge. Linc put his arm around Tassy when she tried again to move closer.

She asked, "Shouldn't we call the fire department or somebody?"

"Not a thing they could do. You can't prop it up without getting under it, and nobody's going to do that now." A sudden thought: "The next-door rentals. Anyone in them?"

Tassy shook her head.

The destruction went on at the speed of a chess match. A foot of bluff would surrender and drop; then minutes would pass; then another big chunk; then more minutes. After an hour of death in slow motion, activity stopped—or, at any rate, paused. The back third of the house now hung in midair above the beach.

Linc looked around at the daylight, then checked his watch. "The café will be open by now. I'll call Millhouse."

Tassy roused and literally shook herself. She started back up to the B and B and Linc followed.

She went to the kitchen and started coffee. "Well, there goes the house sale," she said in a tone artificially flat.

Linc knew she was wrong, of course, but had not yet summoned the courage to tell her the truth. Instead, he continued his act. "Mm, let me just call that attorney, you know, Don Fedderman, right—let me give him a call. His letter does say they'll buy the house in any condition."

"Including kindling?" She shook her head listlessly. "You were going to phone Millhouse."

"I think I'll go see him. There's some things I need to take care of."

Tassy shrugged vaguely. She was back in that nebulous elsewhere, that affectless place where she wandered unreachably.

Linc shook his head and left.

~

At the Seaside Café Linc ate a plain omelet—the breakfast cook vulcanized eggs over easy—drank four cups of coffee, and read what passed for news in the daily that passed for the county seat newspaper. He then called Don Fedderman, reported the situation, and got him to fax up a new letter confirming the offer to buy the property even in its present condition.

When the customers slowed to a trickle he caught Millhouse's eye and the mayor came to sit in his booth.

"I suppose you heard, Jack."

"I've been here since six." But his shifty look gave him away.

"You mean none of your customers told you that Tassy's bluff collapsed this morning?"

"Well, I heard . . . stuff."

"Leaving her deck on the beach and her house sticking out in the air."

"That's terrible."

"Your compassion becomes you. Of course, there were no casualties because some upstanding citizen had got the place condemned even before it became a hazard."

"I had no . . ."

"True. Margaret never consults anyone."

"How do you know it was—?"

"Jack. *Jack!* Well, look at the bright side: You don't have to contest the path closure, because the path was cut into the bluff and has now disappeared."

Millhouse moaned, "So's the beach access."

"Speaking of which, you'd better get Willard to string yellow tape on the fence. That whole site's now a hazard."

The mayor groaned.

"Last item of business: I'm resigning as city attorney and council member, both effective immediately."

"Why?" It was almost a wail.

"Because the city's egregious negligence with respect to Ms. Anastasia Morgan's property is ample grounds for a lawsuit."

Millhouse blanched. "That's just why we need you."

Linc stood up, shaking his head. "Conflict of interest, Mr. Mayor. I'm representing the plaintiff."

Linc dropped a bill on the table, walked out, strolled to the corner, and turned up toward home. Of course, there would be no lawsuit—no need for it—but he liked the way the mayor's eyes had bulged. Cheap fun but he didn't regret it. Despite the morning's calamity he felt almost cheerful as he crossed the porch and entered the house.

Tassy wasn't in the kitchen, so he looked in her new studio. Not there and not in their bedroom either. Glancing down at his driveway from the sitting room window, he noticed her car was missing.

23

I stayed missing all day and into the evening. Linc tried her cell phone eight times and left increasingly anxious messages. Between calls, he went through all reasonable explanations: shopping, visiting, out sketching, just driving around, a doctor's appointment . . .

Doctor's appointment?

Had she gone to get a . . . ? Almost frantic, Linc tried to remember what he'd told her about his feelings. Hell, he'd said babies were bad but babies were good but babies were bad but babies were good. . . . Wait: He'd said a man couldn't know how to make that choice, said he didn't want to weight her decision. Was that wrong? What did she think he was telling her?

What *was* he telling her?

How could he find her? Did she have a doctor? She hadn't said. Maybe a public clinic. They wouldn't take to a nearly hysterical male trying to locate one of their patients. Maybe she *was* just driving around. Call the highway patrol? Call the cops? The missing person thing didn't kick in for twenty-four hours—if it kicked in at all. He could think of nothing else.

Linc sat in the parlor. He didn't eat dinner, he didn't drink bourbon.

After three endless hours he called and left one more message. "Tassy, it's midnight. I'm crazy; I'm worried about you, frightened for you. If you haven't . . . uh, haven't done . . . anything, then don't, oh please don't. If you have . . . if you have . . ." Two deep breaths. "If you have, Tassy, that's okay too. Just come back; just come home." He tried to think what else to say, then finally whispered, "Come home, Tassy; I love you. Good night."

He slept in the parlor, upright in a chair.

~

Knowing that Orson was often up early, Linc shuffled down to the art gallery. The kitchen was lit in the little rear flat, so he knocked and went in.

Orson said, "You look like the walking dead."

"Tassy's gone. She didn't come home last night."

Orson took his arm and led him to a kitchen chair. "Sit down. We'll talk about it." Linc sank obediently.

Orson poured coffee and sat. "Tell the doctor," he said.

Despite Linc's crushing fatigue, his orderly mind put the story together. He explained his campaign to get Tassy to live with him. He summarized their stumbling, haphazard progress from antagonists to lovers. After a deep breath, he confessed that he'd gotten her pregnant, despite his inept attempts at contraception. He repeated the gist of what he'd told her about his feelings.

Orson said, "Mm, whether you've told her or not, have you made up your own mind about the baby?" When Linc nodded, he added, "Well?"

Linc sighed. "I want that baby—oh boy, do I want that baby. I really always did. The minute she told me I felt a kind of—I don't know, joy? Closer to ecstasy."

Orson smiled.

"But she's headed toward fifty. That's dangerous. Mothers lose babies, babies lose mothers, babies have birth defects—Jesus!" He gulped a slug of coffee. "Then there's her life. She's independent; she's a serious painter. What would a baby do to that? She wouldn't be a single mother, not if I had anything to say about it, but I don't know if she'll marry me. I love her; I want to marry her. But does she feel the same?"

"Have you let her know how you feel about the baby and marriage?"

"Yes, he has." Tassy was standing in the doorway to the living room.

"She spent the night here," Orson said.

Looking at Linc, she held up her phone. "A few minutes ago I picked up my messages. Nine of them." As Linc stood up she walked over and stood in front of him. "Especially the last one. The answer to last night's question is, no, I didn't." At the look of relief on Linc's face, she caressed it with her palm. "The answer to this morning's question is, yes I do; yes I will."

Orson mimed shooting a tiny arrow from a tiny bow. "*Twang!*" he said gaily. "You may now kiss the bride." Orson's tone was flip but his voice sounded shaky. Pretending to ignore their embrace, he said, "Well! Now that's all cleared up, let's have breakfast. How about chicken-apple sausages? Hello? You may now *stop* kissing the bride."

Linc and Tassy sat down at right angles so they could hold hands at the table. They stayed that way throughout breakfast, although buttering toast with one hand wasn't easy.

~

Around midmorning Tassy strolled arm in arm with Linc through patchy fog toward the B and B. They paused to inspect her house. The erosion seemed to have stopped, for now, and the house still sat with two-thirds on the ground. Without the weight of the deck in back, it seemed unlikely to topple over.

"I don't know how to cope with that," she said.

"Hm?"

She waved at the wreck of her home. "The whole property thing."

Linc had been walking thoughtfully. Now he said, "I do."

When they reached the big house, Linc led her into the kitchen and sat her down. Then he went into his former one-room apartment, retrieved a folder, and lifted a sheet from the incoming-fax tray. He returned to the kitchen and gave her the folder.

Its contents described the Lost Coast Charitable Trust, newly established to support historical and cultural endeavors on the Redwood Coast. A draft prospectus promised funds to teach art and music in schools, to give grants to local artists, to underwrite public concerts, and to make local history more widely accessible.

Tassy looked up. "These are the people who want to buy my property."

Linc nodded.

"Did you do all this research on them already?"

Linc shook his head. He looked troubled.

"Then what, Linc?"

"I told you that morning how sorry I was for manipulating you. I meant it; *mean* it. But you didn't know about my biggest offense and I was afraid to confess it then." He handed her an additional page listing the foundation's officers. She didn't see names that she recognized, except Donald Fedderman, of Fedderman, Fishbein, and Halsey.

She had also heard of the board chairman, one *Lincoln Ellis?* "Why are you in this?"

Linc gave her the fax. "I phoned Don and asked him to fax a confirming offer. This is it."

The letter acknowledged the recent collapse of the bluff and the total loss of the structure, then repeated the original price offer. She put it together. "This is *your* foundation. You're the one who's buying my house. You're bailing me out *again*!"

Linc nodded. "Listen, I had a good reason."

"You always do—you think."

Linc plowed on. "The big problem between us was money. You were broke . . ."

"And you had oodles, as you said."

"I have oodles squared. I could buy your house out of pocket change, but I knew you'd never sell it to me. Your independence was too new, too fragile. No way you would ever accept help."

Tassy looked down. That was probably true.

"You told Orson and me about old Mrs. Halvorsen. I made the obvious connection. The Narowa wanted control of that beach. You had it; you could sell it."

"Why not directly to them?"

"That might have worked, but I couldn't be sure. That's when I dreamed up the foundation. It buys the property, donates it to the tribe, you have a respectable bank balance. Everybody's happy."

Tassy smacked the folder. "So the rest of this art stuff is bullshit."

"To begin with it was; yes, it was. But then I had another big brainstorm."

"Two in one day, just imagine!"

"I had far too much money and too little purpose in life. The trust can solve both of those problems. I know what I want to do now. I'm going to run the trust personally—make sure it delivers what it promises."

For a long time Tassy looked at him without really seeing. Too much was boiling around in her head. As she thought, she rubbed absently on her stomach.

Finally, she blinked as things fell into place. "I figured something out—better late than never. You can't control me if I don't want to be controlled. You never could. I *am* independent; I've *been* independent. I don't have to be afraid of you."

"Of course not. You never did."

"I go where I want and I do what I want to do."

"Yes, you do."

Tassy took a deep breath. "Okay then, what I want to do is sell the house to the trust and have our baby." Before Linc's grin could bloom, she added, "However, I'm not going to marry you."

Linc turned white. "But you said . . ."

"I know." She rapped the file folder again. "But this has made me think."

"Do you love me? You haven't said that, you know; you've never quite said that."

She studied his tense face. "Yes, I do; yes, I love you. You're probably the first man I've *truly* loved."

"Well . . ."

"And you're *definitely* the first man to love me!"

"Well . . ."

"Hold on. I'm working this out as I go." Thinking, she looked down at the manila folder in her lap, then, "You've done nothing but try to manage me."

"I've admitted that. I can only repeat I'm sorry."

"From the moment we met. You climbed up the path from the beach. First thing you said was, was this an easement? I ought to charge a toll. Remember?"

"I was just making polite—"

"You were so wiped from scattering Ellen's ashes you could hardly make sense, let alone polite conversation."

Linc said, "Okay, I mishandled it. I've admitted that and apologized twenty times. So shoot me: I wanted to take care of you."

Tassy shook her head. "For twenty-plus years a man took care of me—sometime I'll tell you the Range Rover story." When Linc looked puzzled, she waved it away. "I was living his life, not mine. When his life no longer included me, I found I had none of my own. That will *never happen again*."

"Don't you trust me?"

"I trust you, Linc; it's life I don't trust."

They looked at each other awhile, and then Linc said in a tight voice, "All right, I've got to accept that. I don't know how all this would have played out if I hadn't done what I did, but one last time, I'm sorry for how I did it." He stood up and said with false nonchalance, "So. Okay, where will you go now?"

Tassy smiled up at him. "No place. I like it fine right here."

Linc exploded. "Then what the hell are we talking about?" He damped himself down, said, "I'm sorry," and briefly covered his eyes with a hand. "I thought I'd lost you again."

Tassy stood up and embraced him. "Linc, I'll live with you, share with you, love you. Beyond that, we'll have to see how it goes." At his sad head shake she added, "You can give the baby your name, if you want."

"What I *want* is to marry you!"

A long silence, then she said, "Maybe. Maybe someday. We'll see."

Tassy's phone rang. "Hello?"

"Mom! Oh, Mom, what've you *done* to me?"

"Nice to hear from you, Dana."

"I am *so* humiliated I could die! My friends . . . well, we just opened your wedding present."

"Sorry it missed the wedding, but you never told me its date." Momentary silence. "Did you get lots of loot?"

"Yeah: Rosenthal and Baccarat and . . . but *you*, Mom. You sent a set of cheap kitchen pans. You really think I'm gonna *cook*? How *could* you?" Dana was almost wailing.

Tassy was purposely perverse: "Oh, it was easy: Neiman Marcus online, just like you said."

For the first time ever, Tassy heard rage in her daughter's voice. "*You also sent* The Joy of *fucking* Cooking*!*"

"You can't do both at once, dear."

"What?"

"Basic marital advice. Never mind; I've got news of my own."

"Were you trying to make some kind of joke—uh, what news?"

"I'm pregnant."

Long pause. "Not funny, Mother. You're just trying to change the subject."

"You'll have a baby brother or sister. Won't you be pleased?"

"You're serious."

"Mm-hm, want to hear all about it?"

"I . . . no, no, I don't think I . . ." A silence followed that was probably final.

Politely, "Anyway, thank you for your call."

The tone of a phone disconnect.

Tassy pocketed the phone. "That was Dana, my daughter."

Linc, who'd been standing like a man brained with a wooden mallet, said, "Your daughter, right. I'd forgotten."

Thinking about her response to the call, Tassy realized that Dana was now like Linc's Ellen: still missed, still mourned, but filed under finished business.

They studied each other again. Tassy said, "So have we got a deal?"

"A *deal*??"

"Bad choice of words. Can we be partners, Linc?"

Linc nodded slowly. "Yes we can, but I give you fair warning: You said, 'Maybe someday.'" Tassy nodded too. Linc continued, "I'll remind you daily." He kissed her.

"All right."

"Tassy, will you marry me?"

"I just said . . ."

"That was today's reminder."

24

By Labor Day the title to the San Andreas beach had been transferred from the county to the Narowa, but it was not until October 4 that Grandmother chose to inspect this addition to the rancheria. On that date in 1863, a day that would live in obscurity, more than two hundred Indians, mostly women, children, and elders, had been surprised and slaughtered by white men discommoded by their presence in the neighborhood.

Four months before Grandmother, Linc Ellis had waded ashore here in a loopy burlesque of Christopher Columbus and tottered up the bluff path to meet Tassy Morgan. Grandmother's landing was more decorous. Erik beached the Zodiac tender from the family's sixty-foot cruiser and dragged the boat up to dry sand before upending a bucket for Grandmother to use as a step down. The old lady managed the transfer with dignity and set off down the beach. Erik followed.

She stopped midway on the sandy arc and looked out to sea. Sunset was earlier now, and its warm light was kind to her features. She stood there awhile, not looking at much—perhaps not even seeing—then slowly sank to her knees in the sand. Lifting a handful, she let it trickle slowly through her blunt fingers while her grandson watched her, unable to speak.

After another few moments, a stocky gray dog appeared magically and sat down before her. He greeted her, *bark*, pause, *bark*, and then licked her nose once.

"Hello, Wolfie," said Grandmother. "Erik, give me a hand, please." He helped her up and the three of them gazed at the harbor.

Grandmother snorted and started to laugh. When Erik asked what was funny, she pointed at the bay. "The true village site is a hundred yards out there and twelve feet down," she said.

Unable to work out her mood, Erik improvised. "Well, we got what we wanted, Grandmother."

Grandmother said, "It's a start," and wandered away toward their boat.

~

Since property sales and prices were matters of public record, Margaret Nam discovered that the Morgan woman had unloaded her derelict wreck of a shack for an astoundingly good price; and since the sale was apparently private, Margaret had lost a commission of nearly fifty thousand. As if that weren't bad enough, the empty store next to the Hair Place was now filled with a RE/MAX realty office that had stolen two sales out from under her.

Norman had come back—she knew he'd get horny eventually—but their sex was back to the emotional level of tennis and she admitted to herself that sex as a sport wasn't enough anymore. She'd been hoping to build some kind of relationship with Norman until . . .

Norman was tight with the Indians now, since he was the expert on rescuing houses, and they'd hired him to winch Morgan's old place backward onto solid ground prior to demolition. He was probably going to get this new job as well.

And here Margaret sat, suffering a presentation of the new job to the city council by old Mrs. Lagan and Grandmother Halvorsen. Mrs. Lagan mostly conducted the garden club claque, while the tribal chair described the building, pointing to Tassy's colorful design sketches. Margaret couldn't care less about a San Andreas museum, and she cared even less than *that* about some boring Indian village interpretive center, but she'd better pretend to be interested in this civic improvement. Her credibility as a mayoral prospect had hit an all-time low.

Thinking back to her original reason for starting this business, she realized she'd actually won in a sense: Morgan's eyesore was history. But the woman had won every round in their battle, cleaned up on the sale of her worthless slum, hooked up with gigantically big money, and alienated the town from Margaret only months before the election.

Not to *mention* the dozen large abstracts she'd sold the casino restaurant. The whole thing made Margaret feel tired, just *tired*.

~

October served the finest weather on the San Andreas menu, crisp and sunny. The alders turned dramatic yellows, but the rest of the woods were mostly evergreens, so the effect was almost spring-like. Sure, the nights would dip into the forties, but that was as close to winter as it got on the coast, and, as always, no one remembered that floods would engulf them two months later.

Just before Halloween, at the last tortured gasp of the tourist season—such as it was—the town wrapped things up with a gala art show: local paintings, ceramics, jewelry, beadwork, weaving, and sculpture. Almost nothing was sold, as usual.

The big exception was a life-size statue by Bill the Fixer: an opulent nude, lushly modeled, with the start of a bump in the middle. On Orson's informal advice, Bill had diffidently priced it at two thousand dollars and was stunned when a tourist bought it.

Restricted to carving indoors, Bill had used just his slow, tiny chain saw, the electric one with the ten-inch bar. But Tassy had posed uncomplainingly, dressed only in bright pink earplugs, plus a dust mask when Bill wasn't sculpting her face. Linc had thought she looked droll in that costume and took lots of digital pictures. The scream of the saw hurt Beowulf so much that he went on town patrol whenever it fired up.

They'd worked in the other front bedroom, first emptied to simplify sawdust control. Linc wanted to make it the baby's room but Tassy wouldn't commit to that yet.

Printed in the United States
by Baker & Taylor Publisher Services